Dear
Emily

# THE FOREVER FAMILY SERIES
## BOOK ONE

# TRUDY STILES

Cover Art Design by Stephanie White of Steph's Cover Design
Editing by Kathryn Crane
Editing by Murphy Rae of Indie Solutions
Interior Design and Formatting by E.M. Tippetts

E.M.
TIPPETTS
BOOK DESIGNS
www.emtippettsbookdesigns.com

# Synopsis

This book is not suitable for young readers. It is intended for mature adults only (18+). It contains strong language, adult/sexual situations, non-consensual sex, and some violence.

Two women. Carly and Tabitha. They each have suffered life-altering events that have left them both traumatically damaged.

Carly Sloan's life was perfect until her security and innocence were torn from her. The vast repercussions from horrific events threaten to destroy her stability and her chances for a happily ever after. Kyle Finnegan comes into Carly's life at the height of her turmoil. Can he help her find what she desires most?

Tabitha Fletcher has constantly suffered from a very young age. She has been hiding from her past, which was full of sadness, loss, and abuse. She has been so brutally damaged that she has very little hope for redemption. The revolving door of men only leads her deeper into misery.

What circumstance brings these two women together and can they help each other heal? And will they each find what they need?

Redemption.

Love.

Family.

"Dear Emily" is the first book in the "Forever Family" series.

# Playlist

When I write, I MUST listen to music. It helps me concentrate and blocks out all of the noises in my house. If you see me typing with my earbuds in, it means I'm writing. These are songs that played on constant shuffle as I wrote this book and each song means something to me or reminds me of a person in my real life.

The last 30,000 words of this book are dedicated to The Limousines. Both of their albums ("Get Sharp" & "Scrapbook") played on constant repeat.

1). "Don't Stop Believing" – Journey
2). "Cough Syrup" – Young the Giant
3). "Sexy Back" – Justin Timberlake
4). "Moves Like Jagger" – Maroon 5
5). "Chloe Dancer" – Mother Love Bone
6). "T.H.E. (The Hardest Ever) – Will.i.am featuring Jennifer Lopez & Mick Jagger
7). "I'm Not Your Boyfriend Baby" – 3OH3
8). "Pumping on Your Stereo" – Supergrass
9). "Dammit" – Blink 182
10). "Woman" – Wolfmother
11). "The Kill" – 30 Seconds to Mars
12). "You're All I Have" – Snow Patrol
13). "Tear You Apart" – She Wants Revenge
14). "Take Your Mama" – Scissor Sisters
15). "Out of the Races and Onto the Tracks" – The Rapture

16). "Stick 'em Up" – Quarashi
17). "She Hates Me" – Puddle of Mud
18). "Break Stuff" – Limp Bizcut
19). "John the Fisherman" – Primus
20). "Territorial Pissings" – Nirvana
21). "Harlem" – New Politics
22). "Very Busy People" – The Limousines
23). "Don't Change" – INXS
24). "Beating Heart Baby" – Head Automatica
25). "Breakout" – Foo Fighters
26). "We Care a Lot" – Faith No More
27). "Hang em High" – Dropkick Murphy's
28). "Minerva" – Deftones
29). "She Sells Sanctuary" – The Cult
30). "Sail" – AWOLNATION

*For my Emily*
*Mama Loves You*

# Content Warning

This book is not suitable for young readers. It is intended for mature adults only (18+). It contains strong language, adult/sexual situations, non-consensual sex, and some violence.

# Contact
## TRUDY STILES

Website: www.trudystiles.com
Email:authortrudystiles@gmail.com
Amazon: www.amazon.com/Trudy-Stiles/e/B00H3O0OJ8
Facebook: www.facebook.com/authortrudystiles
Goodreads: www.goodreads.com/trudy_stiles
Twitter: @trudystiles
Instagram: https://instagram.com/trudystiles/

# Prologue

## Carly

*New Brunswick, New Jersey*
**Past**
*Age 17*

HE ROLLS OFF of me, and I immediately slip into blackness.

# Prologue (continued)

## Carly

*New Brunswick, New Jersey*
**Past**
Age 17

THE HOT SUN is streaming through the window, melting me into my bed. The sheets are askew, and my body feels fused to the plastic coated dorm-issued mattress.

I'm alone.

And sweating.

An uncomfortable, burning ache and wetness is between my legs. I look down and suck in my breath. In addition to my sweat, dried blood cakes the inside of my thighs. *Where did all of this blood come from? Did I get my period? What am I wearing?* I realize that I'm still wearing the top of my 'Three Little Kittens' costume with a tight black tank top and a strapless black bra underneath. Wait, my bra is gone, but the tank is still on? I then feel something tickle the side of my face. *Is a whisker still attached to my cheek?* Scratching at my face, I find it and pull it off. *Where are the rest of my whiskers?*

I need to stop focusing on these damn whiskers and try to figure out why there's blood all over my thighs and sheets. Panic sets in as I close my eyes and try to piece things together. As I shift my weight on the bed, the burning gets worse. *What happened?*

*Dear Emily*

There *was* a Halloween Party at Sigma Chi last night, right? Where are my best friends, the other two 'kittens', Becca and Callie? We were all together, as far as I can remember. *Where are they now?*

The fog in my brain is thick, heavy. When I touch the top of my head, I find my kitten ears still there. The headband digs painfully into my scalp. My belly starts to churn as the room begins to spin.

*This is my room, right?* I look around and see the picture of my family tacked onto the corkboard next to my bed. This gives me comfort. I see all of them smiling back at me. The picture is from my Grandfather's eightieth birthday party. I remember it fondly.

My entire family is in the picture, all smiling, beaming from ear to ear. My mother Liz and my father, James is sitting on either side of my grandfather holding their glasses to toast. My brother, Jimmy and my two sisters Lyn and Renee are sitting near me, making silly faces. That was a happy day. One of the happiest in a long time. It was only three months ago during the best summer of my life. Endless graduation parties, listless days spent at the beach or the nearest amusement park. I was about to become a college freshman, and my smile in the picture, although goofy, is big and bright.

I reluctantly tear my eyes away from the happy photo and continue surveying my dorm room, which for all intents and purposes is a single. My roommate Ginger basically lives with her boyfriend off-campus. I see her whenever she needs to switch out her laundry and toiletries. We don't even speak to each other, and when she does acknowledge me, she's usually rude and snotty. I'm glad she isn't here that much, it makes life so much easier.

A long tail, poking out from behind the sink catches my eye. It's attached to the black skirt that I wore as part of my costume. I see my fishnet stockings are torn and dangling over the back of the desk chair. One of my black knee-high boots is on Ginger's bed, and the other is nowhere to be seen. *Crap, I love those boots.* There is a black eye patch hanging from my doorknob. *What the hell?*

Seeing these haphazard items of clothing strewn about makes no sense. I usually don't throw my clothes all over the place like this.

*Was someone here last night?* The fog starts to lift as I slowly get up, wobble a bit, and walk over to my sink. I take my skirt out of the sink. It smells like raspberries. I gag a little and remember that I was doing Swedish Fish shots all night.

*Goddamn shots.*

*Callie.*

She was feeding them to me while we pre-gamed before going to the party. *What was I thinking?* My stomach churns and I grab onto the sides of the sink, feeling the sudden urge to puke. I take a few deep breaths and look in the mirror. My dark eye makeup has run down my cheeks, marking my face in a macabre sort of way. My head continues to pound and I turn on the cold water to soak my pink washcloth. I need to feel relief. Taking it back to my bed, I lie down and place the ice-cold washcloth over my face. *Cool. Nice.*

As the spinning slows down, I close my eyes and allow my memories from last night to play back.

*I'm dancing in the basement of the Sigma Chi house with Becca and Callie. We're bouncing around like we're the only three at the party even though there are at least one hundred other people dancing along with us. "Don't Stop Believing" by Journey is blasting through the makeshift speaker system. The music is so loud we can't hear each other. We're just bouncing wildly with silly grins on our faces. Becca is acting out the song, singing with her eyes closed and her arms flailing in the air. Callie is just bobbing her head and screaming the lyrics at the top of her lungs. I am shaking my ass with my hands in the air, jumping up and down, and I can feel the alcohol coursing through my veins. The three of us are having an epic time.*

*I suddenly feel someone behind me, grinding into me. Hands grasping my hips. I jolt and turn around to look into the most incredible whiskey-brown eyes. Well – eye – to be exact. His other eye is covered with an eye patch, and he has a bandana over his head. From what I can see of his hair, it's brown. He's a pirate. The urge to say 'Ahoy Matey' almost overcomes me, but instead, I bite my lip and try to focus on his face. He smiles broadly at me and even though one of his teeth is colored black, I melt. I can't believe he's smiling at me. I'd seen him in the Student Union before, always with an entourage, mostly girls. Usually a different girl is sitting on his lap or is snuggling into his side while a dozen wait in the wings. But now, here on the crowded and sweaty dance floor, he is smiling at me. Me! At least I think he is. His face starts to get blurry. I squint and smile back, trying to look cute. Or seductive. Or both.*

*He shakes his head and laughs as the Journey song ends. A slow song immediately starts and he pulls me close, wrapping his arms behind me. He rests his hands just above my kitten tail and then pulls it while laughing some more. Why is pulling my tail so funny?*

*He moves close and says into my ear, "Hi." He lingers for a moment so I can feel his lips on my neck. I feel flush and my breath hitches.*

*"Hi," I barely whisper. My belly flutters and I shiver in his arms.*

*"I'm Todd," he says through his black-toothed smile.*

*"I know," I whisper again. He's an upperclassman. Todd Mitchell.*

*We dance silently while he burrows his head into my neck. His warm breath continues to excite me and he inhales deeply, taking in my scent. Sweat and booze. I become self conscious and try to pull away a little.*

*"Raspberries," he says into my ear as he tightens his grip on me.*

*"Mmmm, what?" I ask.*

*"Raspberries. You smell like them." He smiles.*

*"Oh, umm, yeah, shots," I slur. "Swedish Fish. I may have had two or twelve." I laugh nervously, "I wasn't counting." I giggle, hiccup, and suddenly feel very woozy and overheated. "I need some air," I say softly as I stumble a little on my feet. I turn to Becca and Callie, but find they are no longer there. Where could they have gone? I haven't been dancing with Todd that long, have I?*

*"Let's go outside." He grabs my hand and pulls me so quickly through the thick crowd that I can't even make out any faces. They all blur together as we whiz past them. This isn't helping my dizziness, in fact, it's making it worse. The stairs are lined with people, and he finally slows down so we can carefully weave up them. When we stop in the kitchen, he grabs two cups of beer from the keg by the door. Handing me one, he grabs my hand again and pulls me outside.*

*As soon as the cool air hits me, the chills start. I'm covered in sweat from dancing, and I'm now shivering uncontrollably. I need to get back inside. I need warmth.*

"*Drink your beer,*" *he practically growls. I shiver again, but take a sip anyway and choke it down. I feel like I'm going to puke and I make the decision to not drink another ounce.*

"*I think I'm done drinking for the night. Too many shots. I'm wasted!*" *I say 'wasted' as if it's long and drawn out. WAAAYYYY - SSSTEDDDD. And I am.*

*Really wasted.*

*I start walking away from the fraternity house toward the street, feeling very unsteady. I need to get home and crawl under my warm, thick comforter. He puts his beer down and takes my hand again. "I'll walk you back to your dorm. Which one are you in?"*

"*Thomas Hall,*" *I stutter. It's nice of him to offer. "You don't have to, I can get back on my own," I say feebly.*

"*It's too dark and late for you to be walking across campus by yourself. Let's go." He pulls me along with him as we make our way to my dorm. Despite my weak protest, I'm glad to have someone to guide me because I'm not doing a great job myself. I stumble a few times and trip over twigs or my own feet. He grasps me, trying to steady me as we walk. These boots are awesome, but I can't walk in them to save my life. I make a mental note to wear my flip flops or something less dangerous the next time I go to a party.*

*We arrive at my dorm; I reach into my pocket, fumbling with my key card and drop it. Shit. I get down onto my hands and knees and giggle nervously. "I'm such a klutz." I push my hands through the tall, damp grass and mutter, "I can't find it."*

*Todd reaches down, immediately finds it next to my knee, and lets us into the building. He pulls me off the ground and my head starts to spin. Too fast, I stood up too fast. "Whoa, everything's spinning," I mutter, trying to keep the alcohol from rising up into my throat. He gives me a minute to get my feet under me and leads me into the dorm.*

*Amber is at the security desk checking IDs. She isn't the most pleasant girl and never has a nice thing to say to me. She rolls her eyes when she sees me and then turns her tits – I mean, attention – to Todd. She heaves her chest out, and her snarl turns to a smile as she purrs, "Todd, are you here to see me? You aren't with* her *are you?" She says 'her' as if I'm a* disease. *Please don't let Todd be fooled by her, the entire basketball team has had her more than once.* I giggle, loud enough for them both to hear me. She stares daggers through me. *Did I think that out loud?*

Todd chuckles. "No, Amber, I'm here with …," He turns to me, and I say, "Carly." He continues. "I'm here with Carly, but it's good seeing you again." *Ew. I hope that doesn't mean he's hooked up with her.*

She sucks in a breath and turns away in disgust. I take this as a small victory and smile like a drunken idiot.

We take the elevator up to the tenth floor, and he helps me find my room. Everything looks the same and it's hard for me to focus as he pulls me down the hall. He again has to help me with my key card, and he opens my door. I fall in, and he follows, kicking the door closed behind him. I realize that I have a guy in my room. *This has never happened before and I suddenly get nervous. What do I do?*

He immediately grabs me and puts his full lips on my neck, probing me with his tongue. I shiver again and moan loudly; his kisses on my neck start to turn urgent and he's sucking, licking, and pulling me against his body. I feel his hardness push into my belly, and I gasp.

He pushes me back onto my bed, pulling my boots and stockings off with a swipe to each leg. He falls on top of me, starts kissing my neck, and works his way down to my breasts. He's frantic, grabbing at my tank top, pulling it up to my neck and unfastening my bra. I'm gasping for air. *This is moving way too fast, and I'm unable to stop him.* He reaches down, pulls my skirt off, and flings it across the room, all while his mouth sucks and bites my breasts. *This doesn't feel good. It's rough and it hurts.*

I whimper a little and he groans, "Mmm, you even taste like raspberries." He takes a nipple in his mouth and bites down while rolling the other between his fingers. I'm startled by the pain, but I allow him to keep going. *Is this how it's supposed to feel?* His hand leaves my breast and travels down between my legs. He pushes my underwear aside and thrusts two fingers inside me. I inhale sharply as pain fills me momentarily. *Now I'm really uncomfortable.*

I start to gather my senses. *This is getting out of control, and I need to slow him down. What the hell am I doing? What the hell is he doing?*

*I'm not ready for this.* I shake my head from side to side and try to *speak against his lips.*

"My God, you are so wet, Candy." *He groans against my mouth.*

"Carly," *I say, trying to catch my breath.*

"What?" *He removes his tongue from my nipple and looks up at me with a smirk.*

"My name is Carly. You called me Candy. Please get off of me." *I beg, twisting underneath him.*

"Whatever." *He grins and all of a sudden his face changes. His whiskey-brown eyes turn dark, and he's no longer smiling. He goes back to sucking and biting on my nipple. I begin to panic. This doesn't feel right and it hurts. Am I sobering up?*

"Stop!" *I push against his hard chest. I need to get him out of my room, now. But first I need to get him off of me. He doesn't budge. It's as if I'm pushing on a brick wall.*

*He continues pumping his two fingers inside of me, burning me, tearing me. He then removes his fingers long enough to rip my panties off. I gasp and try to gain control once again, but I don't think he gets it. He won't allow it.*

"Stop!" *I force the word from my lips. I'm squirming now, and nothing is stopping him.*

*Ignoring my pleas, his pants are now off, and he's grinding against me.*

*What's happening? Can he hear me?*

"No! We can't do this!" *I yell at him and attempt to move out from under him. I try to thrash and buck, but his weight is too much on top of me. I'm powerless.*

*Still ignoring me, he pulls back and, with one thrust, completely fills me. Pain shoots between my legs and I scream. He speeds up with urgency, covering my mouth as a second scream escapes my throat.*

"You're a virgin," *he says through panting breaths. He pins my arms above my head, caging me in with his thick arms on either side of me. Everything burns. He's smiling, and his black tooth is now smudged and looks filthy and menacing.*

*I gasp and can't speak as tears stream down my cheeks. I'm sobbing so hard but I can't hear it. His sadistic grunts drown out all other sounds*

*Dear Emily*

in the room. The urge to vomit hits me, my stomach churning. I can't look at his face anymore and turn my head to see the picture of my family tacked on my wall. I sob harder. They're all smiling at me. I don't look at him as he finishes with one final, deep drive into me. I feel like I'm being torn from end to end with the dull blade of a knife. The burn is radiating all over, down my thighs, and into my chest. I don't want to feel this pain anymore.

He rolls off of me, and I immediately slip into blackness.

# Chapter 1

## Carly

Spring Lake, New Jersey
**Present**
Age 29

Dear Emily,

How do I start a letter to a child I have yet to meet?

A child that has always been in our hearts?

A child that is meant for our family?

Your Daddy and I can't wait for the moment we are able to hold you in our arms for the first time. To lay our eyes on your perfect face, eyes, toes. To breathe in the essence of a new baby, swirling scents of powder and linen.

We can't wait to feel your beating heart against our chests and to listen to your slow and steady breaths. To hear your soft baby noises. To soothe your crying.

We have always dreamed of you, Emily. We've dreamed that someday our family would be blessed with a child. We are so close. Our new family is within reach.

*Dear Emily*

*We are here hoping, waiting, praying.*

*Love and kisses,*

*Mama*


My eyes glisten with tears as I scrawl my signature at the bottom of the letter, touch my fingers to my lips, press them onto her name, and close my journal. I look over to my left where Kyle is softly snoring, sleeping soundly. I mouth the words 'I love you' to him, touch his back lightly, put my journal in my night table drawer, and turn out the soft light by my bedside. I curl my body into his, tuck my head into his chest, and hold on tight.

I love this man with all that I am, and I love the father that he is going to be.

My heart is full of hope.

I've been writing to Emily since the day we found out. The day we received 'The Call' from the adoption agency. I smile and squeeze Kyle tighter as I remember that day with excitement.

*It's the beginning of August, and I am in the teachers' lounge. I am an English teacher at Spring Lake High and I've been preparing my classroom for the first day of school. I have so much to do to get ready and not a lot of time to do it. My cell phone rings, startling me. I see the familiar number from Florida and swallow my iced tea down hard. Nearly choking, I fumble for my cell and answer.*

*"Hello?"*

*"Carly, this is Anna from Home Sweet Home Adoptions. Do you have a minute?"*

*"Of course," I sputter. My heart is racing. I just know this is the call we have been waiting for. My palms are sweating so much that I almost drop my phone onto my BLT. Crumbs fall into my lap.*

*Anna continues, "Is Kyle at work? Can I conference him on the line with us?"*

*"Yes! No!" I'm practically yelling at her. "No, I mean, he's not at work; he's off today. Yes, please try his cell phone." I give her Kyle's number,*

*so thankful that the University is closed for summer break. As the head Professor of Mathematics at Tremont University, he is enjoying some much-deserved time off.*

*The time it takes Anna to conference in Kyle seems endless. I'm rubbing my other hand nervously along my left thigh, so hard that the crumbs on my lap are now ground into my sweaty palm.*

*I hear the line click back, and Anna asks, "Kyle, Carly, are you both there?"*

*"Yes!" I yell into the phone. Why am I still yelling?*

*"Guys, I have such great news for you. You've been selected by a birth mother. Grab a pen and paper and get ready to take notes because you aren't going to remember everything I say and you are certainly going to have questions. I'll give you both a minute."*

*I start scrambling for a pen, find one, and then flip over my placemat to scribble on the back of it. Damn, no ink in this pen. Kyle speaks up. "Hey Car, can you take notes? I'm on the golf course, and the only paper I have is my scorecard." I'm swiping at the table trying to grab the pencil that rolled away while I was eating.*

*"Okay, I'm back," I pant breathlessly into the phone, "and I'm ready to take notes."*

*Anna begins. "Great. As I mentioned before, a birth mother, Tabitha, has selected you. She's having a baby girl. Tabitha has chosen the name Emily already. While this isn't customary, she wanted you to know. Tabitha is twenty years old and is unable to give her baby the life she deserves. She immediately connected with your profile because of your academic background and careers. She also loves that Kyle is a musician. The birth father is listed as 'unknown' since she is uncertain at this time. She's currently in a relationship with Seth, who is one of the potential birth fathers. He's fully supportive of the adoption, and is willing to sign away his parental rights as well. As required by law, we've posted notices in her home state addressing the other possible birth father. If he does not come forward to claim the child, then the courts will terminate his rights. I realize this may be concerning to you, but I assure you that it's common practice. In addition, we don't typically request paternity tests because it's considered invasive. Since Tabitha is only twenty, it is not routine for* amniotic tests to be conducted at her age."

I trust what Anna is telling us about the legal requirements that they must meet, and I move on to feeling my excitement. She chose us, out of how many other potential families?

Kyle taught himself to play guitar about five years ago, and suddenly I'm squealing with delight in my head, thanking the guitar Gods. All of that bad tuning and noise that I suffered through for those months as he taught himself was worth it! It matters! Bad tuning and screeching guitar noises in my head aside.

Anna continues. "Tabitha did not make this decision very easily, and she's still wavering a little bit. But she wanted me to contact you because she wants to know if you will say yes. But before you say anything, let me tell you what we know about her social and medical history."

I'm scribbling down on my placemat, and my pencil is tearing into the paper. The only words I've written so far are:

Tabitha

Seth - possible father?

☺

☺

I'm useless.

"Okay," Anna goes on. "Tabitha is unsure of her family history as she herself was adopted. Depending on who the birth father is, this baby may have Irish, Italian, German, and/or English heritage. As far as her medical history, she's currently being treated for depression and has been taking antidepressants during this pregnancy. She has not consumed any alcoholic beverages and has been taking pre-natal vitamins since she found out she was pregnant."

I look down at the placemat and see that I've scrawled:

Depression

No Booze

Again, I'm useless. I'm certain that this will make no sense to us later.

"So, are you both comfortable so far? It seems that there really aren't any red flags, and this matches your adoptive family planning questionnaire pretty closely."

I can't speak because I'm now just drawing hearts all over the *placemat. Kyle speaks up. "Wow, this is a lot to digest. She picked us? Are you sure? Wow."*

*I can hear Kyle's voice breaking, and I know he's about to cry. Or at least that's what it sounds like. I start to sob and jump in. "This sounds perfect, Anna, just perfect."*

*The call continues with discussion of financial details, match agreements, doctors' appointments, and conference calls to be scheduled. I'm still scribbling nonsense on the placemat when Anna says, "You'll receive a Fed Ex package tomorrow morning containing all of the papers that you will need to sign. Have everything notarized and returned to us within 48 hours. Tabitha and Seth would like to set up a conference call for some time next month, and they'd like Carly to be at Tabitha's next ultrasound."*

*"Yes," Kyle and I say simultaneously. I start laughing. "Yes, yes, this is perfect." Then I start to cry. I'm happy crying. I love happy crying, and I'm doing it at this moment. Kyle jumps in. "Carly, calm down. Breathe. Anna, we are good."*

*I manage to say goodbye to Anna and hang up my phone. It immediately starts ringing and vibrating, almost falling to the floor. It's Kyle.*

*"Hi," I say, smiling through the tears streaming down my face. Then I say, "Oh my God, honey, it's happening!"*

*Kyle takes a deep breath and says, "I'm on my way home. When can you get there?"*

*I realize that I still have several things left on my to-do list. There is no way that I'm going to be able to concentrate on anything.*

*"I'm leaving right now!" I swipe my BLT into the trash, crumple the placemat into a ball, and stuff it and the now-broken pencil into my purse.*

*"Hey, Car?"*

*"Yeah," I reply as I start to run out of the lounge.*

*"I love you," he says softly.*

*The happy tears are back.*

*"I love you too."*

*I smile as I snuggle into Kyle's side. That day was perfect, and the*

*Dear Emily*

feelings come rushing back to me. Tears start to pool in my eyes, and I place my head on Kyle's chest.

I fall asleep listening to the soft beat of Kyle's strong heart.

# Chapter 2

## Carly

*New Brunswick, New Jersey*
**Past**
*Age 17*

*BANG BANG*

*BANG BANG BANG BANG*

What the fuck? It's dark in my room. What time is it?

*BANG BANG BANG*

Make it stop.

"C'mon Car. Open up! We know you're in there!" Becca and Callie yell through the door in unison.

"Ugh! Hold on." I grunt from my bed. I reach over to turn on my lamp, stretch, and sit up. My clock says nine o'clock. At night. I can't believe that I've been asleep for three hours and I feel like shit.

I'm still in my clothes from class five hours earlier. I'm wearing comfy jeans, a long-sleeved, tight-fitting Henley shirt, and flip-flops. I will wear flip-flops until the first snowfall. It truly doesn't matter how cold or hard the ground is. Flip-flops rock. But right now, my feet feel funny since I slept in them. My toes are tingling. I get a cramp in my foot when I stand up and try to slide them off.

I stumble my way over to the door, unlock it, and turn away as they barge in. They aren't alone. Manny is with them too. Manny is hot, proud, and out. He's a gorgeous specimen of a gay man, all six foot three, one hundred and ninety pounds of him. He's dreamy and knows it. He owns it. That's what I love about him.

The first time we all met Manny, he was singing Lionel Ritchie in the shower stall next to us.

In the girls' bathroom.

On an all-girls floor.

He walked out of the shower stall wearing a towel hanging low on his hips. Our jaws collectively dropped as we stared at his perfect abs while he said, "Ladies, nice to meet you. I hope you don't mind, but Shower 4 is now mine. Too much hair and stench downstairs on the ninth floor." He grabbed his toiletry bag and beamed his flawless smile, "Very nice to meet you." He's became a permanent fixture within our group and we couldn't be happier.

Manny storms past me, slams a large brown paper bag onto my desk, flops onto Ginger's bed, and declares, "God, this bed smells stale!" He's practically gagging. She's never here, so I'm sure he just fell into a pile of dust and who knows when she last washed her sheets and comforter.

Next Becca walks in. Becca is gorgeous. Like model gorgeous. She's about as tall as I am at five foot nine inches. But her looks are exotic. Dark olive skin, long dark shiny black hair, and black eyes like onyx. She was the first person that I met during freshman orientation, and we hit it off immediately. We discovered during several deep and very drunken conversations that we both have the same dream when we are sick with a fever. Yes, there is such a thing as a fever dream. It's psychedelic and a mind fuck. Trust me. And she and I dream the same fever dream. Therefore, we are meant to be best friends forever. Fever sisters.

Callie is right behind Becca and skips into the room. She is a surfer girl. Blonde, tan, and beautiful. She grew up at the beach and looks as if she spends every day there still. She's wearing her short jean shorts and tank top. What makes this an odd choice in clothing is that it's November in New Jersey. Not surfer girl weather, and certainly not tank and shorts weather.

I met Callie exactly ten minutes after meeting Becca at orientation when she came in late, skipped into the room, and plopped down at our table. She grinned ear to ear while she squeezed a pink Koosh ball in her hand and started talking over the RA. She said in her not-so-quiet stage whisper, pointing to Becca and me, "This will do – I like you two already! You are both my kind of people. Let's get out of here. Who needs to hear about all of this stuff anyway. It's in the handbook. Let's go get drunk – I have vodka, Everclear, and grape juice." She proclaimed that she's going to be a nurse and smiled from ear to ear. Is this supposed to mean that I should trust her with whatever drink she is going to concoct? She won't let anything mixed with Everclear kill us, will she? With that, she tossed her Koosh ball at the RA, grabbed our hands, and dragged us out of the common room while laughing and skipping. I knew that Callie and I would be forever friends when she held my hair while I puked in the boys' bathroom later that night. Yes, when a friend holds your hair back and can stand the sound of you retching in a smelly, disgusting bathroom, she's a keeper – no doubt.

As all three of them barge into my room, I know that I am going to have to start talking. You see, since *that* night a few weeks ago, I've been aloof. I've tried to avoid being alone with any of them because I've been terrified to say anything. I don't know what to say about what Todd did to me. I'm afraid.

The only thing they know right now is that I left the Halloween party with him that night. I haven't been able to speak about it with anyone. I've completely withdrawn from my best friends, and they have noticed.

Manny gets up with a nauseated look on his face, and I know that he won't be sitting on Ginger's bed again. I begin to arrange my pillows to make more room next to me. He opens the paper bag and pulls out a gallon of pink wine. Don't judge. We are freshmen. It's cheap, and it's pink.

"It's Wednesday, Carly," Manny says, too chipper for my ears at the moment. "Wine Wednesday!"

"What?" I sputter, not prepared for any conversation.

"It's Wine Wednesday. I'm inducting the four of us into this exclusive club. Every Wednesday, Carly's room, nine o'clock. Wine Wednesday." With that, he twists the top off the jug and pours the pink wine into four waiting red Solo cups. He passes them out and nods to all of us.

"A toast. To the Wine Wednesday Club. Where everything we talk about stays in this room. Our conversations are forever in the vault. We agree to listen and not to judge. I love you girls. Now drink to seal the pact."

We all lift our cups. I take a sniff, and it smells sweet. I take a sip, and it's as sweet as it is tart. This is what my grandmother drinks and now I'm drinking it. I feel so cultured.

The room gets quiet, and they all turn to stare at me. I sink further, hoping to disappear into my bed.

Manny continues, "Car, now that we have our pact... treaty... whatever you want to call it, we need to talk. What is going on with you? You haven't gone out to ANY parties since Halloween, and you mope around here all day like your puppy died. Talk. Now." His chipper voice turns stern, commanding.

Becca and Callie's eyes are soft, and Callie's start to glisten as if she's about to cry. *Please don't cry, you're going to push me over the edge.* Becca tries to maintain eye contact with me, but she can't. She chokes on her sip of wine and turns away, swiping at her eyes. *I can't take this, it's like they already know.*

I lose control of my body at this point and start shaking. First, at the shoulders, then my arms, and finally, the rest of my body. I'm about to collapse. Tears aren't yet falling, but I open my mouth in a silent cry. Becca and Callie immediately swarm to either side of me, curling their legs underneath them on my bed.

We sit silently as I try to regulate my breathing, tears threatening to fall. Manny stands in front of us with his arms folded across his broad chest. They're patient. They allow my emotions to build, and I finally let out a wail. The sobbing shakes my entire body. I curl up in the fetal position with Callie smoothing my hair and Becca holding my wrists. Becca moves to kneel on the floor in front of me, her nose practically touching mine. I'm sure she can feel my tears on her face as they roll off my cheeks onto hers. Callie and Becca are warm and close, trying to absorb my grief, anger and apathy.

Manny allows us about ten minutes of this and then grabs all of our drinks and hands them back out.

"The only way this is going to work, Car, is if you talk. So talk," he says.

Callie chimes in. "Honey, whatever you have to say, we're here for you. Please."

Becca's eyes are puffy and red; they're pleading with me. She looks at me and silently nods.

I can't draw this out any longer. I chug the pink wine and then I just blurt it out.

"I was raped on Halloween." I exhale loudly and feel dizzy.

In unison, the three of them suck in their breath and with that most of the air from the room. I don't quite think this was what they expected to hear. Manny's eyes are so wide I can see the bright blue and a large rim of white. His jaw is clenching, and I can see his cheeks pulse with fury. His hands are in fists, and his knuckles are white. Becca is shaking her head and repeating the word 'no'. Callie crawls over to me and wraps her arms around me from behind. She softly whispers into my ear, "It's okay honey. I know, I know, I know." *She knows?* I look at her, and she just shakes her head softly at me and puts her hand on my cheek. "We're all here for you. Tell us what happened, Car. *Please.*"

I take a deep breath and I tell them everything. Everything up to and including the rape. Everything up until I blacked out. Every. Thing. I'm physically drained and exhausted. When I have no more tears to cry, my friends cry them for me.

Manny is the first to say something. "He didn't use a condom."

Statement.

Fact.

"No," I whisper. "No, he didn't." I stifle a sob. I squirm just thinking about having him inside of me, tearing me apart.

Callie immediately jumps in. "Honey, you need to get tested. You need an exam. We'll get you in there first thing tomorrow. It's simple. Discreet. I'll take care of it." Callie is an intern at the on-campus medical clinic. She *will* take care of it. I'm so thankful for this, but terrified at the same time. *What will they find? Am I damaged forever?*

Becca, still holding my hands covered in our joint tears, says, "I'm coming too. We are doing this together. We are *all* getting tested." She smiles softly and squeezes my hands.

I nod. That's about all I can do.

Manny demands, "Carly, you need to tell someone what happened. Campus security. The police."

"No!" I cut him off. "I'm not saying a word to anyone. You are the only ones who can know. I just can't." The tears continue to stream down my cheeks as my friends comfort me. "This has to stay in the vault, Manny. *Please.*" He nods reluctantly and takes a sip of his wine.

We polish off the entire gallon of pink wine as we remain huddled together on my bed for the rest of the night. *In silence.*

# Chapter 3

## Tabitha

*Philadelphia, Pennsylvania*
**Present**
*Age 20*

Dear Emily,

I don't know what to say. I don't feel worthy to be your mother. I'm damaged. More damaged than you could ever imagine. You don't deserve a life with me. You deserve so much more than I can give you.

Please don't hate me. Please don't think that you weren't wanted.

Please don't hate me.

Please.

I gave up my other little girl a few years ago. Your sister, Sara. I didn't know what I was doing then, and I don't know what I'm doing now. I may actually be getting worse.

I'm going to meet Carly in person soon. She's coming to my next ultrasound.

She deserves you and more importantly, you deserve her. She is not damaged. She is perfect in every way.

The first time that I saw her picture in their adoption profile, I knew

22

she would be the perfect mother to you. She is beautiful. I think you are going to look like her. I don't know why. Maybe it's her coloring. She reminds me of what I used to look like. Before...

She is a teacher! Oh Emily, she is so smart, and her smile will make you laugh and giggle. Her presence will put you totally at ease.

She's your Mom and you are so lucky.

I'm jealous of her. Of her life. Of what she is. Of everything that I am not.

I think I hate her a little...

I can't finish the letter. I tear it out of my book, crumple it up, and chuck it across the room. I'm shaking and crying, and my mind is racing. *What am I doing? What are we doing? This is the right thing to do, right?*

My fear and uncertainty have a vise grip on me and I can't escape it. So many doubts. *Too many.*

Seth seems to be handling this so much better than me and this angers me. He has other coping mechanisms that don't involve self-hate and loathing. He's chosen to focus all of his efforts on Kyle and what type of father he's going to be. *Does he wish he was like him?* It's grating on my nerves because all I hear is 'Kyle this' and 'Kyle that'.

"Kyle is going to teach Emily to play guitar as early as possible."

"Kyle is going to get her a piano when she turns seven."

Make. It. Stop.

If I hear any more about what Kyle is going to do, and how great of a father he is going to be to Emily, I might just spit! I know that Seth is enamored by the type of father Kyle is going to be. I actually feel that same way about Carly.

But I'm also feeling jealousy. I'm *jealous* of Carly. Of Kyle.

I'm so angry with myself because I can't cope. Not since Alex...

But Seth seems okay with everything. He isn't experiencing the indecision and fear that I am.

He's okay with the decision to give up our *baby*.

*My* fucking baby.

When I found out I was pregnant, Seth immediately went into full panic mode. He said that he isn't ready to be a father any more than I'm ready to be a mother. A real mother, like Carly.

What makes this even worse is I don't even know *who* the father is. I had unprotected sex with Seth and Alex within days of each other. This situation couldn't possibly get worse for me. For us.

But maybe, deep down, I think I do know. *If only I could be sure without ruining everyone's lives in the process.* If only I could talk to Alex. If only he'd let me explain…

Seth was my savior, *my best friend*. He was here to pick up the broken pieces of me that Alex left behind.

Seth loves me so much, but he's just not ready to take on additional responsibilities. He knows that we can't handle it. *I can't handle it.*

Decision made. We will move on and be happy after it's all over. *Right?*

Carly is perfect. She is going to be the perfect mother, make perfect pancakes, and give Emily the perfect life.

Fucking perfect.

I wish I were perfect.

Fuck.

# Chapter 4

## Carly

Spring Lake, New Jersey
**Present**
Age 29

Dear Emily,

I am so excited to meet you today! I'll see you for the first time during Tabitha's ultrasound.

Oh Emily! I can't wait for you to wrap your tiny fingers around mine. For you to squeeze them and know that I'm here right in front of you.

I have tons of plans to begin furnishing and decorating your room! I hope you like pink because that is going to be a key theme!

I'm overwhelmed with emotion as I write this. I know that Tabitha will not get to experience bringing you home and wrapping you in your soft, fluffy blankets. My heart breaks for her. I can only hope that she finds the peace and happiness that she deserves.

I can't wait to see you today, Emily!

Love and kisses,

Mama

It's eight o'clock in the morning, and I'm so ready for today. Excitement bubbles in my chest almost causing me to squeal. I can't wait to see our precious daughter. I look over at my sleeping husband while a tear silently slides down my cheek as I remember the events leading up to today.

About a month after 'The Call', our home phone rang at the time we planned for our first conference call with Tabitha and Seth.

*Kyle answers the phone after half of a ring. "Hello?" he says and quickly converts the call to speaker.*

*"Hi Carly and Kyle, this is Anna from Home Sweet Home Adoptions, and I have Tabitha and Seth on the line with me as well." I hear the warmth in Anna's voice, and it begins to soothe me, although my feet are bouncing wildly on the floor as I'm planted at the kitchen table.*

*"Hi," I say as my voice cracks. Kyle squeezes my hand and tries to calm me down.*

*Anna continues. "I will be on this call as a silent participant. It's up to you to talk to each other. Ask any questions you want and answer any questions you feel comfortable answering. Okay?"*

*"Yes!" Four voices sound in unison. Tabitha's voice breaks a little and my heart jumps in my chest. Please don't cry.*

*Kyle starts the conversation. "So, Seth? You like music?"*

*I hear Tabitha softly crying in the background, and my heart breaks. I'm glad Kyle jumped in to ask a simple question.*

*"Yes," Seth answers. "I love all kinds of music, but hard rock is my favorite. What type of music do you play?"*

*Kyle chuckles, "Well, I only taught myself how to play five years ago, so I'm still learning. I like to play U2, Foo Fighters, Pink Floyd. I have a wide reach when it comes to likes and dislikes." He's so calm, steady. How is he not freaking out? I'm afraid to open my mouth to say anything.*

*Kyle and Seth continue a conversation about their favorite guitarists, drummers, and bands. They are talking as if they've known each other for years. Laughing like old friends. It's calming me immensely, and I don't hear Tabitha sobbing any longer. Okay, this is good.*

*Once they've reached the end of their epic music conversation, it's quiet for a few moments. The silence seems to last forever and I get the* courage to speak up, "Tabitha?" I hear a quiet voice on the other end of the line say "Yes?"

"Are you okay?" I ask. "Because, you know, it's fine if you're not." I continue. "I can't imagine what you're going through, and the one thing you have to know is that we are so very, very, very thankful. You are giving us a gift. We couldn't be more grateful." I finish. "We absolutely love the name Emily. Thank you for giving her a name."

I hear a quick sob and her voice. "I knew you were perfect as soon as I saw your profile, Carly. You are meant to be her parents."

Then more silence. This is the worst part, we don't know what each other is going to say or do next. Anna jumps back on the line.

"I'm so pleased, guys. This call went exactly as it was supposed to." I can hear the pep in her voice as Kyle and I hold hands across the table and smile at each other.

"The next step is logistics. Tabitha has a doctor appointment scheduled for next Wednesday. Since you are only about an hour away, she really would like you there to see your baby." This is all happening so fast.

Tabitha quickly jumps in. "Yes, Carly, I'd like you there, but...," she trails off for a moment that makes my heart stop. "But it's in a really bad part of Philadelphia, and I understand if you don't want to come into the city." Her voice waivers, unsure.

"Of course I'll come. I have cousins near Philly so I can get some pointers and directions. I will absolutely be there." I say as I smile, my heart racing.

Anna concludes, "So I'll email you the name and address of the doctor and you'll see each other next Wednesday at one o'clock in the afternoon."

And with that, our first conference call is finished.

We hang up our phone and we both take deep breaths, still holding hands.

Kyle speaks first.

"Okay," he says.

"Okay." I'm smiling now.

We jump up, I throw my arms around his neck, and he kisses me so *hard that I can feel it in my toes. He's stroking my hair and pulling me close, devouring me.*

*We break apart to take a breath, and his eyes are glistening when he says, "I can't believe you're going to get to see our little girl next week. I'm jealous."*

*I nod and pull him closer. I keep nodding into his broad chest and squeeze him until he can feel it in his toes. This is one of the best days of our lives and I want to revel in it, and at the same time speed up the clock so we can officially meet our daughter.*

*We remain attached to each other as we go upstairs into our bedroom, where he tenderly and passionately makes love to me all night. We get completely lost in each other and it's perfect.*

I smile as I remember our first phone contact with Tabitha and Seth. I hope that her decision hasn't wavered. I need to see her to know for sure, that Emily will indeed be our daughter in a few short months. I quietly get out of bed trying not to disturb Kyle and rush to take a shower to get ready. I'm anxious to get on the road.

~

I'm dressed and ready to go to Tabitha's ultrasound, and I'm a nervous wreck. I'm going alone. We agreed that it would be a girls-only thing, but I want Kyle with me. I wish he could experience this first with me.

Kyle programs my GPS to get me into Philly by the most direct route. He's anxious, I can tell. He's a little twitchy and laughing nervously. He kisses me tenderly before I leave and says, "Go get 'em, killer." He smacks me softly on my ass and I chuckle. "I'm not going up to bat, dear. I'm going to an ultrasound." He laughs as he closes my car door, placing a light, chaste kiss on my lips. "I love you, say hi to our little girl for me, okay?" My heart smiles as I pull out of our driveway. I watch him disappear in my rearview mirror and my anxiety surfaces again.

The hour drive goes quickly as my mind is racing with the usual questions:

*What if she sees me and doesn't like the way I look?*

*Dear Emily*

*What if she already changed her mind and is going to let me down when I get there?*

*What if she and Seth decided to pick another couple?*

*What if – ugh!*

I have to stop this. If Kyle were here, he would talk me off this ledge and make everything feel alright.

The British voice on my GPS tells me that I've arrived at my destination reminding me that, as usual, Kyle's navigation setup is perfect. I arrive at the clinic about ten minutes early. Tabitha is right. This place is literally in Hell. There's an abandoned building next to the clinic with about a dozen sketchy looking people milling around outside. I see several police officers on foot, patrolling the area and feel a little safer. But not much.

I'm able to park directly across the street from the clinic, thank goodness. The dregs of society are in the surrounding area, and now I really wish that Kyle was here. He has a soft and kind heart, but at six foot four and two hundred and ten pounds of lean muscle, he is certainly intimidating. He makes my five foot nine frame look small and slight.

I enter the clinic and suddenly realize that I have no idea what she looks like. She of course knows what I look like since she's seen our adoption profile, but I'm at a disadvantage. I walk in slowly and scan the room. There is only one couple in the corner huddled together. Okay, she's not here yet.

I sit down and try to relax. I'm early. It's okay. She'll be here.

I hope.

# Chapter 5

## Tabitha

*Philadelphia, Pennsylvania*
**Present**
*Age 20*

I'M ON MY way to the ultrasound and I feel like I'm going to puke. *I'm not ready for this. What is she going to think of me?* She must hate me already, thinking that I'm a terrible person for wanting to give up my child. My flesh and blood. I wring my hands together as the cab prepares to drop me off about a block away from the clinic. I scrounge up change from the bottom of my purse to pay for my fare. I have no fucking clue how I'm going to get home. *Shit.*

I step onto the sidewalk and stare at the clinic that I've been coming to since I first found out that I was pregnant. I begin to feel the same anxiety that I felt on that first visit, and I take a deep breath to try to calm myself.

I'm five minutes late. *Typical.* I can never get anywhere on time. And today of all days. It's a curse. So many things in my life are a curse. *I'm a curse.*

I'm so nervous as I walk up to the door. *What if she doesn't show up? What if she and Kyle decided they don't want my baby?*

I hold my breath as I open the door. As I walk in, I see that Carly is the only person in the waiting room, tapping her feet nervously. Her metallic blue painted toes peep out of her flip-flops. Her long curly hair is pulled away from her face into a loose ponytail with some curls cascading around her narrow face. Her dark brown eyes seem massive against her pale skin. She's dressed casually and comfortably. And she's a nervous wreck.

*Shit.* I made her wait. She probably didn't think I was going to show up. It's written all over her face.

*I suck.*

She raises her head as soon as I walk through the door, and her nervous expression begins to melt. Suddenly, she's warm and bright as a smile transforms her face.

*Perfect.*

I walk in, and she stands, slowly walking toward me as I scribble my name on the patient sign in sheet. The office assistant looks up, nods, and gives me a weird look. She knows. She knows what I'm doing, and she hates me for it. She thinks I'm a terrible person for not wanting to keep my own baby and that I'm a monster. Her eyes burn through me in judgment and I feel like I'm going to puke.

*Stop!* I need to stop these invasive and divisive thoughts. Carly's going to be able to see what a mess I already am.

She doesn't know, and she isn't judging. Is she?

I'm talking to myself. *What's wrong with me?*

I turn to Carly, and she is now only a few feet away from me. She extends her right arm as if she wants to shake my hand, so I extend my hand and she grabs it with both of hers, squeezing. Her eyes meet mine, and they are glistening. *Oh God, please don't cry.* I can't handle this as it is.

"Hi," she says.

"Hi," I say softly, looking away.

We don't have much time to stand here in this awkward stance because the nurse calls me back right away. "Tabitha Fletcher?"

"Y-yes," I stutter. "I'm here and so is my... friend?"

The nurse looks between the two of us, nods her head, and motions for us to go back to the exam room, together.

I lead as Carly follows closely behind, the sound of her flip-flops echoing through the empty hallway.

Once in the exam room, the nurse instructs me to get onto the table and lie down on my back. As she is prepping my stomach with jelly, she begins asking me questions. I'm distracted by the cool, slimy gel and squirm a little on the table.

"How are you feeling today, Tabitha?"

"Fine."

"Any change since your last visit?"

"Nope."

"Any discomfort or discharges?"

*Gross.* "Nope."

"Who is your friend?"

I'm silent for a moment, and Carly looks around the room as if fascinated by all of this equipment. *Did she hear the question?*

"She's the… Um… She's going to be… Um…," I'm struggling with the words and can't seem to say them out loud.

The nurse raises her eyebrow at me and looks between the two of us as the wand hovers above my baby bump.

"She's adopting my baby," I say softly.

"Oh." The nurse replies, and not missing a beat, turns to Carly. "Is this your first?"

Carly replies immediately, "Yes, our first, and a gift. The greatest gift anyone has ever given to us." Her dark chocolate eyes are glistening as she's looking at the monitor. She grabs my hand, taking me off guard and squeezes.

I suck in a breath and lay there silently as the nurse moves the wand around my belly, snapping photos of the baby. My baby. I turn my head away from the monitor; I can't bear to see her.

*Carly's* baby. I can't refer to her as mine any longer, because she's not.

The nurse speaks again. "We already know it's a girl. We found that out at her twenty-week ultrasound. Now that we're getting closer to her due date, we like to keep tabs on the little one and make sure she is growing appropriately."

She smiles at Carly, then at me. *Okay, I can do this. I think.*

She takes some more measurements, wipes my baby bump clean, and takes her gloves off.

"All done. Tabitha, you need to be sure to get your adoption plan in place with Dr. Fisher's assistant as well as the hospital. We want to be sure everyone's wishes are followed." She smiles at both of us and leaves the room.

Carly and I are alone again, and my awkwardness is back. She seems almost relaxed. My stomach is in knots, and I'm petrified that she is silently judging me.

Her demeanor is still. She stands up and offers her hand to help me off of the table. Her hand is warm, and her smile is back.

"Well, that was exciting," she says.

"Yes, it is." I answer. Although it's also bittersweet for me. And terrifying.

As we walk out into the waiting room, I take the printed ultrasound pictures and hand them to her. She seems shocked as she reaches out to take them from me.

"She's your daughter, Carly. You should have these." I press the photos into her palm and pull my hand away quickly.

Her eyes are blinking wildly, holding back tears and she's speechless.

She reaches into her purse and hands me a twenty-dollar bill. She seems embarrassed and nervous about it.

"I want to pay for your transportation to get here and maybe a cup of coffee or something. Here, take this." She quickly shoves the bill into my palm and closes my hand around it. "That's weird, right?" she asks.

Knowing that I need the money to walk out the door, I just stare at her and give her a small smile as I slowly shake my head. "No. I appreciate it. Thank you."

We walk toward the door together and before we walk through, she stops, grabs me, and pulls me into a tight embrace. Her tears are flowing now, and she is shaking as she is holding me. She keeps whispering, "Thank You." She says it at least ten times.

I have no words. I can't say anything. I'm numb.

I push away from her and wipe my own silent tears from my cheeks, nod and walk out the door.

I hail the first cab I see and quickly get in. I don't look back because I know it will break me.

I draw the slightest comfort in knowing that Emily will have a perfect life with Carly and Kyle.

# Chapter 6

## Carly

*New Brunswick, New Jersey*
**Past**
*Age 17*

It's Thursday morning. The Thursday-after-Wine-Wednesday. I'm dragging my ass, immensely hungover. Nausea and dizziness grab me as I look around the room, surveying the damage we did last night. Manny, Becca, and Callie all left my room at various times throughout the night, long after the jug of pink wine was polished off. Our red Solo cups are still piled in my sink and the empty jug sits on my desk, causing my head to pound harder.

I remember that Callie was the last one to leave. Before she left, she whispered in my ear, "I know what you're going through, honey. I love you." She kissed my forehead as I drifted off to sleep.

*She knows what I'm going through?* This will most certainly be a topic for an upcoming Wine Wednesday and I hope to God she never had to experience what I did. I don't wish that on anyone, ever.

Before I started drifting off last night, we agreed to meet at the clinic on campus by ten-thirty this morning. I've already blown off my Biology lab and it looks like I'll miss Sociology too. This is going to continue to be a problem if Wine Wednesday does indeed become a tradition.

I run my fingers through my long curly hair, then wrap it up into a messy bun. I pull on my stretch pants and long-sleeved Nirvana concert t-shirt and step into my flip-flops. I grab a scarf and jacket and head out the door. I'm nervous about where I'm heading and what I might find out when I get there.

The walk across campus is chilly, and I huddle in my jacket to keep warm, wrapping my scarf tighter around my neck. I can't feel my toes and I guess it serves me right, since I'm wearing flip-flops. I'm looking down, trying not to make eye contact with anyone and end up walking right into a wall.

A person.

A wall of a person.

I stiffen as soon as I realize who it is.

*Todd.*

I nearly vomit in my mouth and start to back away. His eyes are like razors as he looks down at me and grins. "Hey. You?" I expect to see a black tooth, but his teeth are back to normal. I see that smudged black tooth every single time I close my eyes.

After what he did to me, he still doesn't know my fucking name.

I stare blankly at him. "Carly, it's Carly. *Remember?* Halloween. *Remember?*" I don't know where my attitude and strength is coming from, but I'm glad I'm not cowering away from him. I can't let him know how much he hurt me.

He stiffens a little bit, chuckles nervously, and says, "Yeah, uh, Carly. Right. Pussycat. Hot night. I'll see you around."

He saunters off, continuing the conversation with one of his buddies.

So I vomit. Not on myself, but in the nearest garbage can.

Fucking pink wine.

Fucking Todd.

I arrive at the clinic just as Becca is walking up. She runs up to me and hugs me and I hope she doesn't smell the puke on my breath. "This is going to be great, Car. Just great. You're going to get tested, get a clean bill of health, and we're all going to be fine. Just fine." She's nervous.

I'm not sure if she's nervous for me, all of us, or herself. I can't quite read her, so I say, "Yeah. I'm not so worried about you guys because you, Callie, and Manny are always so careful. But Todd? I don't know, he probably sneezes venereal disease." I chuckle anxiously and wonder why I'm even attempting to joke about my rape. I'm scared to death.

We walk in to find that Callie and Manny are already there.

Manny approaches us and gives us each a quick kiss. "Ladies, I'm already done. Left my deposit. I'm late for Astronomy. Bye." He flashes a tight smile and waves behind his back. He seems nervous himself and I realize this group STD test pact was a bad idea. *What if we all get bad news?*

I muster up some courage. "Okay," I say. "Let's do this."

We walk into the waiting room, and Callie immediately goes behind the counter. Since she's interning here, she already signed us in, and even completed most of our paperwork. Besides my social security number and my insurance ID, everything else is complete. I glance up at her with a questioning look.

"I got here really early. I'm trying to make it easy and painless for you honey." She smiles, and I try to relax. Yes, she *is* making this easy. What's *not* easy about getting your insides scraped with a cold speculum between your legs?

Right.

Easy.

I barely have time to fill my social security number in when another nurse comes out and calls my name. Callie and Becca look at each other nervously. "Good luck," they say in unison. They both smile softly at me, and I quickly look away. This is worse than what I imagine a walk of shame to be like.

I follow the nurse into the exam room and listen to her instructions. "Take all of your clothes off and put on this gown. Lie on the table and wait for the Physician's Assistant, Jean. She'll be in shortly." She quickly leaves the room, closing the door behind her.

I do as she says and immediately get the chills. The paper gown is open in the back and I'm freezing. It barely covers me and when I sit on the table, I hear a rip. *Crap.*

Jean, the PA, is punctual and comes in almost right away. I fidget on the table, trying to adjust the paper gown.

She has a clipboard with her and a pen with Mickey Mouse ears. *Really.*

This is certainly not a Disney moment. The irony isn't lost on me.

The interrogation begins.

"When was your last period?"

"Last week, the twenty-second."

"Are you sexually active?"

I pause. "Yes? I mean does one time count?"

"Of course. Have you had intercourse?"

"Yes," I say quietly.

"Are you experiencing any discomfort?"

"No. I mean, not now."

I am starting to get shaky at this point because I know where this is going.

"What do you mean, not now? Have you had painful intercourse?"

"Yes," I whisper and a tear slides down my cheek.

PA Jean looks up, and her face softens. She frowns and asks, "Did something happen to you, Carly? Can you tell me about it?"

I'm silent for what seems like forever. She doesn't budge. She only holds my stare longer.

"Yes. I had sex, um, and I didn't want to... "

At this point, PA Jean gingerly places her clipboard on the table next to her and sits down in the chair next to me. She keeps her hand on my ankle and says, "Carly, whatever you say is confidential. We protect your privacy no matter what. You can tell me what happened, when it happened, and let me try to help you."

I tell her. Not everything. I didn't tell her about the dozen Swedish Fish shots I took or that I passed out immediately following the rape.

I *did* tell her that he forced himself on me, in me, and *it* hurt. A Lot. Burned.

I tell her that I had blood on me the next day and lots of dried fluid on my thighs. I tell her that the bruising on my thighs and wrists finally disappeared last week, and I am finally starting to feel normal. *What is normal?*

After a brief silent pause, she takes a deep breath, and her eyes soften even more.

"Carly, first, what he did was wrong. Very wrong and you can prosecute."

"NO!" I can't believe that word came out of my mouth. "No, I can't," I continue. "I want this to be over with and behind me. Everyone saw me leave with him. I'm a freshman! I don't want this to follow me around for four years."

I'm sobbing now; snot and tears are dribbling down my chin and face. I can taste my salty tears, and I'm starting to feel nauseous.

"Okay Carly." Her hand is still on my ankle. "So let's move on, shall we?"

She begins to explain the exam that I'm about to get in detail. I am not ready for this. I don't want to be touched or prodded there. I keep thinking about the burning sensation caused by Todd forcing himself on me. Into me. I'm so apprehensive. I know that Jean isn't going to hurt me, but I feel so damaged and violated already.

She pauses and waits for me to calm down. I do my best and then she proceeds to perform my pelvic exam. I relax as much as I can, and it's over relatively quickly. *Thank God.*

When it's over, she pushes away from the table, takes off her gloves, and makes some notes on her clipboard. Her warm smile finds my face again.

"I didn't see any internal bruising or tearing, so that's good. However, it has been a few weeks, so you obviously healed over that time. We'll take a urine sample to test for pregnancy, but since you had your period just last week, I'm confident you won't be pregnant. I've also taken internal samples and will call you in a week when the results are in. Now, if you're ready, I'd like to talk to you about a birth control method that suits you."

"Birth control?" My heart skips and I tense up.

I hesitate.

"I haven't had sex since–" I stop.

Breathe.

Continue.

"Since it happened, and I'm not in a relationship…," my voice trails off.

"Carly, I don't want to force anything on you that you don't want. Just think about it and let me know. Okay?" She smiles.

She hands me pamphlets on all of the various pills, shots, and implants. I immediately decide to toss this in the nearest garbage can as soon as I'm out of sight. I don't need any of this because no one will ever touch me again.

Then she hands me a business card with a phone number on it. The school counselor. Great. A Shrink. *Just what I need.*

"Make this phone call, Carly. Dr. James is a wonderful lady, and she is a great listener. Please consider it. She can help you deal with all of the questions and feelings you are experiencing."

She backs away slowly, turns, and leaves the room.

*What the hell just happened?*

I clean myself up, get dressed, and walk slowly out of the room. I don't want to see anyone and wish I could just bolt directly outside.

Callie and Becca are both waiting by the nurses' station for me, concern on their faces. Becca is first to reach out and gives me a hug. I can tell she's been crying, and I make a note to add it to the next Wine Wednesday agenda.

Callie looks at me and says, "Okay?" She smiles at me with her eyes. Becca squeezes my hand.

"Okay." I lie.

Callie goes back to work, so Becca and I walk back to our dorm with our arms looped through each other. In silence.

I'm not okay.

# Chapter 7

## Tabitha

*Portland, Oregon*
**Past**
*Age 19*

*Dear Sara,*

*I'm sorry.*

*I'm so sorry.*

*My baby.*

*I couldn't keep you and Tony didn't want you.*

*I'm so sorry. You're better off. You didn't deserve to be born into this life.*

*Forgive me. I can't forgive myself. So please, I need you to forgive me.*

*I love you.*

I'm about to sign the letter as I hear a noise below the apartment. A loud clunking noise barreling up the stairs causing my heart to pound out of my chest.

*Tony.*

I turn off the light, crumble the letter, and shove it under my pillow. It's after midnight. I quickly close my eyes and pretend to be asleep.

I hear the apartment door open, and I can already smell the smoke and filth on him.

He owns the club downstairs where I work. I'm a cocktail waitress in a sleazy strip club, and Tony is my boss, my baby-daddy and my captor. He terrifies me.

When he found out I was pregnant, he demanded that I give up the baby. He's Catholic and doesn't believe in abortion. He also hates children.

But he believes in kicking the ever-living shit out of me any chance he can get.

If I don't have dinner on the table on time. I get the shit kicked out of me.

If I don't roll his dress socks the right way. I get the shit kicked out of me.

It's never-ending and I can't physically handle another beating.

I squeeze the letter under my pillow and think of my daughter. I handed Sara over to an adoption attorney two weeks ago. I don't know where she is or who adopted her. I didn't have a choice. I signed away full parental rights. I was desperate. I needed to protect her from the life that I'm living. Tony arranged it. It's done, and now I feel so empty. Gutted. My baby girl is gone, and I'll never know her. She'll never know me. She'll be better off, but right now, I can't get over the loss of my little girl.

Tony controls me. I'm stuck here in hell, with no way out. He won't let me work in the club again until I get my figure back. I only gained seventeen pounds during my entire pregnancy, and I'm smaller now than I was before the baby. He doesn't like it though. My body. And he reminds me of it daily when he batters me.

I'm pretending to be asleep when he stumbles into the room. *Ugh,* I smell the cigarette smoke, booze, and stale cologne. The usual.

He loudly flicks on the florescent light and kicks the foot of the bed.

"Waaake uuup!" he slur-yells.

My heart pounds harder and I suck in a breath. I start to stir, pretending to wake up from a deep sleep, hoping to draw his sympathy.

I squint and see that he's inebriated.

Completely drunk.

*God help me.*

"Tony," I say quietly.

"Geeet uuup, bitch!" Funny, he pronounces 'bitch' perfectly, but slurs everything else.

"I'm up, I'm up!" I slowly sit up and lean against the headboard. I'm trapped against the bed and terrified of what he's going to do next. *Shit.*

This isn't going to be good.

"I neeeed you to do something for me," he continues to slur, "now!"

He grabs me by my ankles and twists me around so that I'm on my stomach. My arms flail, trying to pull away from him, but it's no use. He forces his weight onto my back, and he is breathing heavily into my ear. My breathing becomes labored with the pressure of his massive body on my back. The stench from the alcohol is overwhelming, and I can practically taste it. I'm nauseous and can taste the bile rising in my throat.

"You're gonna get pretty, right now." He burps; I taste more bile.

"You're gonna go downstairs into the private party room, aaand you're gonna give one of my best customers a blow job." He says 'blow job' directly into my ear with his hot breath and some of his spit drips onto me.

"Tony, no, please!" I beg. Plead. *Holy shit.*

What's going on? He's never asked me to do anything like this before. I've only ever been allowed to be with him. *This can't be happening.*

He gets up, grabs the back of my hair, and pulls me off the bed. The pain shoots through my skull and down my spine. He spins me around, pushes me up against the wall, and a pocketknife suddenly appears. His drunk, shaky hand presses it into my cheek. He slices me as he smiles sadistically.

The cut is deep and the side of my face burns.

My blood is dripping into my mouth, and it tastes like tin and rust. I gag, and suddenly, his hand is wrapped around my throat.

"You do what I say, bitch!"

*Slap!*

My other cheek now burns from his strike.

His hand moves back to my throat. Squeezing. Choking me.

He's cutting off my air supply now, and I gasp, trying to fill my lungs with air. He's going to kill me this time. I need to do something. I can't die like this.

My arms are flailing wildly, and my fingers brush against something on the dresser. Hard, round. Heavy. It's a paperweight. Desperate, I grab hold and swing it at the back of his head as hard as I can. *Thud!*

He drops like a stone.

I gasp and hold my breath, kicking him a little with my foot. He doesn't move.

I don't care if he is dead or alive. I just need to get out of here. I'm trembling as I scramble for my clothes and grab my duffle bag. I stuff everything and anything I can into the bag.

Then I go back to Tony. He's out and he's breathing.

Not dead.

*Shit.*

A lot of blood gushes and pools in his greasy hair.

I reach into his pocket and pull out his wallet.

Empty.

*Fuck. Shit. Fuck.*

I reach into his other pocket.

*Jackpot.*

It's a wad of bills. I don't know how much. I don't care.

I run out of the apartment and into the empty alley behind our building.

And.

I.

Just.

Run.

*Dear Emily*

I'm free.

I'm nineteen years old. I gave my baby girl away two weeks ago. I'm now completely alone.

But I'm free.

I taste more blood as it trickles down my cheek.

I smile.

# Chapter 8

## Carly

*New Brunswick, New Jersey*
**Past**
*Age 18*

*BEEP BEEP BEEP*

I pull the covers off of my head and shoot my arm out toward my night table.

*BEEP BEEP BEEP*

That noise! I slam my hand on top of my alarm clock to silence it. Light fills my room and I know I slept too late.

I turn my head, nine-thirty. *Crap.* I missed Bio. Again.

I sit up, stretch, and look out the window. It's snowing, and it looks so peaceful. I take a deep breath, stretch some more and make my way out of my room to the bathroom. It's quiet in the hallway. Of course, everyone else is in class while I blow off Bio. Oh well, I think Professor Martin likes me. She believed my lie when I told her that I had the chicken pox and was sent home for a week when I missed the last Bio Lab. She's so sweet. She's going to give me time to make up the lab so that I can get full credit for it. *What will be my excuse this week?* I feel bad telling her all of these lies, but I can't bring myself to do much. I need more time.

I relieve myself in the bathroom and turn on the water in the second shower stall. My shower stall. When our schedules sync up, Becca, Callie, and sometimes Manny and I all time our showers together. It's a great time to catch up. It's also a great time for us to innocently check out Manny's abs. We can usually be heard belting out a few tunes (you always sound better singing Bon Jovi in a shower stall). We have assigned shower stalls for each of us. Becca is #1. I'm #2. Callie is #3, and Manny is #4. I wish my friends were here, now. I want to get lost in song and laugh, not deal with what I'm about to do.

I leave the bathroom after I start the water to go back to my room to get my toiletries. It takes forever for the water to get hot.

As I'm walking back to the showers, Denise, our resident advisor, stops me.

"Carly!" She's so chipper that sometimes I want to strangle her, today especially.

"Good morning, Denise." I say as I keep walking, away from her.

"Happy Birthday!" she yells.

*Shit.*

It's my birthday.

I'm finally eighteen years old. I'm one of the youngest in my freshman class. I skipped second grade because I was a literary genius according to the private school where my parents sent me. I've always been the youngest in my class and my group of friends. I was the last to get my driver's license, and I will be the last to turn twenty-one.

"How…?" I start to ask.

"I'm your *Resident Advisor*, silly. I have your housing records. Of course I know that it's your birthday."

"Oh. Thanks." I keep walking to the showers.

"We're having a social tonight in the lounge to celebrate! Be there at seven o'clock sharp. Cookies and hot chocolate! Yay!" She skips away. *Skips.*

I will so *not* be going to the lounge tonight to celebrate.

I step into the bathroom, and it's now filled with steam. I undress, get into the shower stall, and turn the water temperature up. I need to feel the burn to make me forget where I have to be in one hour.

Today I go back to the clinic to find out if what Todd did to me left a mark.

*I don't want to know.*

~

I dress in my baggy jeans and favorite U2 concert t-shirt. My skin is still pink from the shower. I'm about to put my coat on when there is a knock on my door. Callie, Becca, and Manny are all in class. At least, they should be. *Who could it be?*

I open the door and suck in my breath. *Whoa.* Hotness is standing there. Tall. Male. Hotness.

I'm certain that my jaw is hanging obnoxiously open. Standing in my doorway is the most gorgeous guy I have ever seen. Tall, dusty blond hair, piercing blue eyes, and tall. *Did I say tall?*

"Hey," he says. "Are you Carly Sloan?"

"Yeah," I say in my best New Jersey accent. *What?*

"I mean, yes, I'm Carly Sloan, of the Jersey Shore Sloans." *What the hell am I saying?*

*I'm such a dork.*

I can feel my cheeks flush even more than they already were. *Why am I so flustered?*

"Good. Glad I found you. Your RA, Denise, said you were here."

*Why is he looking for me?* Wait, this is a joke. Someone sent him as a joke. A stripper-gram. Birthday jingle. It's a joke. It has to be.

"Okay. Get on with it," I say with an annoyed tone in my voice as I cross my arms over my chest.

He looks confused by my reaction and continues. "Professor Martin was concerned that you missed Biology Lab today and wanted to be sure you were over the chicken pox." He's now smirking because clearly he has figured out that I don't have them. *Crap.* I'm suddenly embarrassed that I thought he was about to break out in song. *Or worse.*

"I'm the new teaching assistant for her Bio Lab, and she was hoping that I could help you catch up since you've been so sick." He now has a full-on grin and his perfect teeth are blinding me. *He's making fun of me.*

"What are you insinuating?" I pause. "And who are you again?"

Dear Emily

"I'm Kyle. Kyle Finnegan. And I'm not insinuating anything. Clearly, you have been so sick the past few weeks you haven't been able to make it to Biology. Professor Martin has a soft spot for you and wants to be sure you get caught up. Wow, chicken pox. Really cleared up fast." He scans my face, his sarcastic tone is obvious.

*Jerk.*

"Yes, they did, as a matter of fact." This lie is going to kill me. "And I didn't get any on my face. I had them in places you can't see…," I trail off. *Shit.*

His blue eyes get darker as he gives my body a once over and he just nods. "Yeah, I'm sure." Another smirk. I'm caught.

"So, what do you want?" I ask defensively as I start to push past him and out into the hallway. "I have to be somewhere in ten minutes."

"Obviously you're not going to class," he accuses.

"No, I have an appointment. What else do you want?" I'm very pissed now.

He pushes a folder at me. "Professor Martin wanted me to bring you copies of her lectures and lab assignments for the past two weeks. And for me to set up a time with you to do the lab assignment from this morning." He shoves the folder at me, and I grab it.

"I don't understand," I say.

"What don't you understand? She wants to help you. Period. So let her. She doesn't do this often. You're lucky she isn't failing you already. Get it?" Now he's getting annoyed.

"Fine," I state in my bitchiest tone possible, unsure of why I'm even causing friction between us. I haven't been alone with a guy since… Todd. But Kyle doesn't seem anything like Todd. His face is serene, gentle. *I need to stop being a bitch.*

"Fine," he states back.

His blue eyes flicker and his face relaxes. *He has kind eyes.* I relax a little and feel drawn to him somehow. I shouldn't be feeling like this after what Todd did to me. *But his eyes are so kind, soothing.*

"I - I have to go now," I stammer, "I'm going to be late for my appointment."

"Here." He hands me a folded piece of paper. "It's my phone number and my lab hours. Along with some suggested times to complete your missed assignments." He places it in my hand and folds my fingers around it.

I quiver when he touches me. It's like an electrical current runs from my palm straight to my belly. *Whoa.* I may just melt, and I don't want him to let go.

"Oh, okay." I can't say much else. I'm stunned and tongue-tied at the same time.

His smile returns as he winks at me. I pull my hand away and stuff the paper into my pocket, my hand trembling.

"Call me to set up the lab work, and I'll let Professor Martin know that you're almost over your chicken pox." He puts his hands into his pockets and walks toward the elevators.

"Wait!" I yell after him.

I run a little bit to catch up. "I'm going your way." I smile.

We ride the elevator in silence, and I can hear his every breath. I'm sure he can hear my heart beating wildly in my chest. Does he feel this, whatever it is? I shouldn't be this flustered over a guy that I just met. *This isn't right.*

We arrive at the first floor, and he gestures for me to get off first. Wow, what a gentleman. My standards may not be that high, but really, I'm touched by his chivalry.

We walk out of the elevator, and he turns back to me, smiling. "Happy Birthday."

"How?" I'm stunned. What is he? Clairvoyant?

"The sign above the door to your room. It said 'Happy Birthday Carly!'"

"Oh. Right. Thanks." *Denise.*

"Talk to you soon?"

"Yes!" I exclaim. I take a breath. "Yes," I say again more quietly. "I'll call you to set up the lab. And thanks for everything." I'm thankful knowing that he's going to keep my secret from Professor Martin, who has the power to fail me.

He walks away as I stand here gawking after him.

*I'm going to be late.*

I start jogging in the opposite direction toward the clinic.

As I'm running up the steps, Callie is walking out. "There you are!" She looks worried.

"Sorry." I'm gasping, trying to catch my breath. Although I try to jog a few times a week, I just ran about a mile at a speed I'm not used to running. I'm totally sucking wind. I picture Kyle and his dusty blond hair and smile. "Something detained me."

"C'mon." She takes my hand and pulls me into the clinic. "Are you alright?" she asks, curious.

I nod and let her guide me into the clinic.

PA Jean is standing in the waiting room. As soon as she sees me, she opens the door to the hallway that leads to the exam rooms. "Carly, we're ready for you."

"Okay," I say meekly and follow her. Callie's soft smile is the last thing I see as I walk toward the exam room.

I hop up onto the exam table, and PA Jean sits in the chair closest to me.

"Carly." She starts talking, and her expression tells me that I'm about to find out something that I'm not going to like. I tense up and blink slowly, trying to calm myself.

Not.

Good.

"As I expected, your pregnancy test was negative."

I sigh and take a breath. "Okay, that's good, right?" I say, my voice wavering.

"However, we found some additional things when we ran your blood work and cervical samples."

*Oh no.*

My heart is racing and is in my throat at this point. I start to sweat and rub my hands back and forth on the tops of my thighs. The friction from my jeans is making my palms burn.

"Carly, you've tested positive for chlamydia. Your levels are quite high, and we need to start treating you immediately. If we even got to it in time," she says through tight lips. *What?* I feel faint and I almost ask her to repeat herself.

"Here are some pamphlets on chlamydia that will tell you what it is. It can be completely symptom-free, but it can cause serious complications to your reproductive tract."

I don't know what to say. I'm stunned. Chlamydia? What. The. Hell. Fucking Todd.

I feel sick.

I stop rubbing my hands on my jeans and take the pamphlet. I don't look at it. I just fold it into a small enough square to shove in my jacket pocket. I start to hop off of the exam table. *I need to get out of here.* "So if that's it, I'll just be going," I say quietly. I can't stay here any longer; the room is starting to close in on me.

"Carly, sit down," PA Jean says sternly.

I do as I'm told and hop back up on the table. I don't make eye contact with her as I stare out the window at the still-falling snow.

"Carly, we need to talk about treatment. I'm prescribing you antibiotics to take for the next thirty days. I'd still like you to consider birth control medication or other methods of protection."

"But…," I stop. What's the use? I should talk to her about it and find out my options.

She continues. "Birth control pills may help counteract some of the side effects of chlamydia. It can help regulate your period and menstrual flow. Sometimes chlamydia can cause scarring in the uterus and fallopian tubes and going on birth control can help ease any discomfort."

"Okay," I'm numb and will say yes to anything. *I just need to get out of here.*

She hands me two prescriptions. One for antibiotics, the other for birth control. She then hands me a paper bag.

"Three months' worth of birth control pills are in here to get you started. Fill the prescription when you need it," she says. "And finally, if you become intimate with anyone while you're taking the antibiotics, please use a condom, in order to protect your partner from infection."

Really? As if I'm going to have sex after all of this.

I grab the bag, hop off the table and walk toward the door.

"Carly?" Jean asks.

I turn to look at her.

"Have you considered talking to Dr. James?" she asks.

"I haven't even thought about it, Jean." I say sternly. I can't deal with this right now.

"Please talk to her, Carly. At least, please consider it?" she begs.

"Fine."

I walk out the door. Through the waiting room. Past Callie, her eyes worried and wide.

Out into the snow.

Happy.

Fucking.

Birthday.

# Chapter 9

## Tabitha

*Philadelphia, PA*
**Past**
*Age 19*

It's been three weeks since I escaped from Hell. Three weeks since I got away from that pig, Tony. Three weeks since I became free.

Five weeks since I gave up my little girl.

*Sara.*

My heart pulls in my chest and I contemplate all that I've been through. I've lived with nineteen years of emptiness, despair. Nothing has ever gone right for me. I wish I could have a normal life. Maybe I can build a new life, erasing all that has happened to me. *Yeah, right.*

I left Oregon in the dust. The wad of money that I took from Tony's pocket was the mother lode.

Four thousand five hundred dollars. More money than I've ever seen in one place.

I know that if he ever gets his hands on me again, he will kill me. I've never seen him carry this much money on him before, so this must have been for something significant. Shit. I don't even care. It's mine now, and I'm so far away he won't find me.

*I hope.*

I took several busses across the country, trying to cover my tracks.

I didn't spend enough time in any one place to enjoy myself or sightsee. I just wanted to get to Philadelphia, Pennsylvania as fast as I could. My hometown.

I was able to rent an efficiency apartment on the north end of Philly. Not the greatest area, but it's some place that I could afford and call home.

*Home.*

I need to make this feel like my home.

I found a job waitressing three nights a week at a diner two bus stops away from my apartment. Again, not in the best part of the city, but it's a job. I also found a second job in a small bookstore. I worked it out so my shifts for both don't overlap. I need to keep adding to this little nest egg that Tony so graciously started for me.

I cringe. What a monster.

I don't know why I spent so many years with Tony. Why I didn't try to escape sooner. Being a prisoner was not my choice, but I could have chosen to fight sooner.

I was desperate and ran away from foster home after foster home. I made it across the country when I was seventeen years old and wound up in Portland, Oregon. The first place I came across was Tony's club. I lied to the manager about my age. He only cared about my tits and hired me on the spot. This was my first mistake.

The moment that Tony saw me working the tables near the stage, he approached me and said that I was something 'special'. Yeah, special enough to fuck and then beat the shit out of on a regular basis. But what did I know? I had a roof over my head and started saving enough money to potentially get my own place.

He talked me into renting the apartment above the club. He knew I needed a cheap place to stay and how could I turn down two hundred dollars per month rent? Little did I know what would follow. I became trapped and had to endure daily beatings and sexual abuse. He stole everything that I had saved and locked me up in the apartment. I became a prisoner with no way out.

I shake my head to snap myself out of it. *It's over now.*

I'm starting my new life. I need to move on.

I touch my cheek where Tony cut me. I have a jagged scar about four-inches long that's still healing. One day, when I have enough money, I'm going to get it fixed and erased. I don't want this souvenir to carry around and wear like a badge for all to see. It's disgusting and a reminder of what I am. Of who I am. *Of what I've done.* I'm marked, damaged.

I'm working at my favorite place on earth, the bookstore. Nothing smells better than a crisp, new book. I could inhale the scent of these books all day. Ah. *Yes, I'm weird.* The bookstore is quiet today as it is almost every day and I'm here by myself while Kirsten, the owner, is out to lunch.

As I'm arranging the latest books to display, I hear the door chimes jingle.

Not turning around, I yell, "I'll be right with you."

I stack a few books on a shelf and turn my head toward the front of the store.

I see a guy standing by the front counter, and he's playing with the bookmarks that are hanging from the metal hooks on the small display case. He's actually *playing* them as if they were *instruments.* He's weaving his fingers back and forth against the strings of the hanging bookmarks, and I swear his lips are moving, silently singing a song to the music he's creating with those bookmarks.

"Excuse me." I stare at his lips while trying to figure out the words he's mouthing.

He stops abruptly and snaps out of the creative trance he's in. I almost apologize for disturbing him and shake my head. *What's wrong with me?*

He turns to look at me, and I immediately start stuttering. "How... how can... can I help you?" His eyes are so dark grayish-black that I can almost see my reflection in them. He's beautiful. Not too tall, just about six feet. Jet-black hair, a little long and spiked on the top. Pale skin. Thin, but not too thin. The tattoos on his arms make them look like he has sleeves under his tight black t-shirt. He's wearing black jeans and black Chuck Taylors.

I have now completely lost the ability to speak, intrigued by him.

"Yeah," he says. "I'm looking for a music book." His voice is soft, soothing.

"Oh," I answer. "What kind of music book? Instructional? A certain instrument?"

He huffs a little. "No. I mean a book that I can *write* music in," he answers, looking down at the floor.

*He's a musician.*

My eyes glaze over, and I don't speak. I just stare.

At him.

"So?" he says. "Do you have any?"

I snap out of it and shake my head back and forth as if to shake cobwebs from my hair.

"Um, no. We don't have music ledgers. I'm sorry." And I really am sorry.

Like really sorry.

I couldn't be more sorry.

I almost say I'm sorry again because that's how sorry I am.

I shake my head.

"Okay, thanks anyway." He turns to leave.

"Wait!" I yell. I don't want him to leave.

*Think, Tabby.*

I grab the three-subject notebook that I was using to take inventory earlier this morning, open it up and rip out the pages that I used. I thrust the notebook at him and say, "Here, use this."

He looks at me funny and turns around. I inhale as he wraps his hand around the end of the notebook, brushing his fingers along mine. His touch is soft, comforting. Across the knuckles of his right hand are tattooed letters that spell E-P-I-C. His rough, calloused fingers feel divine.

"You're giving me your notebook?" he asks almost incredulously.

"Well, yeah." I answer back.

"Cool," he says with a slight chuckle. Then he smiles at me, and my knees almost collapse. "Thanks."

He hesitates before he takes the notebook from my hands, and he stares at me. He's squinting his eyes, trying to figure me out. I realize that I'm doing the same and quickly look away. *Why am I so drawn to him?*

"Well." He pulls the notebook and I release it. "I've gotta run. But…"

"What?" I interrupt him.

He continues. "My band is playing at The High Note on Friday night at nine. Why don't you come and I can buy you a drink? You know. To thank you for the notebook?" He smiles nervously and shifts uncomfortably.

I'm not twenty-one. I have no chance of getting into The High Note. *Shit.* I also realize that I have a shift at the diner that I'm supposed to work.

"Yes. I'll be there." I answer, trying to figure out a way to make it work.

"Great," he says, more relaxed. "I'll leave your name at the door. You should have no trouble getting in."

"Okay," I say quietly.

He smiles. "I'm Alex. Alex Treadway."

"Hi Alex. I'm Tabitha. Tabby. Tabby Fletcher," I stammer, embarrassed.

"Okay, Tabitha. Tabby. Fletcher. See you Friday night," he says as he turns and walks out the door.

*Alex.*

I turn to the bookmarks that he was so magically playing, and swipe my hand through them. I swear I feel a vibration between my fingertips and hear the music that he created.

I think of the tattoo across his fingers.

E-P-I-C.

I smile.

Yes, meeting him certainly was.

# Chapter 10

## Carly

Spring Lake, New Jersey
**Present**
Age 29

Dear Emily,

Time is just flying by! We're getting ready for you my sweet little girl.

Your room has been painted (pink!) and your furniture has been ordered. I already have a rocking chair, and it's the only piece of furniture in your room right now. I'm sitting in it as I write this letter to you. I feel like I can already smell you and feel you in this room.

Tonight, your Daddy painted your name onto the wall above where your dresser is going to be. He spent over three hours on this project because he wanted it to be perfect.

When he was done, he stood back, stared at the letters, and just nodded his head. He said, "Yes, Emily. You belong here."

He's so right, sweetie. You do belong here.

We can't wait.

I'm having lunch with Tabitha today, and I hope she's okay. She's always in my thoughts and it pains me to think about what she's going through. She loves you, Emily. With all of her heart. She wants you to have the *life that she can't give you.*

*We're going to make her so proud and so happy with her decision. We've made that promise to her. Our Promise. We promise to love you and keep you safe forever.*

*Love and kisses,*

*Mama*

I close my journal and lay it across my lap. It's Sunday morning, and Kyle is out jogging. If I'm going to make it in time to meet Tabitha in Philadelphia for lunch, I need to get moving. I wish that Kyle was able to come with me, but Tabitha once again insisted that it just be the two of us. I don't understand why she doesn't want to meet Kyle just yet, but I have to respect her wishes.

I stand up and place my journal on the chair that I was sitting in. I turn around and hug myself with my arms wrapped tight around my sides. I survey the room and close my eyes, picturing the room full of furniture and stuffed toys. Princess dolls and dollhouses. A smiling little girl with brown hair and eyes with the rosiest cheeks and the cutest dimple.

I pause to remember the day last year that we found out we couldn't have children of our own.

*Kyle and I sit across the desk from our reproductive endocrinologist, Dr. Banks. We have now attempted intrauterine insemination three times and in-vitro fertilization five times. All unsuccessful. During our last cycle, Dr. Banks ran some additional tests to try to figure out what was going on. Today we are about to find out those results.*

*"Kyle. Carly." His gaze moves between us.*

*"I'm afraid the news isn't good." His face softens as he gently frowns.*

*We both take a deep breath as Kyle grabs my hand and squeezes tight. He rubs his thumb along my knuckles softly.*

*"As you know, during your last cycle, we tested the embryos that you produced." He pauses to breathe. "Those embryos were all tainted. Tainted with bad DNA and chromosomal abnormalities. The stage that these embryos were in indicates with a high probability that your eggs,*

*Dear Emily*

Carly, are extremely poor quality."

Tears are now welling up in my eyes and about to spill over. Kyle shifts in his seat and moves closer to me, puts his arm around my shoulder and pulls me to him. My shoulders are shaking now, and I'm about to start heaving with sobs. Kyle knows this and just holds on.

Dr. Banks takes a pause and allows my emotions to settle.

Once I've regained my composure, I whisper, "Why?"

Dr. Banks raises his eyebrow. "We've talked about the damage done to Carly's reproductive tract caused by the infection she had when she was eighteen." He turns to look into my eyes. "The scarring is extensive. What I didn't realize was that the scarring also affected your ovaries. I'm almost certain that this is causing a rapid decline in your egg quality, which in turn will produce very poor quality embryos." He pauses to let us digest this statement.

"It's my fault," I whisper. "My fault." I feel as if my insides are becoming cold and hollow. I'm being gutted by an invisible force.

Kyle grabs my hand and squeezes, turns to me and says, "Carly."

I can't listen to this any longer. I stop him. "Stop! I just can't."

Dr. Banks clears his throat. "Carly, there is no blame or fault here. What happened to you back then is not your fault. Believe me. There are other options we can discuss to help you have the family you want. The family that you both deserve."

"No." I state. Matter-of-fact.

"Carly," Kyle says. "Let's hear him out."

I breathe deeply and reluctantly nod in agreement. "Continue," I say softly.

Dr. Banks continues. "We have the option to use donor eggs here. I'm very optimistic that this would work well. The majority of your scarring is in your fallopian tubes, external to your uterus. I'm still confident that you could carry a baby full term."

"Donor eggs?" I ask incredulously. "Someone else's egg with Kyle's sperm?"

He nods.

"No." I state. Again, matter-of-fact.

"Carly, let's discuss this at home," Kyle responds.

"There is nothing more to discuss, Kyle. I'm done with doctors. Done with medicine. Done." I start to stand up.

"Dr. Banks, you have been nothing but patient, kind, and informative, but I just can't do this anymore." I walk toward the door and hold my hand out for Kyle to join me.

He turns to Dr. Banks. "We'll be in touch and thank you."

We walk out the door.

We're silent until we're in the car. He turns to me. "Carly, let's consider what he said."

"No!" I yell. "I can't! We have been going through medical procedures for the past four years. I can't be poked and prodded any more. NO. MORE!"

I start sobbing now, and it feels good. For once, my sobbing feels like a real release. I'm ending this chapter of my life, and I need to move on to what is next. What that is, I don't know at this point, but it isn't more needles or turkey basters.

My sobbing turns to laughter. Holy shit, why am I laughing?

Kyle's eyes are soft, and he reaches for my hand across the center console of the car.

"Carly, are you sure? Because if you are, I will do whatever you want. I love you, and we will get through this. Together."

My laughter is slowing, but I still have tears streaming down my face. He smiles at me, chuckles, and then he shakes his head.

I'm like a crazy person with emotions flooding out of me.

"Yes, Kyle, I'm done."

He smiles at me and wipes the tears from my cheeks with the back of his hand. He then softly cradles my face in his palms and says, "Then I'm done, too."

He leans across and softly places a chaste kiss on my wet lips.

"Thank you," I whisper against his closed lips, resting my forehead against his.

We stay like that in the car for a while, silently inhaling each other.

Then Kyle turns toward the steering wheel and drives us home.

~

*Dear Emily*

That was an extremely difficult day for us. I honestly don't know if and when I will ever get over the emotional loss of not being able to physically have my own child. But it's finally time to move on, and we are, with Emily.

I wipe my eyes and head toward my bedroom. Finding a comfortable sweater and a pair of jeans, I get dressed, slip into my flip-flops, and I'm ready to meet Tabitha for lunch. This will be the third time we've seen each other since her ultrasound and each time, I feel like she may open up more and more. She's so guarded and sad, which is completely understandable. But the more time I spend with her, the more I want to know. *I need to know.* For Emily.

I get into my car and see that Kyle has already pre-programmed the GPS with the restaurant information. Only Kyle would do something so thoughtful. It's so easy to love him as much as I do. I look around and see if I can spot him getting closer to home, but he's nowhere to be seen since he's still out on his run. I want to shower him with kisses and thank him for being the most thoughtful, perfect husband. I frown when I realize I won't be able to do that until later.

I also wish he were here to give me one last pep talk before I leave for Philly. My stomach is in knots and my anxiety is through the roof. I look one more time to see if he's back from his run and sigh. I reluctantly put the car in drive and let the GPS guide me to Philadelphia.

My mind races as I begin my trip. I'm consumed with worry. It doesn't get easier with each visit and my anxiety begins to take hold.

*I hope Tabitha is okay.*
*I hope she'll want to see me.*
*Is she as anxious as I am?*
I'm scared.

# Chapter 11

## Tabitha

*Philadelphia, Pennsylvania*
**Past**
*Age 19*

IT'S FRIDAY!

Somehow, I managed to switch shifts at the diner with Dottie. She would do anything for me and I love her for it. She has a bunch of kids at home and a husband who works just as hard as she does, but as soon as she saw how excited I was about my plans tonight, she called her sister to take care of the kids and took my shift.

I'm so nervous and excited to go see Alex at The High Note tonight. *What am I going to wear? Who am I going to go with?* I have no friends here. What I wouldn't give for a girlfriend right now. Someone to help pick out *the* perfect outfit. Do my makeup. Fuss over my hair.

But...

I have no one.

I'm on my own.

My mood suddenly switches and I stiffen.

I'm sitting on my bed with my iPod on, earbuds in my ear, listening to Rage Against the Machine. This is bringing my mood down, but I need anger. Angry lyrics. I need to get out *my* rage. To feel my rage.

I'm a mess, my mood is everywhere. My mind is racing trying

to think of happy thoughts and at the same time, I want to punch something. Pull something. Pull my hair out. Scrape this scar from my face. *Scream.* I don't like feeling like this, with no control over my sadness and anger.

I try to relax, so I close my eyes. All I see is Sara. My baby girl. I miss her. I miss feeling her kicking feet in my belly, her baby hiccups tickling my womb. I start rocking back and forth on my bed, and I rip the earbuds out of my ears. I need to stop. No more rage.

I remember the week before Sara was born. Tony was in an exceptionally good mood, which meant that things were going to turn real bad, real fast.

*We're having dinner at the club. The only place that I am ever allowed to eat. I push my food around on my plate. I have no appetite.*

*Tony is smiling across from me and pushes a packet of papers in front of me.*

*"What's this?" I ask him.*

*"Open it," he commands and sneers. He licks his lips like a snake would if a snake had a human tongue. Ick. My skin is crawling just looking at him. How did I let him get me pregnant? Touch me? Control me? Own me? What am I even doing here? Why can't I muster the courage to leave? To escape?*

*I pull the packet closer and see across the top: Adoption Agreement. I stop reading.*

*I look up at Tony, and he's smiling. Big.*

*"Adoption agreement. For what?" I ask incredulously.*

*"Your baby." He emphasizes 'your' as if he didn't force himself into me repeatedly, getting me pregnant with his baby.*

*"What? I thought…," I start to say.*

*His look becomes menacing. "You thought what, princess? That you were going to have this baby, and I was going to pay for the two of you to live upstairs over my club?" he says with dripping sarcasm.*

*"Tony, I…," I can't speak. My throat is closing up as if I'm being strangled. He can't do this! He can't take my baby from me! I need to get away. Get out of here.*

*I push the papers to the floor and watch them scatter in all different directions. I get up and start to run away when he grabs me by my bicep and pulls me back.*

*His face is inches away from mine, and his cold, dark eyes are shooting into my own. "You WILL sign these papers, princess. You don't have a choice. I OWN you, and I OWN the right to have you and ONLY you. This baby is not welcome in my life, and I'm not ready for you to be gone. If you don't sign these papers, you will regret bringing that child into my home. Do. You. Understand?" His hot breath is smothering me, and I try to back away. He's too strong. I can't fight him.*

*He just threatened me. But worse, he just threatened my baby. I have to protect her. But how?*

*Maybe signing these papers will get her far away from here. From Tony. From me. Maybe this will be the best thing for her. I can't subject her to a life above this god-awful club. I can't subject her to the almost daily beatings that I receive from Tony.*

*I need to protect her, even if it costs me my life.*

*I have to do it. I have to do what Tony wants.*

*He grabs me by the back of the neck, pulls my hair, and forces me to the floor to gather all of the papers that I scattered just moments before.*

*After I pick up all of the papers, he hands me a pen and pushes the papers around to find the pages that I need to sign.*

*I sign the consent to adoption and revocation of parental rights. Paper after paper I sign until my wrist hurts and my hand is shaking. I feel as though a knife is twisting into my gut as I sign away all rights to my daughter.*

*"Now," he says. "The next thing you have to do is smile when the lawyer meets you in the hospital. You need to tell him that this is what is best for your precious little girl. That you want her to have a good and loving home. Do you understand me?"*

*"Yes," I whisper.*

*"Yes what?" he snarls.*

*"Yes, I understand, Tony."*

*He lets me go.*

*"Get the fuck out of my face. You look like a pig," he says.*

*I leave the bar, walk upstairs to our apartment, and look around.*

*He's right. I am no good for this baby. Even if I were to get away. Escape this hell. What could I provide her? How could I take care of her?*

*I sink to my knees on the living room floor while holding my belly. I start to sob uncontrollably while rubbing my hands on my baby bump. I can't even talk to her to tell her that everything will be okay. I don't know that it will.*

*I continue to sob, keeping my wails to a minimum. I don't want Tony to hear me. What have I done? What am I going to do?*

*The choice has been made. I curl up on the floor, holding my belly and whisper to my baby, "I love you, and I'm doing this all for you."*

Remembering Sara and my old life sends me into a downward spiral. I pick up my iPod and throw it across the room. Why didn't I run then? I could have tried with Sara. I should have tried. But I didn't. I'm a coward. I curl up on my pillow and let my rage slip into darkness.

~

I'm sweating and tangled in my sheets. It's dark with a hint of light from the street peeking through the curtains. I roll over and look at the clock.

Ten forty-five PM.

*Shit.*

I'm *late.* So late that I've probably missed Alex's entire set. I panic, wondering if he's waiting for me and disappointed. I don't want him to be upset with me.

I throw on my boots and run out the door.

I don't even know what I look like. I'd been crying, and I must be a mess.

I arrive at The High Note ten minutes later and there are only five people outside waiting. I get to the back of the line and shove my hands in the pockets of my jeans. *What am I doing?*

The five people in front of me aren't getting into the club. They sound frustrated and are huffing and puffing. The bouncer repeatedly tells them that they are at capacity, and their names aren't on 'the list'.

The list!

My name is on that list.

I clear my throat and say, "Excuse me?"

The bouncer looks up and scowls at me.

"I'm on the list." I crack a small smile as the people in front of me grumble.

He looks down at his clipboard. "Name," he says sternly.

"Tabitha Fletcher. I'm with Alex."

He scans the clipboard, running his finger up and down and he finally stops, resting on a name.

He looks me up and down and waves me forward.

The rest of the people in line are agitated and are now throwing insults my way. I tune them out and walk up to the door.

Mr. Bouncer lets me in. That's it. Easy. No ID needed.

I almost chuckle as I walk in. *What right do I have to be so cocky?* None.

My smile evens out as I start to scan the crowd.

The music is what hits me first. It's deep and melodic. Heavy base, steady drums, haunting voice. I feel the music in my chest, beating in time with my heart.

I look up to find the stage.

Alex.

The lighting is dark and dim, and he seems like a shadow on the stage. He's holding the microphone with two hands, his guitar hanging from his back, and his eyes are closed. He's singing deeply with such emotion. I don't hear the words. I only see his lips moving. Like he was doing the other day with the bookmarks.

I'm so drawn to him and the melody. I stand still and just stare. I begin to sway with the music until I hear the words that he is singing.

*Jaded... I'm jaded*

He breathes.

*Alone and damaged*

His voice is reverberating throughout the bar.

*I need hope...*

*But I'm hopeless*

*Tattered and used*

*No end in sight*

He begins screaming the lyrics.

*Jaded*

*Weary*

The music stops. The drums beat one last time.

He whispers, "Alone."

The lights go out completely; the crowd screams for more. Alex has left the stage.

Jaded, damaged, and alone. He could have been singing that directly to me.

For me.

*About me.*

It's my anthem. How could he know?

How could he know that I'm damaged?

I touch the scar on my cheek. My fingertip is cold as I run it up and down the four-inch length. I can feel my scar burning now as my emotions start to wrestle with my brain. I stand here as I rub my cheek and stare at an empty stage.

I don't know how long I've been standing still when I feel a soft pressure on my lower back. Someone's hand is gently pushing me toward an open booth.

I turn to look.

Alex.

I shiver as I look into his eyes. His gaze is intense and freezes me into place. We stand there, staring into each other's eyes for a moment, then he nudges me softly, and somehow my feet start moving. He removes his hand, I sit down in the booth, and he slides into the bench across from me.

"Hey, Tabitha Tabby Fletcher," he says. He clearly likes to say all of my names. His smile helps me begin to focus and I realize where I am.

"Hey," I respond. "Thanks for getting me in here tonight. And you can call me Tabby." I tense up and smile thinly. I'm so nervous. "I'm sorry I got here late. I lost track of time." I lie. I can't tell him that I had a total bipolar melt down and passed out from exhaustion.

"I feel bad...," I look away, embarrassed. Does he suspect that I'm crazy?

"Hey." He chuckles. "No worries. I was actually worried about *you*. I thought you might blow me off." He looks me in the eyes again, and I am now lost in his gaze. I can't believe he was worried about me blowing him off. *Is he interested in me?* I tense up even more, unsure of how to proceed.

"Wow, your music is incredible. What I heard of it anyway. Just wow." I can't get anything else out of my mouth. I need to tell him how his song found its way into my soul, all one minute that I actually heard. I need to tell him that he must have written that song for me. I can't go all fan-girl at this point. He'll head for the door. He doesn't seem like the 'groupie' type and I'm certainly not one. I feel small and awkward.

I'm overwhelmed by his presence. He is nothing like Tony. His demeanor is soft, edgy. He's intense, but not in an intimidating way. He also seems guarded, like me. *What could he be hiding?*

There is so much I want to ask him. *Need* to ask him. I just need to know *him*.

"How did your writing go the other day? You know, with my notebook?" What a stupid question. *I'm an Idiot.*

He looks away from me, and his eyes are now darting all over the bar. Shit. He doesn't want to talk about his music.

He waves his hand in the air to get the attention of the waitress across the bar. She makes her way over and immediately heaves her chest out in front of Alex, entirely ignoring my presence.

"Yes, sugar, what can I do for you?"

"Two ice waters please," Alex replies.

She seems surprised by his order. "Anything else?"

"Nope." And he immediately looks back to me.

The waitress walks away in a huff, but manages to shake her ass as she goes along.

"You're not twenty-one, are you, Tabby?" He asks.

"No," I say softly.

He laughs heartily for the first time. "Neither am I. I'm only nineteen, and besides, I don't drink." His laugh quickly fades and his expression turns serious, as if he just told me a secret that he didn't want me to know.

"Oh," I say. *Wow, I'm really carrying this conversation,* I think sarcastically to myself. I must seem like flat soda to him.

"Where's the rest of your band?" I ask, quickly looking around the bar for any sign of them.

"Who knows? They're probably in the back. We aren't a very social group." He shifts in his seat, uncomfortably. "We'd rather sit in the back room between sets than be out here with these people. They all think they get us, but they don't…," his voice trails off.

I boldly reach across the table and grab his right hand. "'E-P-I-C'. Nice tattoo. Does it signify something major that happened in your life?" I ask as I run my finger along his knuckles. I smile into his eyes. I can't believe how brazen I'm being. His hand is cool to the touch and mine begins to shake while holding it.

He quickly puts his left hand in view, and I see 'F-A-I-L' across his other knuckles. "Oh," I say quietly. "It goes together." *Duh.*

"Yeah," he answers. "It's my band's name. Epic Fail. But it means a bit more to me." His eyes become heavy, sad. Now I'm intrigued, and I want to know more about him. Immediately.

Our waitress interrupts us by slamming our ice waters between us. He pulls his hands from mine and pushes back against the booth, away from me.

I quickly grab my water and begin drinking it.

He shifts his eyes around again, looking everywhere but at me. *What the hell?*

I guess my advances weren't appreciated. I shouldn't have touched him, held his hand. Does he just want to be friends with me? That's fine I guess. I read this whole thing wrong. Of course. *Ugh.* Besides, who am I kidding? It's only been a few *weeks* since I gave up Sara. Since I ran away from Tony. This can't happen. It shouldn't happen. *I'm not ready.*

I take a deep breath and push back into the booth on my side. "Well, Alex, it's late, and I had a rough day. I won't keep you any longer. I'm sure you have to get ready for your next set or something." I take another sip of water, almost choke on an ice cube, and start to get up from the booth.

He grabs my wrist and my defensive flinch is automatic. His touch burns me, and I feel it all over. I start to tremble and pull my hand quickly from his grasp. *Why did he do that?* I start to back out of his reach.

"I'm sorry," he says. "I didn't mean…"

His eyes are searching mine, hoping for me to tell him it's okay. I'm backing away now, and I can't stop myself.

"No, I'm sorry," I say as I start to turn. "Thanks for the water."

I'm now running.

Out of the club.

Why did I freak out like that? What is wrong with me? He's not Tony, and he wasn't trying to hurt me. Right?

I sprint down the block toward the city bus that's idling at the corner. I look behind me. No one.

*Shit.*

Why would I expect he would chase after me? He doesn't even know me.

I don't even know me anymore.

I get onto the bus, swipe my card, and throw myself into the first seat. I involuntarily touch my scar, drop my head back against the seat, and close my eyes.

The bus pulls away, and I don't look back again.

A total epic fail.

Pun intended.

# Chapter 12

## Carly

Philadelphia, Pennsylvania
**Present**
Age 29

I ARRIVE AT the restaurant where I'm meeting Tabitha and sit at a table with a lovely view of the city street. I'm early again, and I've already ordered my drink, unsweetened iced tea with a lemon twist. My favorite. It reminds me of my Aunt Frankie.

My Godmother, my angel.

This was her favorite drink, and she always had a pitcher brewing. I smile. I miss her so much. What would she think about everything that Kyle and I are going through? I remember the last conversation that I had with her.

*I leave work early one night and decide to stop in to see my Aunt Francis, 'Frankie'. She had just made the most difficult decision that she could make. She is stopping chemotherapy. She has leukemia. It had been in remission, but it came back with a vengeance. She can't take the medicine, doctors, and nausea any longer. She is now placing her fate in God's hands.*

*I arrive at her house around four thirty PM and find her in her favorite room, the sunroom. She's sitting on her comfy couch with a full glass of iced tea in front of her, untouched. I sit down next to her, and we quietly stare at the news on the television. We sit like this, in comfortable silence.*

*After a while, she turns to me and whispers, "Carly, I'm afraid." A single tear rolls down her cheek.*

*I look up at her and say, "Don't be afraid, Aunt Frankie. There is nothing to be afraid of. Your Dad will be waiting for you with open arms." Really? I don't believe a word I'm saying. I'd be terrified if I were in her place.*

*I'm terrified of death. Finality. Nothingness.*

*Hell, I'm even afraid of being buried, closed in a casket. I know I'll be dead and won't know where I am, but the thought of being closed in and buried six feet down seriously disturbs me. I have no rational thoughts about death and only think of it in terms of something macabre.*

*I'm afraid of losing everything and everyone that matters to me. I'm afraid for her and for what she's going to miss out on. What she's going to lose. Her family. Her children. Her grandchildren. Her future. This isn't fair. I take a deep breath as I try to conceal my own sadness and panic.*

*She asks how my last in-vitro fertilization treatment was. She already knows that it didn't work because she speaks with my mother, her sister, at least once a day.*

*"It didn't work, Aunt Frankie." I frown as I briefly explain our latest trials and tribulations.*

*She smiles softly and says, "Car, you will have a family. I just know it. You and Kyle are meant to have loads of happy, bouncing babies." She holds my hand. Her grip is loose, and her hand is so cold. She seems so hollow and frail. She's given up her own fight. Yet, she has such hope for me. I can't begin to understand where her hope for me comes from and wish desperately that she would turn that hope into something positive for her own healing and recovery.*

*"The family you dream of is around the corner," she says softly. "I just know it."*

*I continue to hold her hand as we watch the latest news in silence. I spend about an hour with her, and I am reluctant to leave. Eventually, I get up and kiss her cold, sunken cheek. "I love you, Aunt Frankie," I whisper to her.*

*She died the next day.*

My eyes are full of unshed tears as I think about Aunt Frankie and the fight that she lost. She believed in my ability to be a terrific mother. I smile as I think of all that she fought for, and I can only hope to make her proud as Kyle and I raise Emily.

I look around the restaurant and I see a family sitting at a table across the room. They all look so happy. Their little boy, who couldn't be more than two, is sitting in a high chair, and he's thoroughly covered in marinara sauce. He's got spaghetti wrapped around his little fingers, and he's smiling ear to ear. His parents are softly talking to each other while their little boy is enjoying his meal. Perfect. Simple.

I didn't notice Tabitha slip into the chair across from me. She is smiling tightly and quietly says, "Hi."

"Oh, hey!" I say quickly.

She realizes that she interrupted me eavesdropping on the family across the restaurant. "I'm sorry," she says.

I smile quickly and shake my head. "No worries. I was just watching that cute little boy over there. He's a mess!" I giggle a little as I gesture toward the family.

She cranes her neck to see the family that I'm stalking. "Adorable," she says.

We sit awkwardly and quietly for several minutes before she speaks up.

"Are you ready? I mean, ready for the baby?" she asks.

"Yes!" I exclaim. "We're *so* ready, Tabitha. Gosh, the room is ready and even painted pink." I take my phone out to show her the pictures I took of Emily's room. She scrolls through the photos while turning my phone to get a better look at the room.

"Wow, it's awesome," she says. "I love her name painted in white on the pink walls. It's such a nice contrast. Her crib is beautiful." It's an off-white crib with flowers carved into the woodwork. We've already set up the bedding. It's a gorgeous Wendy Bellissimo pattern with flowers and safari print. It's a perfect combination of girly and modern. I fell in love with it as soon as I saw it and immediately ordered everything from the collection. I definitely tend to over-do it sometimes. Callie and Becca were there to support my impulse purchases and purchased several stuffed animals to match the pattern.

She hands me back my phone and turns to the waitress who just arrived at our table. We order our meals and sit quietly facing each other. *What are we going to talk about?* We've just about exhausted most safe topics, like decorations and such. I'm feeling slightly awkward that I just showed her pictures of her daughter's room. I hope I didn't make her as uncomfortable as I feel.

"So, how are you feeling?" I ask.

"I'm good. I'm getting more and more tired as the days go by. I'm huge. I wasn't this big with my first pregnancy." She sucks in a breath and immediately looks away, realizing what she just said.

*What? First pregnancy?*

"Oh," I say. She just dropped a bombshell on me. Another pregnancy?

"I should explain." She stops to gather her thoughts and looks worried.

"You don't have to explain," I say, trying to let her off the hook. But I want to know. *I need to know.*

She takes a deep breath and says, "It's okay. You should know about it. Someday, Emily should know." She pauses, trying to remain calm. "I had Sara, my other little girl, two years ago. I had to give her up." Her eyes are darting all over the restaurant. She's nervous and I should stop her from sharing this story. I'm so confused and disturbed by her revelation that I start to fidget in my seat and rub my hands on my jeans.

"I couldn't keep her. I was in a really bad place. I don't even know where she is, who her parents are. I didn't get to choose them like I did you." She begins to ramble, trying to explain herself further, "I didn't tell the agency about this because, well, it's embarrassing. I mean who gives up *two* children?" She looks down at her napkin and she starts pulling it apart subconsciously. Tearing little bits of paper from the napkin and leaving them on the table. She chose us, though, and that's what matters.

"I'm sorry, Tabitha. I can't imagine," I say truthfully.

*Dear Emily*

"It's okay, really." She stops and looks at me, trying to convince herself too. "I know that Sara is in a better place. Happy. Safe." She pauses as she says 'safe,' as if she means to emphasize its significance. Her eyes are glistening, and I need to change the subject. I'm feeling selfish right now. What if remembering her first daughter makes her change her mind? *Shit!* I start to feel vulnerable.

"You did what you thought was best, I'm sure."

We sit in silence for a few minutes as the waitress brings Tabitha her drink.

"So, what else do you have for Emily?" Tabitha asks quickly.

She changes the subject to indicate that our conversation about Sara is over. I stiffen a little as I answer.

"What *don't* we have?" I chuckle, nervously. "I'm a bit compulsive when it comes to getting her room ready. Her room, as you saw, is completely furnished and decorated. We have tons of pink clothes, blankets, and stuffed animals. Kyle thinks I'm nuts to go so overboard, but I don't know any other way." I'm honest. If I could buy all of Babies-R-Us, I would. I want Emily to have everything. To give her all of the comforts she deserves. To give her all of me.

Tabitha smiles a big smile this time. She almost seems relieved.

"That's awesome, Carly. I'm sure that Emily will be so happy in her new room."

Now I feel bad. I'm flaunting everything we're giving to Emily. Everything that she *can't.*

I change the subject.

"So, how did you and Seth meet?" I ask. We've talked about him before, but only briefly and I'd like to know more. He seems to be great support for her, so I feel this is a safe topic to bring up.

She takes a deep breath. "He kind of saved me. I mean, not *literally*, but he was just always there for me." She looks away and smiles softly. "I was in another relationship when I met Seth, and then I did something stupid to mess that up. Seth was my friend and then just became more."

I nod and smile at her. "I'm glad, Tabitha. We could all use someone to help us through the tough times." I'm afraid to ask my next question, but I persist. "Is Seth the father? Don't answer that if you don't think

77

you can." I immediately regret asking this and wish I could take it back. I don't have the right to ask.

She shrugs her shoulders and her mouth tightens as if she's contemplating her next words carefully. "I don't know, Carly. He could be. The other relationship I was in… well… the timing. I don't know." She's struggling with her answer and I immediately feel terrible for prying too much. "The other potential father, Alex, and I met after I ran away from an impossible and dangerous situation in my life. I had just given up Sara and moved across the country, back to Philly. We had a very powerful connection, and we were together for over a year until I messed up." Her voice trails off, and she looks away. "He could be Emily's father. I just don't know. I've said too much I think."

Her tone makes me think that she does know. That she thinks Alex is Emily's father. She speaks about Alex differently than she does Seth.

As she's sharing this story of sadness and regret, I'm starting to feel nervous that she could change her mind.

"I'm sorry." Am I? I mean, I am sorry for her situation, but I wonder selfishly if this child would be ours if the situation were different. If this guy Alex were still in her life, would Emily be coming into ours? I shake my head. I shouldn't be thinking these thoughts.

"I really am sorry, Tabitha. I don't know what else to say."

She's quiet for a few moments. I can't tell if she's about to stand up and bolt out of the restaurant.

"Are you okay? I'm sorry if I pried too much," I say, trying to comfort her.

She nods and continues, "I've had a very tough life, Carly. I didn't share this with the adoption agency because I'm profoundly ashamed of my choices. I've been running my whole life, and I want to put the running behind me to make something of myself. This is my first step. I'm making this choice for me and for Emily. I need to make sure she has a good life and then I need to straighten myself out. Seth's not ready to be a father, but he's ready to help me. I need to let him."

"Oh." I say quietly.

The waitress returns with our lunch order and places it in front of us. I have a salad with grilled chicken and Tabitha has grilled cheese and French fries.

We eat silently for a little while as we both watch the family across the restaurant pack up their belongings. The mother picks up the little boy who still has a red stain on his face from the marinara sauce. She's laughing as she holds him up and away from her as she surveys his messy state. He's giggling and his father starts to tickle his chin. They're so happy, and I can't wait to experience the same euphoria.

We watch them leave the restaurant.

I turn to Tabitha and say, "Emily will have that. Unconditional love, comfort, laughs. She will have all of that. Kyle and I will give that to her. We'll give her everything."

She laughs a little. "As long as you let her smear marinara sauce all over her face and let her get spaghetti in her hair." She continues laughing, and for the first time I let out a breath of relief. She's actually picturing Emily with Kyle and me, and I'm relieved.

"She'll have such messy spaghetti and sauce, I promise!" I'm picturing our little girl, and I start laughing.

Our lunch is finished, and the waitress quietly clears our plates. We sit across from each other, quiet and contemplating. But unlike at the beginning, we are comfortable in each other's presence now. The painful silence that we once looked at each other with is no longer there, and I almost feel content.

I remember the photos that I brought from home and say, "I have pictures of our family if you'd like to see."

"Yes! Wow! I'd love to see as many pictures as possible," she answers.

I pull out a small album that I made of both Kyle's family and mine. I go page by page, showing her pictures of my parents, brother and sisters, nieces and nephews. Kyle's family is small with just one sister. Both of his parents are deceased. I tell her stories of birthday parties, anniversaries, and weddings. She is engrossed and hangs on my every word. She seems almost jealous, but I shake off that feeling.

She listens to me tell silly stories about our families for almost an hour. Time really is flying by. Thankfully, the awkwardness from earlier has eased a bit, allowing us to really connect. Today has been the most revealing of all of our conversations, and I feel like I still need to digest everything I've learned.

As we end our conversation, she says, "Carly, you and Kyle are going to be perfect parents to Emily. Just perfect. I couldn't be happier for her, you and Kyle." She trails off.

I reach across the table and grab her hand. I squeeze. She squeezes back hard and just nods at me.

I pay the bill, and we quietly stand up and walk out of the restaurant. I hand her a card that I wrote for her. A thank you, pour out my guts, heart and soul kind of card. I put two gift cards in there. One for Target and the other a Visa gift card. She needs to pay bills, pay rent, and buy clothes and food. I want to help her, and this is the way I can.

She doesn't open the card. She tucks it into her bag.

Before she turns away, she throws herself into my arms and hugs me tight. I can feel her lightly sobbing against me.

"Thank you," she says.

"No. Thank you. You're giving us this gift, and you're the one that deserves thanks, love and hugs. Everything." I squeeze her back, and she pulls away.

She wipes tears from her cheeks and smiles.

She turns away, hails the first cab she sees, and waves to me before she gets in the car.

She's gone before I know it, and I'm standing alone on the sidewalk. I wrap my arms around me, hugging myself.

My smile is huge.

This *is* happening.

It is.

Emily.

I smile even bigger and walk to my car.

I get in and turn on the stereo. "Lightning Crashes" by Live is playing. I get chills immediately. This song reminds me of my Aunt Frankie. They sing about the circle of life, and I realize that somehow, my Aunt's life has come full circle and she has guided Emily to us.

Happy tears stream down my cheeks, and I press my foot to the floor, racing to get home to tell Kyle about my day.

# Chapter 13

## Tabitha

Philadelphia, Pennsylvania
**Present**
*Age 20*

I DON'T HAVE the energy to walk up the stairs to my apartment. I'm drained, physically and emotionally. I trudge up the stairs, hoping that it's empty. Seth's support has been comforting, but I don't want it today. I can't bear to go through everything that happened at lunch. This is all becoming far too real and I don't have the strength to cope.

I walk through my door and kick off my shoes. *He's not here.*

I feel like shit; I'm still scared, sad, and jealous. I can't help the jealousy. Jealousy is such an ugly feeling that hangs over me like a dark cloud. Jealousy turns to resentment, and I need to squash this now. I can't allow those feelings to consume my thoughts.

But I can't help it.

Why can't I be like Carly? I'd be strong and confident. Blissful. Happy.

Nope. I can't.

Her latest card made me cry big, ugly tears. I cried the entire cab ride home. Her notes are always thoughtful and touching, grabbing my heart. She can't help expressing her and Kyle's gratefulness for the gift that I'm giving to them. Every time I get a letter, I always have the same reaction. They gut me. I don't know why I did, but I opened it in the cab, knowing exactly what I was in for. As soon as I opened it, two generous gift cards fell out onto my lap. *She is constantly giving me things, helping me.* This letter, in particular, really got to me.

> *Tabitha,*
>
> *We're never going to stop saying 'Thank You.' Never. Ever.*
>
> *We already feel Emily's presence in our home. I can almost smell her baby scent. I'm sitting in the soft rocking chair in her room as I write this card to you. I close my eyes and picture Kyle sitting in this same chair, cradling her in his arms, softly patting her bottom and gazing into her eyes.*
>
> *He's going to be a great father. Kind, loving, protective.*
>
> *Thank you, Tabitha, for giving us that gift.*
>
> *For giving Kyle the gift of fatherhood.*
>
> *For giving him a future of adoring his little girl.*
>
> *Taking her to ballet classes and soccer games.*
>
> *The father/daughter dances that are in their future.*
>
> *The dance they will share at her wedding.*
>
> *Thank you. Thank you. Thank you.*
>
> *Love,*
>
> *Carly*

*Shit.* I shouldn't have read this in the cab. I choked on my sobs the entire way back to my apartment. The cab driver must have thought I was insane.

I was wiping the tears dripping down my chin with the back of my sleeve while he looked at me through the rearview mirror with pity.

I can't help but picture *Alex*, not Seth, in those same situations with my daughter. *Alex* with Emily in a soft rocking chair. *Alex* holding her close while dancing at a father/daughter dance. Emily standing on his toes as he dances with her.

*Alex* walking her down the aisle, giving her away at her wedding. These things will never happen. Not with Alex. Not with Seth. Emily will only know one father, and that's Kyle.

I lie down on my couch and reach for the gift cards. She can't stop herself from giving me things. Her generosity is overwhelming. I've known Carly for a few short months, and she has given me more than I ever received over the years from bouncing from foster home to foster home.

She's going to be a great mother. I need to keep telling myself this in order to accept the decision that I've made.

I don't remember my own mother, and I'm not sure I even want to. What kind of mother leaves her daughter in the ambulance bay of a hospital? I was naked, wrapped in a newspaper and placed on the ground. A speeding ambulance could have pulled in and easily crushed me. That's how much that bitch thought of my well-being and safety. Fuck. I'm lucky to even be alive, no thanks to her. The hospital staff gave me the name 'Tabitha' because I was abandoned on Halloween. My name seems fitting, although my 'mother' was the witch, not me.

My first home was with a single woman, Trina. She was a nurse in the emergency room and helped take care of me during my early days. She adopted me shortly after and raised me from the time I was found at the hospital until she died in a car accident when I was seven. *She* was the only mother I ever knew. She was cruelly taken away from me.

From that point on, I moved from home to home. I was never in a place for more than a year at a time. I was labeled difficult, introverted and disturbed. Each foster family had their own reasons for taking me in, mostly selfish. My presence in their homes kept food on their tables and kept the monthly support checks flowing.

When I was seventeen, I hit the road. I stole money from the last family I was with. They deserved it. Their eighteen-year-old son was a complete pervert and made it his mission in life to interrupt too many of my showers. The last time he walked in on me getting changed, he had a full erection and a grin on his face that made my skin crawl. Later that day, I bolted and took buses across the country until I eventually wound up in Portland, Oregon. Where I met Tony. I shudder, remembering all that I suffered with him.

I hear the front door open as Seth walks in with takeout food. He knows by now that I don't cook and makes it easy for me by always showing up with takeout. As much as he does for me, I feel nothing as he walks through the room. His warm smile should comfort me, but I'm numb.

"Hey babe," he says as he places the greasy-smelling food on the small table in my kitchenette. "How was lunch with Carly?" He doesn't seem to mind being excluded from our frequent visits. I think he's mostly relieved. It's so much easier for him to disconnect from what's happening.

I swipe my eyes to make sure that all of the tears I cried while thinking about Alex and Emily are gone. I feel like I'm betraying Seth by having those visions of another man with my daughter.

"Fine. Good, actually," I reply.

"Great. I knew you two would continue to hit it off. I'm really glad."

He starts to divide the food onto two plates and gestures for me to join him at the table.

"No, I'm not hungry. I had a grilled cheese for lunch."

I walk past him to grab a glass for some water.

"Okay. Suit yourself," he says as he digs into the huge burger in front of him.

I have no words right now. It must be hormones or something, but I just can't stand being in his vicinity at the moment. I need to leave because I don't want to take anything out on him. Today has been overwhelming and I don't feel like re-living it.

I grab my jacket and head toward the door.

"Where are you going?" he asks.

"Out."

"Wait. I just got home," he says confused.

"Seth, what do you want from me?" I yell at him. I don't know why or how my anger escalated so quickly, but it did.

"Tabby, I want to talk to you. I want to be near you. You haven't been around for the past week, and when you are here, you're not yourself. What's up?"

Seriously? He's asking me what's up?

"Seth, what the fuck do you think?" I gesture toward my large belly and just stare at him.

He huffs a little and puts his burger down on the plate in front of him. He stands up and walks toward me, then wraps his arms around my waist and puts his face into the side of my neck.

"Babe." He breathes in and squeezes me tighter. "I know this isn't easy. It can't be. It's not supposed to be. But I'm here and you need to lean on me. You can't continue to go off on your own to deal with this. It's not healthy, and it's eventually going to take its toll on you and me. Let me help you."

He lifts his head and looks into my eyes. His eyes are glistening, and I know he's feeling this just as hard as I am. I just haven't let him express it. I've been keeping him at bay because I don't want to face the reality that he wouldn't want me if I were to keep this baby. I'm being selfish.

He continues, "We're in this together, regardless of the situation. I know this baby might not be mine, but you are. Mine. You have been for a long time, longer than you can imagine. You can't know what it's like to see you go through all of this. Trying to go through it alone. I'm here, and I'm not going anywhere. We'll get through this together. I know you may not believe me, but I'm sad about what we're doing. I realize that I'm giving up the chance to be a father to this little girl, but I'm not ready. I want to build a life with you, on our terms, without feeling regret or angst over this child. It wouldn't be fair to her to be with us when we haven't figured ourselves out. I'm being selfish here, but I want you and only you. And I want you to heal. I need you to heal. I'll be there, with you, when Emily is born. We'll say goodbye to her together. I'll never leave you the way *he* did." He can't say Alex's name. Ever.

Seth can't be a father right now, and I can't be a mother, not until I fix myself. I can't commit my life to raising a child. I'm too damaged.

I pull away from him. He stares into my eyes, and I start to soften a little bit. He loves me so much. Why can't I give myself completely over to him? He's been with me for the past eight and a half months. He's tried to help mend my broken heart. We were friends first, and then he told me that he fell in love with me the very first time we met. Back when my heart was beating only for Alex. I've been so unfair to Seth, allowing him to protect me, help me, when I know he's suffering too.

It's a shame he fell so hard for me because I'm not sure I can love anyone again. Ever.

# Chapter 14

## Carly

*New Brunswick, New Jersey*
### Past
*Age 18*

I'M STANDING UNDER a hot stream of water as I rinse the conditioner through my long, thick hair. Once I'm satisfied that it's gone, I turn off the water, grab a towel, and step out of the shower. My shower. Stall #2. As I wrap myself in the towel, I realize that I left my clothes on my bed back in my room. *Dammit.* I look around to see if there's anything else I can cover myself with and see nothing.

I grab my toiletries and walk out of the bathroom in my bare feet, dripping water behind me as I quickly make it back to my room. I freeze when I turn the corner and see a guy about to knock on my door.

Kyle.

*Crap*

It's too late to hide from him since he's already turning his head to look at me. Then he grins. Big. I'm so embarrassed and I want to disappear.

I'm practically naked as I walk up to him. His gaze slowly travels up and down my body, and I begin to flush everywhere.

"You really shouldn't walk around in a towel, Carly. You never know who you might run into." He's smirking and I get chills just looking at him. Well, I am soaking wet, in a towel.

He continues as if I'm not practically naked in front of him. "Professor Martin will be happy to know how healthy you are now." His smile grows as he continues to take in the soaking wet sight of me.

I'm flustered and don't know how to react. *Is he flirting with me?* "Excuse me, but I I need to get into my room," I say, nervous.

"Why of course," he says as he steps aside chivalrously. He gestures toward my door and bows his head as he looks up at me and winks.

Geez! Enough with the winking, and the smile, and those perfect cheeks. He has a little dimple in the center of his chin that I just want to lick. Shit! What is wrong with me? *What is he doing to me?* I shouldn't be feeling this way. I should be more guarded, *careful*.

I walk past him and nervously start to shut the door. "I need to get dressed." He puts his foot in the door to prevent me from closing it. I immediately tense up, worried that he's going to force his way in.

"I'll be out here. We need to get you caught up in Bio, so hurry up and get dressed." He smiles and pulls his foot away so that the door shuts softly. I take a deep breath. I'm overreacting, right?

I find my clothes that I left on the bed. I shimmy into a pair of flannel lounge pants and a long-sleeved t-shirt. I towel dry my hair and let it fall onto my shoulders. I look at myself in the small mirror above my sink and take a deep breath. I say silently to myself, "Kyle is not Todd. He isn't going to hurt me." *He's different.*

I nod at my reflection and walk toward the door. I'm so tense, and I hope it's not visible to him. I take a deep breath and try to relax as I reach for the doorknob.

I open the door, and he's leaning against the wall. When he looks at me, I feel that flush again, and my cheeks must be bright red at this point.

"Wow! It's hot. I can't cool down after that shower." I lie. I cooled down. Then I saw him outside my door and heated right back up again.

He laughs. "Yeah, must be the shower." Cocky, isn't he?

I step aside, allowing him to enter my room. I'm taking a chance and letting my guard down somewhat.

"Nice room," he says, looking around. His eyes immediately find the picture of me with my family on my corkboard. He nods toward the picture and asks, "Family?"

"Yes," I answer. "My parents, grandfather, brother, and sisters."

"You have a big family. That must be nice. It's just my sister and me. My parents are gone." His voice trails off, and he clears his throat as if he didn't mean to tell me that little tidbit about himself and he wants to take it back.

"Oh." I gasp slightly and place my hand near my throat. "I'm sorry."

"It's okay. I mean it's really not okay that my parents are dead, but it's okay in that I've had time to deal with it. My mom died when I was little, and my dad died a couple of years ago. You just learn to live without them. You know?"

No, I actually don't know. I haven't seen much death around my family or me. Yes, I've had some grandparents pass away but as sad as it is, it was their time. They lived a full life. I can't imagine losing one parent, much less both.

I take a deep breath and ask, "So, what's up? Why are you here?"

He looks surprised at how quickly I changed the subject.

"You never called. Biology lab is Thursday, and that's two days away. What are you waiting for?" He seems annoyed with me, like I disappointed him somehow. *I have been avoiding him.*

"Professor Martin isn't going to keep giving you chances, Carly." He says sternly.

"I'm sorry," I say. "I've had a lot on my mind, so much going on. I haven't been focused on Bio or much of anything else, really. You're right. I'm taking advantage of a situation, and it's going to bite me in the ass." I look down at the floor and say, "I'm sorry."

I move to sit on my bed and look at the empty chair at my desk, silently suggesting that he sit there.

He takes my nonverbal cue and sits down at my desk.

"We need to make a plan, Carly. Do you have time now?" he asks.

"Well, yeah, I guess so," I answer. "Um, why don't we go down to the lounge where we can be more comfortable?" I'm suddenly feeling uneasy about being alone with him in my room. I don't think he'll do anything like Todd did, but I can't calm my nerves. I can't sit here with him alone, wondering what could happen. I don't trust myself, and I'm not ready to trust anyone else.

"Okay, great!" He exclaims enthusiastically. He jumps up and opens the door.

"After you," he gestures. Still a gentleman.

We walk down the hall to the empty lounge and settle at the large table in the corner. We have a pleasant view of the courtyard, and I sigh in relief.

"Let's get started. I have an outline of things that you missed while you had the 'chicken pox.'" He curls his long fingers into air quotes as he says chicken pox and smirks at me again.

"Whatever," I say, rolling my eyes and chuckling a little bit.

We spend the next two hours going through notes and lessons, then make a plan for me to make up the two labs I missed. He is so patient with me and helped me through the lessons with ease. He is so smart and dreamy. I need to snap out of it!

We finish studying for the night, but he doesn't seem ready to leave.

He reaches out, touches my curly hair, and brushes it off of my shoulder. I'm unprepared for his touch, and I flinch slightly. I want desperately to lean into his hand, but I hold back.

"It's still wet."

"Yes, when I air dry it, it takes a while. There's just so much of it." I answer with another full-body blush.

"It's nice," he quietly replies.

"Thanks."

We're staring into each other's eyes in silence.

"So, tomorrow night. Let's do this again?" he says, more of a question than a statement.

"Sure," I answer quickly, and then realize that tomorrow night is Wednesday. "I mean, no! I can't. It's Wednesday," I say, as if he knows what Wednesdays are to me.

"Yes, tomorrow is Wednesday, Carly," he affirms.

"No, Kyle, you don't understand. I have plans tomorrow night. Actually, every Wednesday night. With my friends. It's Wine Wednesday." I state matter-of-factly.

"Wine Wednesday?" He asks. "What is that?"

"Oh, it's just me and my best friends. We get together on Wednesday nights, drink cheap wine, talk, and gossip."

"So gossiping and drinking cheap wine is more important than your catching up in Biology? Hmph."

Really? He's annoyed with me?

"Listen, Kyle. I understand you want to help me catch up and keep me in Professor Martin's good graces, but Wednesdays with my friends are non-negotiable. I can find another time tomorrow to meet you in the lab." I feel bad and he looks disappointed in me. He doesn't understand how much I *need* tomorrow night with my friends. It's been the only thing that's made me feel safe, loved.

"Fine. How about over lunch? The lab is free from noon to one o'clock, and we should be able to get both of your lab projects done in that time." He stands up and starts walking toward the door.

"Kyle," I say, stammering a little bit. "I'll see you tomorrow at noon." I smile softly and look up at him. I don't want him to leave and I can tell he's disheartened. He turns to reach for the doorknob of the lounge and looks back at me. He holds my gaze longer than I'm comfortable with and I blush again.

"Great, Carly. See you tomorrow." He opens the door slowly, still staring into my eyes, almost through me. "Sweet dreams." He winks as his lips curl up a little, and just like that, his smile is back.

Dreams?

I look over at the clock on the wall and see that it's after midnight. *Whoa!* He was here for hours. Time flew by, and I didn't even realize it.

"Goodnight."

He turns away again and is gone. Out the door. *Damn.*

I gather my notes and make my way back to my empty room. I throw myself back onto my bed, into my comforter and pillows and stare at the ceiling. He must think that I'm a selfish brat. And was he flirting with me? I don't know what I'm doing. I wish he didn't have to leave. I want to lick that dimple in his chin, his lips, his neck.

I want to feel his strong arms around me and breathe him in.

Am I even ready for that? I want him to touch me, but I don't know

if I can even handle it.
 I can't figure this out on my own.
 I need my friends.
 And some pink wine.

# Chapter 15

## Tabitha

*Philadelphia, Pennsylvania*
**Past**
*Age 19*

LAST NIGHT WAS horrible. I royally fucked things up. I mean, who storms out of a bar without an explanation? I froze up and had to get out of there as fast as I could. Alex must think I'm crazy.

I *know* I'm crazy.

Loud, rustling noises pull me out of my funk. Kirsten is moving boxes of books from the stock room to the front.

"Tabby, we need to get these books inventoried and onto the shelves some time today. It shouldn't take you more than an hour or two," she says as she drops the third box of books onto the floor.

"No problem. Are you here much longer?" I ask.

"No, I have a dinner date with my parents. They're in town for a few days and demanded some quality time with yours truly." She smiles and hands me the keys to the store. "You don't mind locking up, do you?"

"Not at all," I answer.

"Great. Thanks honey, see you on Friday." With that, she turns and leaves the store.

"Great," I say sarcastically as the door closes behind her. I look around at all of the books that I need to inventory, that Kirsten just dumped on me. I see the clock and realize that I'll be there for at least four more hours. *At least I have plenty of time.*

It's another perfectly quiet day in the bookstore. We typically only see a handful of customers in a given day, but today is especially tranquil. I'll be able to tackle the new books and maybe I'll have time to sit back, relax, and read a bit.

I spend the next hour arranging the new books that Kirsten dropped on the floor. I'm holding the last book up to my nose and inhaling the scent that I love as the door opens and chimes.

I place the book on the shelf and turn toward the door.

"Alex," I say, surprised.

"Hey," he replies. He softly smiles as he walks toward the lounge. "I'm glad you're here today."

"Oh?" I ask.

"Well, yeah, Tabby. You ran out of the bar last night totally spooked, and I need to explain myself. And to find out if you're okay."

"I'm fine, Alex. Really," I lie.

"If you were fine you wouldn't have run out of The High Note as if you saw a ghost when I grabbed your wrist. I'm sorry. I clearly did something to upset you, and I'm just so sorry." His eyes move to the scar on my cheek. He stiffens and looks away. I can see his jaw clenching and his cheeks pulsing.

I'm silent for a few minutes and walk toward the lounge where he's standing.

"I don't know why you're here or why you invited me out the other night, but I am in no state or frame of mind to move forward with this. Whatever 'this' is."

I move my hand, gesturing between us. I look into his eyes so that he understands I'm serious. I can't do this.

He shrugs his shoulders and says, "I don't know what you're looking for, Tabby, but I'm just hoping to have coffee with you." He smirks as he sits down on the leather couch and crosses his leg over his knee. "I could use a friend right now, and I have a feeling you could too."

Wow. He's right. I don't think I've ever needed a friend more than I do right now. I have no one. I'm alone. Alone in the present and alone with my past.

Alone with my demons.

I lower my eyes and look at the floor. My cheeks start to flush, and I frown. I *really* want to be more than friends, but I know I can't handle it. I can't give myself to another person so freely. Tony ruined me. My pain is too fresh. I don't have the ability to trust anyone. But can I trust Alex?

"Okay," I say softly. "Friends." I want to say 'for now' so I can leave the door open for more, but I can't.

He snaps his fingers and then slaps his hands together. "Great! You, Tabitha Tabby Fletcher, have yourself a new *friend*." He smiles and my ears start to tingle. I'm blushing again, my chest burning with embarrassment. Yeah, this friend thing isn't going to work out.

He jumps up, and I flinch a little. I can't help my response to sudden movement, and I'm not sure if I ever will.

He strides over to the door and starts to walk out.

"Wait, where are you going?" I'm surprised he's about to bolt out of here.

He leans out the door, grabs a cardboard cup holder with two large iced coffees from the ground outside, smiles, and winks at me.

"I took a chance and thought you'd agree to an iced coffee with your new *friend*," he says, pointing his thumbs back at himself, grinning ear-to-ear.

I melt. My chest starts to burn, and my heart is pounding. *Friends.*

He grabs one of the iced coffees and extends it toward me. I grab the cup and our fingers brush against each other, mixing with the condensation from the cup. My fingers are damp, and he rubs his thumb along my knuckles as he hands the cup to me. *Friends.* Friends don't do that.

I pull my hand away quickly. "Thanks, Alex." I look into his eyes. There is heat between us and his glassy eyes turn liquid and soft.

We stare at each other for what seems like hours. I finally look away and step back to find a seat in the lounge area. I practically fall into the chair.

"So, tell me about your band," I say, not making eye contact.

"What do you want to know?"

"Everything," I state simply. I smile at him and put the straw in my mouth. I bite down on the straw almost bending it. It's a habit I have. I bite every straw immediately as if I'm marking it as my 'property'. I look up at him and wait for his next words as I continue to chew on the end of my straw.

"Where do I start?" He takes a deep breath, then takes a sip of his iced coffee. He pauses and starts, "Dax, our drummer, and I grew up together. He and I are practically brothers. His family took me in when things went bad with my Pops. Tristan, our bassist, is Dax's cousin, and he was the only bassist we knew, so he just stuck around." He chuckles a little and shakes his head. There is clearly an inside joke that I'm not in on.

"Then there's Garrett. He plays lead guitar, and he's just Garrett." He smiles at me. "That's our band, Epic Fail. We've been together for almost five years. We don't always get along, but we all actually 'get' each other."

"Well, from what I heard the other night, you really make great music together," I say softly. I'm sorry that I missed most of their set, and I want to hear more from them. From Alex.

"So, Tabby, what's your story? Where did you come from?"

I'm silent for a few moments. What do I tell him?

That I came from an ambulance bay at Temple University Hospital?

That I don't know who my parents are?

That I'm a depressed, pathetic, damaged and distraught nineteen-year-old that has no hope?

Fuck. Me.

I stumble a little over my words. "I'm from Philadelphia. I was born here. My mother... Well, she left me at Temple University Hospital shortly after my birth. I think my birthday is Halloween; at least that's what the doctors and nurses estimated when they took me in. I was named after a famous television witch who I know nothing about." My eyes start to water, and a tear is threatening to spill out. I start blinking rapidly. *Don't cry.*

Alex is silent, and his face softens. He just stares at me.

I start shifting in my chair.

"Anyway, I was raised mostly by my adoptive mother, Trina, until I was seven. She died in an accident." I pause. This is too hard to replay.

My tragic fucking life.

He puts his iced coffee down and shifts forward in his seat. "I'm sorry, you didn't have to tell me all of that." He frowns and I can tell he feels bad.

I'm nervous, so I just keep talking. "There isn't really much else to tell. After Trina died, I was placed in several foster homes that just never took. I left my last foster home when I was seventeen and moved, well, ran away to Portland, Oregon. I got a job, met someone who wasn't very nice to me, and now I'm here. End of story." I stop and look away. I said too much. I can't talk about Tony. Or Sara. I just can't.

He takes a deep breath and looks at me. "I'm sorry, Tabby. I'm just so sorry."

"Did that 'someone' give you that scar?" he asks quietly and his gaze shifts to my cheek.

"Yes." It is so hard to admit that I let someone do this to me. To mark me. To defile me. Tony made me ugly, inside and out.

He stares at me, and I feel the warmth from his eyes and, as uneasy as I am sharing private and intimate details, his eyes soothe me.

"I didn't have the best parents either." He pauses.

"My mother died when I was five and she was the only light in my life. My pops raised my sister and me on his own. He tried, but he was a mess. My sister left home as soon as she could afford it, and my pops, well, he never understood it. He started to take it out on me." He stops abruptly, and I'm certain he isn't going to continue. Maybe he has his own scars. Marks.

After several moments of silence, he continues. "It wasn't good with my pops, and I got out of there too. Dax's family took me in when I couldn't take it anymore. They are my family, and it feels like they always have been. Other than my sister, I really don't have any blood family left."

I take in all that Alex has shared. He's not *unlike* me at all. He has experienced pain and loss. He is damaged too.

"I'm sorry." Tears form in my eyes because I truly feel his pain and his heartache. I know what it's like to barely have a family. To have no one. I just want to wrap myself around him and for us to tell each other that all will be okay. To feel it and know it for sure.

I wish I could feel his warmth and comfort. I need that so badly. I thought I'd be afraid of intimacy, considering what I've been through, but with Alex, it would be different. Tender. Gentle.

It wouldn't be like it was with Tony.

We sit silently for a little while as we both take turns sipping our iced coffees.

"Tabby, I can't begin to imagine the pain you hide behind or what caused it. But I can try to understand if you want to share more. I can be here for you."

God, if only he knew. He can't possibly be ready to hear about my pain. I'm a damaged, beat-down shell of a girl. Of a woman. I've given up so much to have this freedom. I've given up my child. My soul. What would he think of me if he knew? He'd think I'm a coward. I just can't open myself up like that. I thought I could, but I can't.

"Thanks, Alex. I appreciate it." I hesitate and decide that I'm not going to say any more. Scare him off. I don't want to lose the only friend I've had in years.

So, I change the subject. "When's your next gig? I'd like to come and see the whole show this time." I smile slightly and try to make it seem genuine.

"Next Saturday. We're back at The High Note. You should come early; meet us for a bite to eat. Meet the guys. What do you say?"

I have a shift at the diner in the morning on Saturday, and I'm off from the bookstore.

"Sounds great." I fumble for my phone and set up a reminder for my alarm to sound hours before I need to be there because I can't be late again.

"Why don't you meet us there at seven thirty? We can have some dinner and chill out before our gig. We go on at nine PM." He pauses, waiting for me to confirm.

"Okay, Saturday it is." I'm excited, and I feel like he might be too.

"Great, Tabby. You won't regret it. The guys, well, they can be intense, but I'm guessing you can handle that. They'll like you, I'm sure." He smiles and tilts his head. Some of his locks fall to the side of his eyebrow, and I just want to run my fingers through his hair. To let my hand linger and feel the pulse in his temple. To bury my head in his neck.

As I'm picturing my intimate contact with his hair and scalp, he gets up and starts walking toward the door. He turns to me before he leaves. "See you Saturday, Tabs." He smiles and slowly walks out the door. *Tabs.* He created a nickname for me and I almost melt.

I need to focus. He's clearly affecting me in ways that scream 'more than friend'. But, I need to take this one step at a time and learn how to be close to someone again.

Learn how to trust again.

Learn how to be me.

I don't even know who I am.

# Chapter 16

## Carly

*New Brunswick, New Jersey*
**Past**
*Age 18*

*BEEP, BEEP, BEEP!*

*Arg!* I slam my hand on my night table, trying to silence my alarm. This has become a ritual for me and the mornings have become harder and harder to face.

I turn off my alarm and squint at the clock. *Seven-thirty AM.* I have some time to get some things done before the lab re-do with Kyle.

I slowly get out of bed and trip over a pile of laundry in front of my bed. *What the hell?*

I had piled these clothes by my closet. *Ginger!* She must have been here at some point and moved them. What is she trying to tell me? I didn't think the clothes were in her way.

I pick up my clothes and throw them into my empty laundry basket by the door. I commence my morning ritual, washing my face and brushing my teeth. I tie my long messy hair into a ponytail and step into my flip-flops.

"I will be productive today," I say to myself in the mirror.

I swipe some change from my dresser, grab my clothesbasket, and head down to the ninth floor laundry room. I've got my MP3 player blasting in my ears, and I'm skipping down the stairs. Blink-182 is piping through my head and "What's My Age Again" is giving me an extra boost. Just what I need for the long day ahead of me.

I hop into the laundry room and place my basket on top of an empty washer. *Yes! It's free!* As I'm sorting my laundry and singing along to Blink, I hear the door slam shut behind me. I speak over my shoulder without turning around. "Sorry, the last washer is claimed." I'm smirking at my small victory.

I hear a huff and something crash to the floor. I rip my earbuds from my ears and spin around, my defenses high.

"Kyle!" Shit, he scared the crap out of me. "Was that necessary?" I chastise him.

"Sorry," he mumbles after dropping his own clothesbasket. "I just thought I'd get to a machine since it's early, and it's the only time today I can get a load done. And well, now I don't have an opportunity since you have that machine." He points to the one that I've claimed. Yes, it's *mine!*

"Well, clearly, I was here first." I'm cocky now and giving him attitude over a washing machine. Geez, I need to chill out.

He sulks and bends to pick up his basket. "I guess I'll go down to the fifth floor."

Man, that sucks. Everybody knows that the fifth floor washing machines steal your quarters, so no one ever uses them anymore. He'll have to go down several more floors just to get his laundry done. Suddenly, I feel pity for him. I mean, who wouldn't? I absolutely hate having to travel more than one floor to do my laundry.

"Alright, I have a compromise." I smile slyly.

"What?" He's curious now, raises his eyebrows, and scrunches his chin. I melt a little when I notice his incredibly perfect dimple. I flush as warmth spreads through my chest.

"Well, I was going to do my whites first, so if you have any that you'd like to throw in with mine, I can share."

He looks at me cautiously. I haven't given him my ultimatum yet, and he looks skeptical. "What's in it for you?" He asks, curious.

"Well, we're supposed to make up two of my Bio labs today at lunch time. Can we postpone until later in the week?" I take a quick breath and don't pause too long because I don't want him to interrupt. "I mean, I know they're due tomorrow, but I could really use some time today to catch up on other things and I have a date night with my friends." Shit, now I just sound like a selfish ass.

"Really, Carly. You are going to *allow* me to wash my underwear with yours so I can turn the other way and lie to Professor Martin *again* so you can get some beauty rest and drink wine with your friends tonight?" Well, when he puts it that way...

"But, I..."

"No, save it, please." He picks up his basket and turns to leave. "I'm done covering and lying for you, Carly. Get your shit together on your own. And stop being so damn selfish!" He starts to raise his voice. "I've been doing what I can to help you catch up because you had the 'chicken pox,'" he uses finger quotes again, "and now you're just completely taking advantage. Is this how you plan to get through college? Using people? Lying? Jesus, what the fuck was I thinking?"

*Oh no.*

"Kyle...," I have no words. He is so right. I've been using him. Using him as a shield to avoid my scholastic responsibilities. Using him as a crutch.

"Wait!" I yell as he's turning to leave. "Please, Kyle, I'm sorry. You're right. I need to get my shit together."

I walk toward him and take the basket from his hands. He doesn't fight me and allows me to take it. I put it down next to mine and start to toss his whites and lights into the washing machine with mine.

I want to explain to him why I've been so delinquent, but I can't tell him everything.

"Listen. I've had some things happen recently that caused me to put school and classes on the back burner. You're absolutely right; I need to get focused again. It starts with Biology. Today." I smile, hoping he warms up to my slight admission of guilt and ownership.

"What do you want from me?" He's clearly not fully invested in my plea.

I drop the quarters into the slots, start the washing machine, and turn to face him again.

"What I want is your help with my Bio labs like you promised. I will do this load of laundry, washed, dried, and folded. I don't iron. That's my deal. Do you accept?" I'm smiling big now. He can't turn me down; I'm turning on my charm.

His eyes brighten a bit as he smiles. His smile...

"Deal. But you have to meet me at noon; we have two labs to complete. And you're doing *all* of my laundry." He's chuckling now. *Good.*

"Fine. Deal." I shove my hand out to shake on it. He grabs my hand and wraps his fingers firmly around mine. I feel our connection as my entire right arm is now tingling, and my cheeks are burning. *Please don't let go.*

He looks into my eyes, and his smile gets bigger. "Great. My room is 909. When this load is done, swing by and get the rest. Oh, and it may take you a couple of trips." He laughs out loud and turning to leave the room, calls over his shoulder. "I haven't done laundry in two weeks, so you may be here a while."

*I guess I deserve this.*

"See you soon!" He saunters out of the laundry room and heads down the hall.

I flop into the chair across from the washing machine and turn up my MP3 player to "Dammit", the next Blink-182 song on my playlist.

Yeah, seems about right.

~

Several hours and loads of laundry later, I'm finished. I lug the overflowing basket of Kyle's clean laundry to his room. His door is slightly open so I gracefully kick it open and throw both his laundry and myself inside the room.

He's sitting on his bed with a girl next to him. An extremely gorgeous girl leans into his side. I clearly just interrupted something. My heart drops in my chest. He has someone. *Oh no. I was hoping...*

"Oh," I say. "I was just bringing the rest of your laundry." I drop the basket in the open doorway and leave. I can't get out of here fast enough. I feel awkward and sad. Do I even have a right to feel this way? He's nothing to me, right?

"Wait! Carly!" He's calling after me. He's now in the hallway behind me and seems apologetic. "I'll see you at noon, right?"

"Yes, see you at noon."

I turn to the stairs that lead to my floor.

We're just friends.

Friends that do laundry together.

Nothing more.

*Then why does my heart hurt?*

# Chapter 17

## Carly

Spring Lake, New Jersey
**Present**
Age 29

Dear Emily,

I can't believe that soon you'll be here, in our arms, in our lives. Just a few weeks away!

We're ready for you sweetheart. So very ready.

We love you so much already.

See you soon.

Love,

Mama & Daddy

I finish jotting down this quick note to Emily, and when I hear the garage door open, I close my journal. *Kyle.*

I tuck the journal into my night table, and walk down the stairs to meet him. Portraits line the stairway, and I notice the smiling faces of our families. This is a wall of hope. A wall of love. Our family is about to become a forever family. An open spot at the bottom is reserved for our first family portrait with Emily. I touch the bare wall and smile.

Kyle emerges from the garage as I enter the kitchen. His arms are full of groceries and goodies from the wine store. It's Wednesday, and we're expecting our friends for our weekly get together.

He places the groceries on the granite counter top of the center island in the kitchen and reaches out to me.

"Hey babe," he says softly as he pulls me into an embrace. He drops his lips to my neck and places small kisses just under my ear. He knows how much this drives me crazy, and I'm already on fire from head to toe. His onslaught of kisses and nips are building into a frenzy. I start to wiggle in his arms.

"Kyle," I sigh. "They're going to be here any minute." I giggle as he wraps his arms around me and begins to playfully tickle my ribs.

I'm just about out of breath from laughing so hard when our back door flies open.

Kyle and I release each other quickly, and he turns, adjusting himself to hide his arousal.

"Becca!" I exclaim.

Becca enters the kitchen a little slowly with a huge smile on her face. "It seems I've interrupted something. Someone is always interrupting something with you two." Laughing, she places canvas bags onto the center island next to the bags that Kyle brought in earlier.

"Oh, it was nothing," I lie. If we had continued our antics any longer, *I* would have been on the center island next to the groceries.

"Well, as long as nothing interferes with Wine Wednesday!" She laughs and skips toward me, pulling me into her arms. We hug each other tightly, and she kisses my cheek.

"Hey now! That's my girl!" Kyle says while laughing, pretending to be jealous.

She unpacks the bags that she brought with her. Cheese, crackers, and two bottles of wine are placed on the counter. "So, how was your lunch with Tabitha today?" She asks casually.

"That's a topic of discussion for later, chick!" Callie exclaims from behind us. We didn't hear her come into the kitchen.

She hugs Becca then me and places her satchel on the counter.

"Girls, seriously, what's with all of the food? There's enough here

*Dear Emily*

for the entire weekend. Did I miss something?" Kyle is surveying the goodies as he's pulling out crackers and eating them.

"Hey, we can't come empty handed." Callie states.

We arrange all of the snack foods onto serving trays and bring them into the family room. We have an oversized leather sectional couch that can comfortably seat up to eight people. When we host Wine Wednesday, we've been known to fall asleep together on this couch; it's that comfortable and spacious.

We start to take our places on the couch when the doorbell rings.

Kyle answers the door and is immediately pulled into a bro hug. *Manny is here.*

Me, Callie and Becca squeal with delight. Our night has officially begun.

"Ladies," Manny states, looking around the room.

"Manny!" We shout almost in unison. We all jump up and take turns hugging him. He gets to me, lifts me into his arms, and squeezes tight. "Hey Car," he says softly into my ear.

I smile as he puts me down onto the floor.

He hands Kyle a large bag and walks past him, stating, "You can take care of that, right buddy?"

Kyle huffs and brings the bag into the kitchen. He really is so tolerant of our friends.

I flop back onto the couch between Becca and Callie when Manny hands me my glass of pinot noir. Our collective taste in wine has exponentially increased.

"Becca, who is that guy with you in that picture on your Facebook page? He is *hot*!" Manny is always so subtle.

Becca looks around the room and we all silently stare at her, awaiting her answer. I don't remember seeing the picture on Facebook, but I have admittedly been preoccupied lately.

"What picture?" Becca asks elusively.

"Seriously, Bec. C'mon!" Manny is insistent.

She's silently looking around the room, hoping we all drop the topic. Too bad for her, we're all waiting intently for her answer.

She takes a deep breath and begins, "Well, his name is Lance and we just met a few weeks ago. He's a personal trainer and owns his own fitness company. He's… very nice."

Manny's jaw drops and Callie asks, "Personal trainer? Are you a client?"

Becca doesn't answer immediately, and Kyle enters the room with a tray of snacks.

"Kyle!" Becca says a little too enthusiastically. "Here, let me help you with that." She jumps up and reaches for the tray. She seems happy for the distraction, and I'm sure she hopes the subject will change.

"Becca?" Callie interjects. "What's the deal with Lance?"

Becca's smile is now infectious, and she answers, "Ask me again in a few weeks." She winks at Manny who is still dumbfounded.

I laugh out loud at this vision and turn to Becca. "Honey, you just tell us all about him when you're ready." I reach out and squeeze her hand and her eyes soften.

"Becca, I'm with Manny. I want to know what's going on!" Kyle says. He is smiling playfully at all of us as his eyes sparkle. I want to jump into his arms and squeeze him until he can't breathe.

"Guys, seriously, I don't want to jinx things. Lance is really great, and we're taking things slow. Okay?" Becca is a bit more forceful in her delivery, and we all look around the room at each other.

I nod. "Sure Bec, tell us when you're ready, but I think I speak on behalf of all of us when I say, 'Damn, girl!'"

We all laugh and Manny claps his hands and stands as he applauds her. "Becca, good for you. If he's hot and you don't want him any longer, send him my way. You know how much I love fit men."

Kyle settles onto the couch and wraps his arms around me. He leans into my neck, inhales deeply, and kisses my shoulder. I melt into his arms. I need to get my physical response under control. After all these years, his touch still makes my belly clench. His kiss travels up my neck and he places a wet kiss on the side of my neck. I inhale deeply and lean back into him.

"Guys, seriously, get a room," Manny bellows.

I giggle and place my hands on Kyle's legs.

"Becca, we're happy for you, and we certainly don't need details on your love life. We just want to know if you're happy," Kyle says while nuzzling into my ear. My entire body reacts and comes alive.

Becca can't hide her huge smile and her eyes light up. "Thanks, guys."

That is the end of that.

Becca is private to begin with, so I understand her reservations about sharing a relatively new relationship with our crazy group. She's looking away, and we all react to her silence.

"So, Carly, anything new with Tabitha?" Manny asks nonchalantly.

I pause briefly as Kyle squeezes my waist.

"I had lunch with her last week." I take a deep breath. I want to share with my best friends how happy and confident I am that this is going to happen, but a small part of me is guarded and worried that Emily is not going to be ours. When we had lunch together, I saw something so slight in Tabitha's eyes that indicated something, like regret. I shake my head. Regardless of how much I think this adoption is going to happen, I still have to guard my heart.

"It's good, for now…"

My friends all stare at me. The concern on their faces is evident, and I'm waiting for the next statement. I'm afraid to share my fears, worried they may indeed become reality. It already feels like Emily is part of our family and I'm terrified that may never happen.

"Car, what's up?" Callie asks.

"I don't know, guys, it's just…," I start, pause, and start again. "Well, I'm just worried. I'm worried that Tabitha is going to change her mind. That's normal, right?"

Becca speaks up. "Yes, it's completely normal. Why wouldn't you have those feelings? I mean she is giving up her *baby*. If she didn't have second thoughts, I'd think she was crazy. Seriously, it's okay for you to be worried. But just try to keep everything in perspective. You've had some good interactions with her, and she seems to be committed to her plan. Just hang in there."

"You know," Callie chimes in, "I totally agree with what Becca is saying. Tabitha needs to go through all of the emotions of what's about to happen to accept the finality of it. It's like she's going through the grieving process but she hasn't yet lost her child. Her emotions are going to be all over the place, and so are yours. Ride this out and I just know it's going to happen, honey."

"It's a done deal." Manny turns to Becca. "What's not a done deal is you and Lance. C'mon, Becca." Manny is now whining. "Give us the scoop!"

This is why I love my friends. They let me share my insecurities and make me feel validated and at ease.

Manny fills our wine glasses, raises his own, and toasts. "Cheers! Carly and Kyle, as you begin the life that you've always dreamed of and welcome a little girl into your home. Becca, may you enjoy many sleepless nights with your hunk of a man. Callie, just for being you and a constant pillar of support in our family." He puts his glass to his lips and takes a sip.

"Cheers, Manny!" Callie says, "The Wine Wednesday founder and chairman."

We all clink our glasses and finish off what wine we have left.

I settle back into Kyle's chest and rest my head into his shoulder.

Kyle chuckles behind me and whispers in my ear. "It's going to be fine, Carly. Emily is our daughter, and nothing is going to happen to change that. I can feel it. I *promise*." He kisses my neck lightly and now all is right with the world.

I believe him.

His promises are always forever.

# Chapter 18

## Tabitha

Philadelphia, Pennsylvania
**Present**
Age 20

Dear Emily,

I'm getting ready to say goodbye to you, little girl. Carly and I had lunch again today, and the more time I spend with her the more comfortable I am with my decision. We had a wonderful lunch, and I saw what type of mother she's going to be. She and Kyle are going to be perfect parents for you. You'll be a part of a perfect family.

I have some things that I'll be giving Carly and Kyle for you.

I'm finding it hard to part with a blanket that Trina made for me when she adopted me. It's a knitted blanket with pink, green, and yellow blocks in a checkerboard pattern. It's still so soft. The corners are worn because Trina told me that I used to rub the blanket between my fingers to soothe myself to sleep. I want you to have this blanket always. A piece of me.

I also want you to have two pictures.

Alex and Seth.

One of these men is your father. They each hold a special place in my heart and someday I will try to share with Carly and Kyle as much *about each of them as I can.*

*I hope you understand some day why I made the decision that I have.*

*I love you, sweet girl.*

*Hugs,*

*Mommy –Tabitha*

Man, this is getting harder and harder every day. In about three weeks, my baby will be born and then she'll be gone. I feel like I'm on a death march over the hill and around the bend I'll be slaughtered. I'm walking over that proverbial hill, knowing full well that my life as I know it will abruptly end. I won't have Emily. She'll be gone.

I sob as I sign my name to the letter. My tears fall over my cheeks and the scars of my past. I swipe at my eyes and place the letter into a large envelope along with the others I have written.

I rub my baby bump as I feel Emily moving and kicking. She's been so active these past few weeks. It's as if she knows something is up and can sense the anxiety that I'm feeling.

"Everything will be okay, baby," I whisper as I rub my belly.

I'm startled as my phone rings. "Hello?" I answer quickly.

"Tabitha, hi. It's Lisa from Home Sweet Home Adoptions." Lisa is my social worker and has held my hand throughout this entire gut-wrenching process.

"Hi, Lisa."

"I'm calling to check in on you to see how you're doing? I understand that you've had several meetings with Carly since your conference call. How'd everything go?" Lisa asks.

"Good, Lisa. I'm happy with how things are progressing. I'm just… I'm just so sad. I'm afraid of this pregnancy coming to an end. But I know that I'm doing the right thing for Emily and for me."

"Tabitha, any time you need to talk about anything, I am here. I'm here to help you come to terms with your decision and handle your emotions. You have my cell number and can call me anytime."

"Yes, Lisa, I know. And thank you."

"The other reason for my call is to move forward with some of the logistics. We have your hospital plan all set, so the staff at University Hospital is aware of your plans for adoption. There will be a social worker, Michelle, to help you through everything you need to do."

As she's speaking, I'm realizing how much more real this is. I'm starting to panic again and I try to relax myself.

"Michelle will work with Carly and Kyle to make sure that all of your wishes at the hospital are followed."

"Okay," I say softly.

"Next, we have to work with your attorney to start posting legal notices for the absentee potential birth father. These are going to be posted in area newspapers for the next thirty to sixty days. This notice is typically a formality, but when we deal with situations where a birth father is unknown or absent, we're required by law to post these notices. It gives him the opportunity to come forward and claim his child."

"I understand. You know that I tried to reach him once. He's finished with me, Lisa. So post what you need to post, but he won't come forward. I'm sure of it."

"In addition, you'll be receiving a package shortly for Seth. As he's currently involved in your life and since he's a potential birth father, he'll need to sign his revocation agreements as well. You mentioned that he would do this, correct?" she asks.

"Yes, he'll sign them right away. He's very sure of his decision, Lisa." I wipe tears from my cheeks.

"Finally," Lisa continues. "Carly and Kyle have signed an agreement consenting to open communications throughout Emily's life. They've agreed to send pictures and letters to you at least twice a year until she turns eighteen. They've also openly stated that they will consider future visits with Emily if you so choose. I know this is a lot to think about right now, but I have to tell you that I've seen open adoption arrangements such as this work splendidly as long as both sides maintain certain boundaries."

Wow. I hadn't even thought about any of this. I honestly don't know how to react. Would I be able to handle seeing Emily when she's older? Knowing that I didn't raise her? What would she be told about me? This prospect scares me, and I'm not sure what to say.

"Do you have any questions, Tabitha?" Lisa asks.

"No, you've covered just about everything that I need to know. I'll call you if I think of anything. Thanks, Lisa." I cover my mouth and stifle a sob as I hang up the phone.

This is becoming far too real, and I'm not sure that I'm ready for what's next.

"Hey Tabby," Seth says softly as he stands in my bedroom doorway.

"Oh!" I'm startled. I didn't hear him come into my apartment.

"What's wrong, babe? Why are you crying?" He walks over to the bed and sits close to me. He places his hands on my knees and slowly circles his thumbs.

He's so sweet and just wants me to be okay. I know this. I take a deep breath.

"Seth, this is just so hard. You know? I feel like the next few weeks are going to be so difficult. The last few weeks with my baby girl." I place my hand back on my belly and lower my head.

"Babe, she will always be with you. Always. But we're doing the right thing. Emily will have a better life with Carly and Kyle. We aren't ready for this, Tabby." His voice is kind and soothing, but his words aren't encouraging. He doesn't feel this with me. He can't possibly understand. I'm giving up a piece of me. *Another* piece of me. First Sara, now Emily. Seth has fully admitted that he doesn't want this child. And what if she is Alex's? What would Seth do then? We couldn't handle this either way. I'm not strong enough.

"Thanks, Seth. I'm ready to move on, but I'm not ready. I can't explain it. This is nearly impossible. Emily doesn't belong to me anymore; she is Carly and Kyle's already. I can feel it. Somehow, I already know how right this situation is, and I'm beginning to accept it fully, but I'm feeling as if this is it for me. My last chance to be a mother."

I stop and stare into Seth's eyes, hoping he can understand where I'm coming from. He maintains eye contact and slowly reaches up to touch my face. He brushes his thumb over the faint scar on my cheek and wraps his fingers into my hair, slowly massaging the back of my neck. His touch sends butterflies through my body.

My body physically responds to him.

Aches for him. *Aches for something.*

But my mind is elsewhere.

He leans into me, and I let him come close as his tongue sweeps across my lips. His nose swipes across my cheek as he inhales and says my name. I take a deep breath and yield to him. His lips gently touch mine again as his tongue presses further into my mouth. I finally kiss him back and press my body into his. His fingers move tenderly down and press into my lower back, softly caressing me. They're so light that chills travel up my spine and radiate through my belly.

His lips are now all over my face. My neck. The swells of my breasts. He's breathing heavily, and his hot breath counteracts the chills that just started and heat is now pooling between my thighs. His fingertips softly touch my breasts and he begins circling my right nipple as his mouth travels to the outside of my shirt and his tongue teases my other erect nipple.

He slowly lifts me so that I'm straddling his waist and we are facing each other. He stares into my eyes, pulling me toward him. I feel his erection beneath me, and I grind my hips into him. I immediately feel a jolt through my core as my body reacts to his firmness. I press against him with more force. I need him inside me now.

My panties are getting wetter and wetter. I place my head into his neck, then lick and bite the sensitive area below his ear. He moans into my neck and pulls me so that my lips are back on his. He's attacking my mouth, our tongues entwined. Our breathing is heavy as we continue savoring each other.

Slowly, his mouth leaves mine as he lifts me up a little so that he can give my breasts more attention.

"Take your top off, Tabby," he commands. I remove my hands from his hair. Doing as he asks, I lift my shirt over my head and throw it to the floor, and then slowly reach behind my back and unclasp my bra, letting my engorged breasts fall free. I then place my hands back into his hair, bringing his lips back to mine. Pressing my tongue firmly into his mouth, slowly entwining it with his, he kisses me passionately as his hands travel down my back.

His fingers find the outline of my panties as they start to travel under the elastic, touching my sensitive skin. I gasp as he pushes my panties aside entirely and strokes my core. I can't control myself as I pant loudly, feeling his fingers swirl in the wetness that is pooling between my legs. My walls clench and spasm around his finger as it slowly enters me.

"God, Seth!" I yell between moans. "Please," I beg.

"Please what, Tabitha?" He growls and nips at my earlobe.

"I need you inside me!" I'm begging. I need him. *I need to feel.*

He pulls his finger out of me and pushes me away. He stands and opens his jeans and quickly pushes them down his legs. He kicks them off, then removes his boxer briefs and his cock springs free as he lies down onto the bed.

"Come here, Tabby." He gestures for me to straddle him.

I remove my panties and drop them to the floor. My belly is so large at this point that I feel awkward, but I try to crawl seductively across the bed with a smirk on my lips. He grabs my wrists and sits up with his back against the headboard.

"You are so fucking gorgeous. So beautiful." He pulls me to him, taking my breast into his mouth. His tongue is quickly sweeping, lapping over my already hard nipple. As he softly bites down, I start to break apart.

He pulls my hips up, then pulls me down over his throbbing cock. As he slowly slips into me, my walls start to pulse around him. Slowly guiding my hips up and down, the heat continues to push into my core. I need him. This release.

I'm climbing already and can feel my walls contract further around him. My breasts are now heaving, and he can barely keep his tongue on my nipple. Barely brushing his teeth across the top of my breast, Seth plants his mouth onto the side of my neck. He grabs my hips firmly and starts to pump faster and faster into me.

Our breaths are heavy, and I feel my release building quickly. He drives faster and harder, and I break apart just as he is fully seated inside me. I can feel him pulsating with his own release as mine continues.

*Dear Emily*

Our fluids mix and consume us both.

"I love you, Tabby." His breath comes in short pants as he softly bites my earlobe.

He slowly pulls out of me and rests his head onto my shoulder. I suddenly feel the emptiness, the longing for him to fill me again. My need isn't love, though. It's physical, the need to be possessed. I lean into his chest as he lies back down on the bed, pulling me with him. I slide next to him and burrow into his side, still gripping his neck.

I feel terrible thinking this, but I don't think I love him. I don't think I can love anyone. I just can't return the sentiment. I'm not ready to give myself fully to him or anyone. Yes, we've fucked. Made love. But I can't yet give him my everything, my soul.

I remain silent as he pulls the blankets over us. He leans over and kisses the top of my head.

"I'll still love you tomorrow, and the next day, and the day after that. I'm not going anywhere, Tabby. Ever. I'm here for you for as long as it takes for you to be fully here with me." He turns the light off and breathes deeply.

I feel tears pool in my eyes and I squeeze them shut. I don't believe him. If circumstances were different and I decided to keep Emily, he would bolt. I just know it. Or at least I try to convince myself that's what he would do. I have to think the worst to accept the reality.

I'm just not sure I can ever be fully connected to Seth.

To anyone.

I start to drift off to sleep, listening to his steady breath beneath my cheek.

It's not Seth's face that I see as sleep engulfs me.

It's Alex's.

# Chapter 19

## Carly

*New Brunswick, New Jersey*
**Past**
*Age 18*

THE COLD AIR envelops my face as I walk out of the doors of Thomas Hall. I'm finally awake and out on time. I'm so pleased with myself as I stride across campus on my way to meet Kyle to make up the Biology labs.

This morning sucked big time. I'm so disappointed that I found Kyle with a girl. Of course he has a girlfriend, why wouldn't he? *Why do I feel this way?*

I need to get through these next few hours so that I can make up these labs and be done with him. I'm so embarrassed, I read his signals wrong and got my hopes up. I wish it was different, and that I was ready to feel the way that I am.

"Hello, Pussycat." I hear a voice behind me. Todd nudges me with his shoulder as I slow down. "Where are you going? Maybe I can take you there?"

I feel sick to my stomach as he glares into my eyes. "I'm… I'm meeting someone in a few minutes, Todd. I can't talk to you. Not now, not ever."

He roughly grabs hold of my arm as I start to walk away. "Kitty-

Cat, I haven't stopped thinking about you and your tight body since Halloween, and I'm ready for seconds." The wild glint in his eyes sends chills down my spine. He is dangerous, and I need to get away from him immediately.

I yank my arm away and turn to run.

"I'll be seeing you around, Pussycat."

I am now full-on sprinting as I look back over my shoulder. He's still standing where I left him. Staring. Menacing.

I make it to Manning Hall with five minutes to spare. My heart is pounding. I'm so rattled by Todd. *Is he stalking me?* As I run up the stairs to the Biology lab on the second floor, my flip-flops catch on the bottom step. Losing control, I fall forward and I feel a strong arm grab me around my waist. I'm about to scream when I hear a kind voice.

"Easy there, killer," Kyle says through a wide grin. He pulls me back into his chest as I steady myself. "Flip-flops? Really, Carly?" He's chuckling now as he shakes his head.

"What?" I ask, gaining my composure. I look around for any sign of Todd, worried that he followed me. "Flip-flops are comfortable. They didn't cause my fall. I just, uh, tripped on the first step. Lost my footing." My cheeks are burning from embarrassment, and I pull away from him. I rub the tender spot on my arm where Todd grabbed me.

"Right. Whatever you say."

He gestures for me to go up the stairs first. "After you."

We walk upstairs, this time without incident, and arrive at the lab.

"I'm sure you just want to get this over with, right?" I'm anxious and embarrassed.

"Yup," he says quickly. "We have two labs to get you caught up on. The first is determining blood type, and the second is comparing plant and animal cells."

This is not the least bit appealing to me. I'm taking Biology as my science elective toward my degree as a secondary education English teacher. This class is a necessity, but I just want to teach English.

I toss my backpack onto one of the empty tables and sit on a nearby stool. He takes a set of keys out of his pocket and unlocks a cabinet along the wall. He starts to gather equipment we'll need for our lab work.

"You know, Carly, you can at least act like you want to be here," he huffs as he places a microscope on the table in front of me.

He pushes a few papers around on the table and gets the rest of the materials. I watch him as he places some drops of water onto each of the papers and turns to grab something else.

He places some slides on the table and grabs my right wrist, turning my palm facing up. Suddenly, I feel a sharp pain on the tip of my finger and scream, "What the fuck!"

Ouch! Motherfucking OUCH!

He's still holding my wrist tightly with one hand while he places a stick against my now bleeding fingertip, collecting droplets of my blood. He does this three more times until he collects a total of four samples and places them on the paper on top of where he placed the water. He finally lets go of my wrist and presses a cotton ball onto the tip of my finger.

I'm burning all over, mostly from anger. "A heads up would have been nice!" I yank my hand from his grip, remove the cotton ball, and put the tip of my finger into my mouth. *Relief.*

"Hey, if I told you what I was going to do, would you have let me?" He lifts up the paper with my blood droplets on them. He starts to move the paper slowly in circles so that the blood mixes with the water and enzymes.

I remove my finger from my mouth with a loud pop. "Seriously, Kyle. You don't just do that to someone without warning. I mean, look at this!" I hold my finger up so he can see that it's still bleeding.

He chuckles and looks down at the paper in his hand.

"Type O. Congratulations, you're a universal donor." He smiles and pushes some worksheets across the table to me. "Complete this lab sheet while I get the microscope and slides ready for the next assignment." He turns and I look down at the paper. I start to answer the questions, following the procedures that he just performed on my now throbbing finger.

After several minutes, my notes are captured on the sheet in front of me. I guess that was easy, but I certainly won't admit it to Kyle.

"Next up is a comparison of plant and animal cells. Are you ready, or do you think you'll need me to call you an ambulance?" He smirks sarcastically.

"I'm fine," I huff.

He pushes another worksheet to me and gets the slides set up. "I swear I did this exercise in fifth grade. I'm sure I can tell the difference between plant and animal cells." I feel like I'm completely wasting his time.

The microscope is now in front of me and he is standing behind my stool. He reaches both arms around me as he places a slide on the tray. He leans over me, his chest pressing into my back. "Now, take a look and tell me what you see." His mouth is practically touching my ear as I shudder. How can I possibly concentrate? I surprise myself with my reaction. All I want is for him to kiss my neck and wrap his arms around me. This is completely wrong. He has a girlfriend and I'm damaged.

I start to take notes as he switches the slides on the tray. I'm comparing cell structures, membranes, and nuclei. He is still behind me, talking very softly into my ear. I can feel my hair brushing up against his lips. "You see, the nucleus of a plant cell is located in a different area than an animal cell. The plant cell has a very defined outer membrane while an animal cell does not." He's trying to make sure I grasp these elementary concepts while he presses his chest into my back.

My heart is racing so fast that I'm sure he can feel it against his chest. I don't want to, but I pull away slightly. He can't know how he's affecting me. I mean, he has a girlfriend; he shouldn't be this close to me.

He's causing me to react to him. Forcing me to let my barriers down.

And I am.

Big time.

"I think I got it, now, Kyle." I pull a little further away from him and he gets the hint. He takes one last deep breath, as if he's inhaling me, and pulls away.

He takes the sheet that I've been taking notes on and peruses it carefully.

"Yes, Carly, you definitely got it. Good job." He smiles tightly and starts to gather the supplies from the table.

He puts everything back into the cabinet and locks it.

He takes both of my lab worksheets and puts them into his backpack. "I'll give these to Professor Martin tomorrow morning when I see her. I'll tell her that you're now all caught up and you remain a stellar student." He says this with little emotion and zips his backpack closed.

"Thanks, Kyle," I say breathlessly. He has really affected me and I can't seem to compose myself.

"So I guess we're all set? Even? I mean you helped me with these labs and kept my chicken pox secret from Professor Martin. And I did your laundry. So we're straight? Right?" I'm actually sad that our little arrangement is now over.

He reaches out and grabs the hand that he pricked earlier, raises up my forefinger, and swipes his thumb across the tip. "Feel better?" His big smile is back and I almost melt while he is grasping my hand.

"Yes, it feels better. I can only feel a slight heartbeat in the tip of my finger now. Not the throbbing I felt before." I'm completely blushing now and I pull my hand away.

"Good. And I'm not sure if we're even. Yet." His eyes sparkle and he smirks at me.

"What do you mean? We are square. Even. Done." I stammer incredulously.

"Dinner. Then we're square." He states.

"I don't think so, Kyle." He's kidding, right? Dinner, as in a date?

"Hey, we both need to eat and since I still clearly have some leverage over you, you aren't in any position to argue. I'll pick you up at your room at five o'clock."

I huff again and throw my backpack over my shoulder.

"Okay," I say feebly.

We walk out of the lab, down the steps, and out into the cold afternoon air. I look around anxiously, trying to find Todd lurking. I move closer to Kyle as we walk, needing his protection.

"My friends are coming over tonight, so we'll need to eat quickly, and then you'll need to be on your way. It's Wine Wednesday, Kyle."

"So we'll do dinner earlier then," he smiles. "Actually, how about a late lunch. Starting now?"

"Um, okay." I say.

We walk toward Thomas Hall into the cold wind.

We enter the building and Amber is at the security desk again. She's like a freaking fixture here. She perks up when she sees Kyle and heaves her tits out as usual. Her smile is huge when she says, "Kyle... How are you? How's the Teaching Assistant gig going? Professor Martin has you covering so many of her lectures. Lucky you."

"I'm great, Amber, and yes, I am working hard." He dismisses her flirtatious advances and places his hand on my lower back, directing me toward the cafeteria.

For once, I don't let her antics bother me. "Bye, Amber. Always a pleasure!" I smile back at her as I look over my shoulder.

We enter the cafeteria and the attendant states, "We're closing in five minutes. Hope you're taking your food to go."

I completely forgot that they close down to prepare for dinner.

I turn to Kyle and say, "We can do this another time."

"No, let's get our food and take it upstairs. Your place or mine?" He winks and smiles.

"Mine, I guess. My roommate is never there so we can spread out and enjoy our food," I answer. And maybe I can test myself being alone with him. Build up my courage to trust again.

I go over to the salad bar and load up on my favorites. I then grab a whole wheat roll and a bottle of water and head to the cashier. I see that Kyle's tray is piled with tons of food and I giggle. "Do you think you have enough?"

"Well, you clearly forgot to get dessert. One of us needs to remember," he replies.

We check out just as the cashier and staff is getting ready to lock the doors.

We make it to my room and I wonder if we should go to the lounge again. It's safer, more open. I shrug my worry off a little and we place our trays on my desk. My desk is situated at the foot of my bed, so I sit on the edge of my bed and offer my desk chair to Kyle. I fold my legs like a pretzel in front of me as I pour the dressing onto my salad.

"So, who's your roommate? Her side of the room seems, well, unlived in," he says.

"Ginger, and she doesn't really live here. Her boyfriend lives off-campus and she's there all the time. The only time I see her is when she needs to switch her laundry."

*Shit. Laundry.* I frown as I remember walking in on Kyle with that girl earlier this morning.

"Oh," he says as he takes a bite from his sandwich. He finishes chewing his food and continues, "Speaking of laundry. Thanks. I mean, you really rocked it this morning. I don't think I've had all of my laundry washed, dried, and folded since I started school this semester. I guess after this meal, we'll be even." He smirks and takes another bite.

My heart sinks. I'm glad that we're going to be even, but that means this is it for us. I'm caught up in Biology and his laundry. And he has a girlfriend.

"Yeah, no problem. It's all good."

I stab my salad and spear a cucumber with my fork.

We finish eating our lunch quietly.

"How's your finger?" He asks casually, looking into my eyes.

"My finger?" I hold it up so the tiny pinprick hole is facing him. "It's okay."

"Good," he smiles and then laughs. "Your reaction was priceless." He shakes his head as I picture him stabbing my finger with a pin.

"Yeah?" I say. I reach across the desk and grab his hand, pretending to stab him with my fork. "How would you feel right now if I meant to stab you with this?" I threaten playfully.

He removes the fork from my hand and tightens his grasp around my wrist. "You'd never be able to pull it off due to my ninja-like reflexes," he jokes and releases me.

I place my hand out and ask, "Can I have my fork back, please? I need to finish eating my salad." He smirks and places it gently in my palm, leaving his hand over mine for a moment. I miss his touch and battle with my senses. *He has a girlfriend.*

"So, where did you learn your ninja skills?" I ask.

He shrugs his shoulders and smiles as he breaks apart the giant chocolate chip cookie on his plate. "I'm just a natural, I guess." He starts to laugh and takes a bite. "Want some?" he tilts the piece of cookie toward me, offering a piece.

"No, thanks. I'm full."

"After a salad? Really? Here." He takes the other half and places it onto my tray. "I insist."

I take a sip of water and reach for the cookie. "Thanks for sharing," I say, taking a bite. "God, this is so good."

We finish our dessert in silence, mostly because we can't shove enough of the cookie in our mouths to satisfy ourselves. That was the best chocolate chip cookie I've ever had.

"What made you want to be a teaching assistant?" I ask, curious about how he wound up with Professor Martin.

"It helps pay the bills. And I like Biology," he says as he wipes crumbs off his lap.

"Why would you waste your time trying to convince me to get my act together? You could have just let her fail me." I feel guilty about how I've monopolized his time.

"I'm obligated to. It's my job to help students who fall behind. Professor Martin doesn't like to fail anyone and she insisted that you needed help." He looks at me funny, confused. "I told you this before, she has a soft spot for you and that's where I came in."

"You helped save the day," I mutter, embarrassed that I became a pet project for the teacher.

"Hey, to tell you the truth, I wouldn't be here if I didn't want to be."

"Yeah, but I was wasting your time." My guilt over my delinquencies is catching up to me. "I'm really sorry I was so difficult. I didn't mean to be. I've just had a lot going on…,"

"I get it. I'm glad I could help and now you certainly won't fail." He smiles and stacks our trays and dirty plates together. "Study partners?" he asks, surprising me.

"I thought you were done with me? Our *arrangement* is over, right?" I ask, confused.

"I'd like to make sure my time investment pays off. Professor Martin is going to watch your progress closely, and I want to make sure my positive influence shines through."

"Does this mean I still have to keep doing your laundry?" I ask, suspicious.

"Only if you want to. But having lunch together every once in a while might be good enough payment. What do you think?"

I think he's sending crazy mixed signals and I don't know what to say. *Is he making a regular date with me?* Not if we're study partners, right? Maybe regular lunch is just that. Lunch. To study together.

"Okay, I guess," I say hesitantly.

He smiles huge and reaches across the desk to shake my hand. I reluctantly place my hand into his as he wraps his warm fingers around mine and grips tightly. "It's a deal. Now you have to get an 'A' in the class, or my reputation as a teaching assistant will crash and burn."

I slide my hand out of his grasp and wish that I didn't. His hand felt warm. Safe.

My entire body begins to relax and for the first time in forever, I'm at ease. Comfortable. *And so tired.*

I yawn. I guess waking up at the crack of dawn today is really catching up to me.

"Tired? I don't mean to keep you up." He chuckles.

"Yes, I'm tired. I was up at the ass-crack of dawn doing laundry, remember?" I cover my mouth as I yawn again.

"Considering you need a nap before your 'wine' thing tonight, why don't you go to sleep? If you don't mind, I'm going to clear our trays away and get some work done."

"You mean you're going to stay here, while I sleep?" I ask.

"Sure, unless you're uncomfortable. I could use the quiet and you could use the sleep, so I thought it would be a win-win." Well, he does have a point. I need to convince myself and believe that Kyle isn't a threat. This is impulsive and reckless.

But I don't want to be alone. My altercation with Todd earlier today has me rattled and I don't want Kyle to leave me. Determined to battle these demons, I stretch out and grab the afghan my Nana made me when I was a little girl. "It's okay. You can stay and study. Don't let me sleep too long, I should study a little too before my friends come later."

"I'm rubbing off on you already. You'll pass this class with flying colors," he says as I burrow into my soft, welcoming pillow.

"Sweet dreams," he says as I drift off to sleep.

~

I open my eyes and notice that my room is almost dark. My desk lamp is off and the light from the windows tells me it's almost dusk. I hear soft snoring from across the room and see that Kyle is asleep on Ginger's bed. He's stretched out with his jacket pulled up to his shoulders and his biology book is next to him. I watch his chest rise and fall and am comforted to know that he's still here.

My trust grows as I realize that I fell asleep several hours ago and he didn't hurt me. *He's not Todd.* I stretch and listen to his deep breathing. It's soothing and is drawing me back into my own dreams.

I sigh as I feel myself slipping back to sleep.

~

*I'm restrained beneath him and I look up and see the smudged black tooth and crooked smile. He's holding my wrists so tight that my fingers are tingling from the lack of circulation. His hot breath is burning my nose and my mouth is open in a silent scream. He's laughing as he bites my nipple with pure menace. He's pushing his hips into me, keeping me pinned to the bed. He tears off my panties and starts to thrust his fingers into me, tearing me, burning me.*

*I start to scream and he shoves his hand over my mouth, muffling my pleas for help. I try to bite his hand but the pain and shock of what's happening to me is too much. I feel him press himself into me and I can't take him in. I'm raw and burning. Thrashing. Fighting. Sobbing. Crying.*

*"No, no, no!"*

"Carly, wake up, Carly!" I hear a desperate voice and feel tears pouring out of my eyes and down my cheeks. I shake my head back and forth and I feel his weight on top of me.

"No!" I'm finally able to scream and I buck my body up against his. "Carly! Carly! It's me, Kyle!"

I'm sobbing so loudly now. He shifts his weight off of me, slips next to me, and starts to whisper in my ear. "It's okay." His voice is soothing and I'm starting to come out of it. "I'm here. He can't hurt you. I'm here." His fingers are softly running up and down my arm and he's pulling me into him with his other arm.

I gasp as I realize that I'm no longer dreaming that awful dream about Todd. Reliving what he did to me. I'm here with Kyle. In my room. Safe.

"Kyle." I'm crying and the sobs overtake me.

"Shh, it's okay. It was just a dream."

He pulls me closer.

I let the sobs and tears work through me and try to regulate my gasping to match Kyle's soothing breaths. Several minutes go by. Kyle remains silent.

What did he just witness? Did I talk in my sleep? *Does he know?* Please, God, he can't.

"Carly?" Kyle asks quietly.

I exhale. "Hmm?"

"Are you okay? I mean that was just a dream, right?"

I stiffen up, feeling a little weird that he's now laying next to me. I don't answer him quickly enough and he continues, "What you said… did someone do something to you to make you dream like that?" I can feel him become rigid behind me and he pulls me even closer into him.

"No, Kyle." I lie. "It was just a dream." Seeing Todd today must have triggered it.

"I don't believe you." Clearly, I didn't convince him.

"The things you were saying, the way that you were thrashing around. Carly, it was real for you," he states.

I lie there silently and grab his hand to move it from my waist. He flinches at my touch.

I muster my courage and start talking sternly. "Kyle, first of all, what the hell are you doing? You were supposed to be studying. Second, this is none of your business."

I pull away and sit up on the edge of my bed. I can't talk about this. He has no right to know. I feel violated and embarrassed at the same time.

He's silent for a few moments and drops his head, shaking it slowly back and forth.

"I'm so sorry. I shouldn't have." He stops and looks up at me.

"You just looked so comfortable and you were sleeping so soundly that it made me tired. I went to go lie down on your roommate's bed and passed out."

He's stammering, clearly nervous. "When I heard you yelling in your sleep, I thought you were being attacked. You were thrashing around so much, like it was really happening to you. The look on your face, the tears...," he stops and breathes deeply. "I had to wake you up, get you out of the hell that you were in. I'm sorry, I was out of line." He shakes his head and sits up.

"Kyle..."

A loud banging noise commences on my door. I hear voices. Becca, Callie, and Manny.

"Car, open up. We're here!" Manny is yelling through the crack in the door.

Kyle's eyes dart to mine. "Wait," he says too late as I unlock the door and let it swing open.

Manny, Becca, and Callie walk in and collectively gasp.

Kyle jumps from a reclined position on my bed to his feet and stammers, "Uh, hey. I'm Kyle."

"Well, sorry to interrupt, Kyle." Manny giggles.

"Wait, it's not like that–," I start to say but I'm cut off.

"Carly, I should get going. Thanks for letting me study and crash here." Kyle grabs his backpack and pushes through the crowd gathered in my room.

I follow him into the hall as I walk past Manny, Becca, and Callie.

"Kyle. I wish you didn't see me like that. It's not what you...," I hesitate going any further. "I'm sorry," I say.

He looks up at me, softly touches my cheek, smiles, and says, "I'm here if you want to talk about it. Whatever that dream was about."

"I don't think I can." I say as he pulls his hand away and shrugs.

"Listen, my friends are here and it's Wednesday. I'm sorry I'm such a mess and you had to see that," I say. "Thank you for everything today, Kyle."

He lightly touches my arm causing me to flinch slightly and he quickly pulls his hand away. "I'm sorry, Carly. For everything that you've been through. I'm so sorry." He just made a huge assumption and I don't correct him.

He smiles, turns away, and walks toward the stairwell.

I walk back into my room.

Manny, Becca and Callie are standing each with their hands on their hips. Callie looks worried, Becca is smiling and Manny yells, "What the hell was that, Carly?"

And Wine Wednesday has begun.

# Chapter 20

## Tabitha

*Philadelphia, Pennsylvania*
**Past**
*Age 19*

I'M DAYDREAMING AS I take clean plates from the industrial dishwasher and place them in the cabinet. It's two o'clock, I'm working at the diner and the afternoon lunchtime rush is over. I've been working since seven this morning and I'm exhausted. I need to get the caffeine flowing through my veins or I'm going to drop.

I absolutely cannot be late tonight. I'm meeting Alex at The High Note and I don't want to disappoint him. He's taking a chance on our potential friendship and me. I can't let him down as I've done with so many other people in my life. If I'm going to make a fresh start, I need to commit to this. I'm also taking a chance on *me*, going out on a limb and doing something to better myself. I need to begin surrounding myself with good, kind people. *Safe people.*

"Tabby, you have a customer in booth eight," Dottie says as she packs her bag to leave. "And he is a cutie-pie."

I close the cabinet door, grab my apron, and head out to the dining room. I see that my customer is alone, so I grab one menu and place setting and set them on his table.

"Good afternoon," I say. "Would you like something to drink?"

He looks up at me and grins. His smile seems so genuine and my cold exterior starts to melt. I typically don't interact or become too friendly with my customers, or anyone for that matter. But this guy seems so warm and inviting. *Maybe this is progress.*

"Lemonade, please," he says smoothly. And he flashes that smile again. I don't move to get him the drink because I'm drawn to his softness and the kindness in his eyes. I can tell immediately that he doesn't have demons dwelling in his head. Not like me. He's pure and untainted. People like me spread melancholy. He exudes comfort.

He clears his throat and says again, "Lemonade."

"Oh, sure, I'll get that right away for you." I turn abruptly and go behind the counter to fill up a large glass with ice and lemonade. My hands are shaking a little and I don't know why or how to stop them. Maybe it's all of the caffeine that I've already consumed today. Or maybe it's just my nerves. I'm not used to attention from anyone unless it's a rude comment or a smack to the face. Tony always made sure that I stayed on my toes. Kept me in line.

I take a deep breath, walk back to his table, and place the lemonade in front of him. I start fumbling for a straw in my apron and drop them all to the floor. As straws scatter everywhere, he starts to chuckle. I bend down quickly, scoop most of them up, and shove them back into my apron pocket. I have a flashback to when I scattered Sara's adoption papers and immediately flinch, thinking that he will pull my hair like Tony did.

I'm embarrassed by my flub and try to pull myself together to take his order. "Have you decided on your meal?"

"Yes, but first, I need to know your name."

"Why?" I ask. *I'm not worth knowing.*

"Well, it would have a lot of relevance when I ask you to join me for a late lunch." He flashes that electric smile again. I begin to get suspicious of his motives, and surprised by his request.

"Sir, I'm working? I can't just sit here with you." I wouldn't even know what to do with myself. *Is he flirting with me?*

He laughs openly and says, "Seth. Not Sir. Seth Tyson. And you can sit down, I'm the only person in this entire diner." He gestures to the bench across from him.

"*Seth*, I really don't have time for this. It's not appropriate. Can you please give me your order?" I pull out my pen, ready to write down his request.

He replies persistently, "I'll give you my order as soon as you agree to join me."

I exhale loudly and shift on my feet. *Seriously?*

His eyes search my face, and he raises his eyebrows. "Well?" he pushes.

I'm actually starving. And there is no one else in the diner. *Maybe I should do this. See if I can actually make a new friend.*

My internal battle is silenced for now and I say, "Okay."

He looks surprised that I actually agreed, "What's your name?" he asks. "I should know this if I'm going to be eating with you."

"Tabitha," I say and begin to regret my decision. I shouldn't do this. I don't want to lead him on. "I'll agree to have a *snack* with you, but that's it."

"Excellent. Sit down and let's discuss our meals." He's very excited and I get the feeling he thinks my friendly gesture may mean something more. Why does he even want to spend time with me? *I'm gross. I'm poison.* I will drain his happiness faster than he can blink. He has no idea what he's doing by inviting me to have a snack with him.

I quietly move my order pad between us and position my pencil to take his order.

"What would you like to eat?" I ask.

He raises his eyebrow and stares into my eyes. His gaze is penetrating yet soft. He seems soothing and protective. Not judgmental.

I shake my head to rid myself of these thoughts and wait for his answer.

"I'll have the grilled cheese with tomato and an order of fries with gravy on the side."

My hand shakes a little as I write down his order. *Why is he making me so nervous?*

"Anything else?" I ask.

"Only for you. What are you going to eat, Tabby?" His tone is very light, almost fun. And he just called me by my nickname. It seems that Seth doesn't have a care in the world and is playing the part of a Good Samaritan. Well, I don't need any handouts or false attention. *This is a big mistake.*

"I suddenly don't feel hungry," I state. "Thanks for your order and it will be out shortly."

I get out of the seat and abruptly leave the dining area. I can feel Seth's eyes burning into my back.

Why is he flirting with me? Can't he see the badge on my face? The reminder of the damaged and messed up person that I am?

I press my fingers harshly into my scar and close my eyes. I need to feel the pain of this mark on my face. I need to be reminded of the person that I am. What I gave up for my freedom. I scratch my nails down the scar until it burns.

I remember how much my initial trust in Tony wavered and how he made me feel when he took me in.

*Tony walks me upstairs above the bar and opens the door to the apartment. "I'm glad you like this apartment, princess." He places both hands on my shoulders and starts to massage firmly. "This is your home and you will never want for anything again. I'll take care of you."*

*I don't know Tony's age, but I believe he's significantly older than I am. I left Pennsylvania at seventeen and turned eighteen while traveling through Nebraska or one of the middle states. Although I'm still a teenager, I don't think he knows. Or cares.*

*His hands travel down my back and spine and he places them on my hips.*

*"I'm so happy that I can help you. We can do so much for each other, princess," he whispers into my ear.*

*His hand lightly taps my ass and he pushes me into the bedroom. "I'm glad you like your room and that you're settled and comfortable. What's mine is yours." He smiles, turns, and leaves the room.*

*I find the duffle bag that I had hidden under the bed and open it up, looking at the few belongings that I brought with me. The vibe that he's giving off is wrong, dangerous. Should I leave now? Run? I don't feel good about this situation, but what can I do? I have no place to live and I just* started my new job. I need to ride this out, build up some savings. I will make something of myself. Then I can leave.

"Princess…," Tony calls from the other room.

I hide my bag back under the bed and walk through the bedroom door.

"Yes, Tony." I respond.

"We need to work out your hours as soon as possible. There are three other new cocktail waitresses starting this week and your schedules need to be coordinated."

"No problem." I turn away and walk back into the bedroom.

"Don't wait up for me, princess. I'll be late tonight." He turns and walks out the door.

Oh. Shit.

Several hours pass and although I'm apprehensive, I'm pleased with myself. I've unpacked my one duffle bag, showered, and eaten a healthy meal. I'm so happy to have a home. I'm nervous about my situation, but I convince myself that this will be my ticket to a new life. I need to save every dime that I make. I need to be sure that I can make it on my own.

Several hours later, I hear a key jiggling in the apartment door and I slowly back away. Not knowing who it could be, I'm nervous and cautious.

Tony stumbles in, chuckling. He has a girl behind him and she's giggling as her ample breasts are bouncing up and down.

"Hello, princess. Trixie and I are going to bed. You'll be okay out here on the couch, right?" He doesn't wait for my answer as he pushes past me and shuts the door to 'my' bedroom.

I have no idea what's happening, but I thought this was my place. I can hear Trixie's giggles escalate into pleasure and her noises turn animalistic. Tony is grunting like a gorilla as I curl up on the couch using one of my hoodies as a blanket. I cover my ears with a throw pillow and hope this ends quickly.

I fall asleep on the couch wondering if my recent choices were wise and if I should have stayed with the Lohman family in Philadelphia. Even Richie Lohman didn't make my skin crawl like Tony does. As many times as Richie walked in on me naked or ogled me around the house, I *didn't feel the way I do now. Alone. Confused. Afraid.*

*I shake my head slowly, thinking about the pervert and hoping that I made the right choice.*

*Ding, ding, ding!*

I snap out of these awful memories and realize that the bell is ringing and Seth's food is up.

*I need to get myself together.*

I grab the plates and walk quickly over to his table.

His head is bent down looking at a magazine as I drop the plates in front of him. "Do you need anything else?" I ask.

"No, but I thought you were eating with me."

"No. I'm not hungry," I lie, avoiding eye contact.

I turn to walk away and he grabs my arm lightly. I gasp and pull my arm from his grasp. My hands shake and my breathing picks up. *Why would he grab me?*

Seth seems flabbergasted. "Tabby, I'm sorry. I didn't mean to make you feel uncomfortable. I just thought that since you were alone and this place is empty, you'd want to keep me company." He looks down at his grilled cheese and tomato sandwich and shakes his head slightly. "Did I hurt you?" he asks, worried.

I suddenly feel bad. He seems so nice, genuine. And I'm wearing my crazy on my sleeve for all to see.

"It's okay, Seth. I've just had a long, hard day." *A long hard life.*

I watch him as he pushes his French fries around the plate. He's worried and I feel bad. He did nothing wrong.

"Really, Tabby, I didn't mean to upset you. I thought I'd try to get to know you, I shouldn't have pushed you. I arrived in Philly six weeks ago and I have yet to crack the social scene. I could use some pointers." He smiles and I begin to relax. "I'm just looking to make a new friend."

"Ha!" I laugh. Why would he think I know anything about this city? "I've been here for just a few weeks and I've literally had conversations with like four people, other than here at work. I know absolutely nothing about the social scene in Philadelphia and quite honestly, I wouldn't know where to begin. I work, sleep, work, and sleep again. I can't be bothered with anything else." *My anxiety would get the better of me.*

His face softens more. "I guess we're both in the same boat. Maybe we could learn things about Philly together? As friends?" *I'd like that.*

Encouraged by the prospects unfolding in front of me, I say, "I work in a bookstore over on Spring Street. Why don't you come check it out and maybe I can get you on the list for a book signing or two?" I smile at him and his bright eyes comfort me.

"I think I'll stop by on Monday," he says. "I look forward to our adventures in the city."

I nod and smile, turning away to walk back into the kitchen. I can feel his eyes on my back, peering into my soul.

*What is happening?*

And why am I excited about it?

~

Several hours later, I finish up with my last customer and stare longingly at the clock. Twenty more minutes and I'm so out of here. Seth has been gone for hours and I kind of miss him. He was genuinely nice without a hint of mystery. I wonder if he'll show up at the bookstore on Monday. I actually hope that he will. I'm proud of myself for letting my guard down and trusting my instincts. *I just hope they're right.*

I'm worried that I'm getting my hopes up for good things to happen. I'm not sure it's best for me right now to think of the possibilities with either Alex or Seth as friends or *more*. I need time to heal. And I'm not sure either one of them will help me get there.

I remove my apron and tuck my tips into the back pocket of my jeans. I made forty-five dollars tonight and that should be enough to pay my cab fare, cover charge and maybe a drink of soda or two.

"Goodnight." I call to Jeffery, our evening cook. "See you next week."

I walk quickly out of the diner and hail the nearest taxi. It's a short ride to The High Note and I'm anxious the entire way. Thankfully, there is no line when I arrive. Also, the bouncer isn't even posted outside yet. I walk right in and begin to scan the crowd and tables for Alex.

A hostess steps in front of me and says, "Can I help you?"

"Yes, please. I'm meeting someone here for dinner. He's in the band playing tonight. Maybe I'll just take a seat and wait for him."

"Sure. How many people are you expecting?"

I shrug my shoulders, "I'm not sure. Maybe the whole band?"

"Follow me. I have the perfect booth for you." She leads me to a semi-circular booth that could easily fit up to six people.

"Thanks," I say as I slide in toward the center of the booth.

"Your waitress will be right over to take your drink order. I believe the band is in the back right now. I'll let them know you're here." She smiles and skips away.

I try to relax as I look around the bar. Since it's only seven-thirty, it's fairly empty. A few families are scattered at various tables enjoying their dinner. There are four men sitting at the bar and from the looks of them, they've been there a while. One of them actually appears to be asleep on top of his folded arms.

I chuckle quietly to myself and shake my head a bit.

"Something funny?" I hear Alex ask. I didn't even see him walk over.

I turn my head quickly to look at him.

"I'm just people-watching. Take a look at that sleepy guy at the bar." I nod toward the bar and Alex turns to observe.

"Lenny is here every day at four o'clock. He spends at least half of his paycheck before he takes his daily nap. He's a great guy, but clearly is on a toddler's sleeping schedule." He laughs heartily and I join him.

He slides into the booth next to me, leaving much of the seat open on his left.

"Did you order anything yet?" he asks.

"No, I was waiting for you. And I'm actually on time." I'm so proud of myself.

"I noticed."

Our waitress is now standing in front of us.

"What can I get you both to drink?" She pauses and then focuses her attention on Alex. "Hi, Alex," she says quietly and I swear she bats her eyelashes.

"We'll both have ice water please. Can we also have some popcorn?"

"Sure." She smiles and slinks away.

"So, Tabs, how was your day?" he asks in a chipper voice, his eyes shining.

"Well, I worked at the diner today, so it was about the same as every other day I work at the diner," I state vaguely. I smile at him as he slides closer to me and laughs a little.

He looks at me and continues to smile. He's so much more relaxed today. Maybe he's happy with our decision to walk down the 'friends only' path.

"You need to spice up your life a little bit, Tabby. If working at the diner excites you, we need to get you some better hobbies." He's so right and I wouldn't even know how I would do that. *Maybe he can help me.*

I notice several guys walking toward our booth. They all have varying degrees of smirks on their faces and I can only assume that this is the rest of the band. *I'm not ready for this.* I'm not yet fully comfortable being around Alex and now three more are about to invade my space.

Two of them slide into the booth to my right and one slides in next to Alex. I'm pinned in the back center of the booth and I begin to panic. I'm boxed in. *Trapped.* I'm already planning my escape route. Sweat drips down the back of my neck as my heart pounds in my chest. *I need to get ahold of myself.*

Alex senses a change in my demeanor and he softly places his hand on top of my thigh. I tense up at first, and try to relax underneath his touch. I know he's trying to calm me down, to soothe me. He slowly moves his hand in a circular motion above my kneecap. I loosen up a little bit and at the same time, feel a tingling sensation travel from my thigh to my core. *What is his touch doing to me?*

"Hey guys," Alex speaks quietly. I think he realizes that I'm feeling overstimulated and he's trying to keep the introductions quiet and low-key.

"This is Tabitha. But you can call her Tabby. And only I can call her Tabs." His introduction is short and sweet and I find it odd that he claimed a nickname just for him. I tense again at this thought. I don't want him to have any control over me, much less my name. He once again senses my tension and he gently squeezes my thigh, his thumb circling just above my knee. I start to squirm, my discomfort growing. *I'm not used to this kind of tenderness.*

"Hey Tabby," the guy next to Alex says.

"Tabitha," says the guy on the end.

"Tabs," says the guy sitting directly on my right. As he calls me by the name that Alex claimed, he rubs his leg up against my right knee. I'm sure this is incidental contact, but this action causes me to move closer to Alex as I move my leg away from his.

Alex begins the formal introductions. "This is Dax." He gestures to his left. "Tristan is on the end." He nods his head toward the end of the booth. "And Garrett is next to you." He tenses up as he concludes Garrett's introduction as if he knows he brushed up against me under the table. I'm suddenly startled by his possessiveness.

He turns fully toward Garrett and says, "Dude, I told you her name was Tabitha. Got it?"

*Whoa. What the heck?*

Garrett seems amused and looks like he's about to say something, but slowly moves away from me and picks up his menu. *I don't like him.*

Our waitress is back with our ice water and popcorn. She motions to the rest of the guys. "Hi boys," she says, smiling. "Anything to drink?"

They order two pitchers of beer and request frosty mugs. Then they proceed to order every greasy appetizer on the menu.

She leaves to fill the order and an awkward silence hovers over the table. I don't know what comes over me, but I feel the need to blurt something out.

"So, Alex told me how you all met. That's great." I fumble for some sort of conversation starter. I'm stuck between these guys; I might as well *try* to make it interesting. I need to divert my attention away from being trapped.

Dax turns, looks at me, and smiles tightly, "Well, Alex told us nothing about you, Tabby. So why don't you fill us in? Where did you come from and what have you done to make Alex so possessive of you already?"

*Whoa. What did I do to deserve this attitude?*

They're all staring at me, waiting for my reply. I stutter a little bit, "Well, I… I'm originally from Philadelphia. I spent a few years out west and made my way back here just recently. Nothing much to tell to be honest." I'm already feeling a cold vibe from Dax. There is no way I'm going to open up and share anything about myself.

"Short and sweet," he replies. He still has a bit of a smirk on his face and his eyes lock on mine as if he's trying to read me or catch me in a lie. He seems protective of Alex and I think he wants me to know that he's got his eye on me.

I shift in my seat and accidently brush up against Garrett's leg. He inhales deeply and chuckles a little bit.

"No need to make the chick uncomfortable, Dax. Everyone knows that you have Alex's back and will pretty much squash anything or anyone that hurts him. *Right?"* Garrett turns toward me as he says this.

What the hell is up with these guys? I don't know what I was expecting, but I certainly wasn't expecting this kind of treatment.

Tristan is scanning the bar area and quickly jumps up. "I'll be right back; I need to say hi to someone." With that, he takes off toward a redhead sitting at the corner of the bar. Clearly, his priorities are in order. At least he didn't waste any time taking jabs at me to make me feel more uncomfortable than I already do.

Alex is remaining oddly quiet during this interrogation. *Why isn't he speaking up to come to my rescue?*

I feel the need to defend myself. "Guys, I have no intention of hurting anyone. I'm Alex's *friend*. Nothing more." I look over to Alex who is staring down at the table.

The waitress arrives with several frosty mugs and a couple of pitchers of beer. "Your appetizers are on the way. Cheers!" She turns on her heel and walks away.

Garrett begins to fill up everyone's mugs. "Tabitha, beer?"

"No thanks," I reply. "I'm good with my water."

He pushes a full mug toward Alex. Alex puts his hand up abruptly to stop him. "Garrett, you know I don't drink."

"Dude, she didn't even card us. Take advantage." Garrett's smiling as he tries to convince Alex to drink.

"No. Thank. You," Alex says forcefully.

"Suit yourself. More for us," Garrett says as he raises his mug to clink with Dax's.

I wonder how Alex is even friends with these guys. They don't treat each other with respect. Hell, they don't even seem to like each other. Yet they're in a band and spend almost all of their free time together. I don't get it.

I'm so nervous that I'm picking apart a cocktail napkin, tearing pieces off and making little balls in front of me.

Tristan slides back into the booth next to Garrett and grabs his mug full of beer.

"To new *friends*," he says as he nods in my direction. "Cheers!"

I raise my ice water along next to all of their mugs.

"Thank you," I say. "Cheers."

Alex remains silent through the entire discussion.

I feel his hand on my thigh again just above my knee. He starts softly rubbing my kneecap and he leans in to me so his mouth is pressed into my hair, against my ear.

"Tabitha, I'm so sorry," he whispers as his warm breath lingers on my neck. "I'm sorry." This gives me the chills and I shiver. I'm sure he noticed and now I'm embarrassed by my reaction. I just can't help it. I have a physical reaction to his presence. I'm starting to burn all over and I just can't yet tell if I like it.

I don't want to pull away, but I have to. We don't need to get any more grief from the guys. I can't endure this discomfort any longer. I need to get up but I'm trapped.

I lean back into the booth so that Alex's mouth is no longer dangerously close to my ear, turn to look at him and smile. I mouth the words, "It's okay." But really, it's not. I don't like being made to feel like I'm such a virus. I already hate myself and what I've become. The icy reception I'm getting from these guys is just adding to my issues and I just can't take this anymore.

"Excuse me," I quietly say. "I need to use the restroom." Dax smirks at me, slides out of the booth, and Alex slowly follows him. I now have my escape route.

I scoot out of the booth and start walking toward the bathrooms. Dax grabs my arm and pulls me close to him so he can speak into my ear. I tighten up and try to pull away. "Don't hurt him, Tabitha," he says and quickly lets go of my arm. My arm aches and I worry that it's going to bruise. *Did he mean to handle me so forcefully?*

I'm flustered as I practically run into the bathroom.

I lock myself in a stall, sit down on the closed seat, and put my head into my hands. This is too much. Is Alex even worth all of this grief that I'm getting from his friends? *I have to get out of here.* Run. Again.

I spend about ten minutes trying to calm down, but I can't settle myself. I step out of the stall, wash my hands, and splash some cold water on my face. I look into the mirror at my pathetic face. "You are such a coward," I say to my reflection. *Why did I let them talk to me that way?*

I'm upset with myself and need to escape. I open the door and walk out, right into Alex.

"Whoa!" I exclaim. "What are you doing back here?"

He reaches out, grabs my hand softly, and leads me into an empty room. This must be the lounge where the band hangs out while waiting to perform.

As the door shuts, he turns me around so that my back is pressing against it. He places his hands on either side of my head and leans in close, our lips barely touching. My heart is pounding, unsure of what's happening. I'm scared. He's staring into my eyes, almost burning holes through my head. I inhale deeply and he slams his lips into mine. His kiss is rough and hungry. His tongue immediately parts my lips and assaults my mouth, intertwining with mine. I tense up and try to pull away. I can't catch my breath and begin to panic. *Why is this happening? What does he want?*

He pulls back and looks into my eyes again. "Tabitha," he says softly and licks his lips. He then bites down on his lower lip as he continues to stare. "Please tell me that I didn't just go out of bounds with that." He looks worried.

I'm still stunned silent. I wish that we could start over, where I'm more receptive and more of a willing participant. *Did I want him to kiss me?* I've known that I've wanted *something* since the first time I saw him in the bookstore making 'music' with the bookmarks. I was drawn to him immediately. But I can't stop thinking about Tony, or what he would do to me if he witnessed this. What he would do to Alex. I panic even more and I start hyperventilating. I clutch at my chest. It feels like an elephant is sitting on me now. I haven't had a panic attack in a while. Alex backs up, confused by my reaction. The look on his face changes to concern and as I'm gasping for breath, he starts to panic as well. I feel my eyes glaze over and I'm dizzy.

"Tabs?" His eyes are wide, scared. I'm choking, coughing, and gasping for air. I lean back into the door. My heart is racing and my chest is burning. My vision gets blurry and I start to slide down the wall. As my ass hits the floor, tunnel vision takes over and I can barely see Alex.

Or anything.

I slip into blackness.

# Chapter 21

## Carly

*New Brunswick, New Jersey*
**Past**
*Age 18*

LET THE INTERROGATIONS *begin.* After Kyle leaves, I go back into my room to face my curious friends. They glare at me, accusingly, as I enter the room.

"What?" I ask casually, trying to hide my discomfort. I don't know what happened with Kyle and me today and I'm not sure I'm in the right frame of mind to even figure it out.

"What do you mean *what?*" Manny demands.

I know he's going to be persistent, but I don't want to talk about it.

Callie looks at me sternly, "Car, seriously. Why was he on your bed? Doesn't he have a girlfriend? Are you even *ready* for anything serious?" She's worried for me.

I don't want to be read the riot act, but it looks like I'm well on my way. *I didn't do anything wrong.*

I pick up the gallon-sized bottle of wine, screw off the cap and lift it to my lips. I'm not above chugging this God-awful shit. And that's what I do. Chug. This is not an easy feat as wine is spilling out of my mouth, dribbling down my chin. I must look ridiculous.

Becca approaches me and takes the jug from my hands. I use the back of my sleeve to wipe the wine drizzle from my lips and face. I'm a mess.

"Carly, what is going on? Please talk to us," she says.

Manny grabs the jug from Becca and begins to chug some himself. I laugh at this gesture as he shoves it into Callie's face. "Bang it!" He yells his term for chugging.

Callie doesn't have time to think as Manny forces her to chug as we both did. So she 'bangs' it.

After several rounds of this, half of the jug is gone.

This chugging ritual relaxes me. Or maybe it's the wine. *Yeah, I'm pretty buzzed.*

"OK guys," I slur a little and begin to ramble, "I get that you're concerned. But seriously, nothing happened with him. We had been studying all day together. I got super tired. Shit, I was up at the crack of dawn doing our laundry. I fell asleep and then he did, too. That's it! I had a bad dream; he tried to calm me down. Then you guys showed up. End. Of. Story." I hope that explanation makes them happy because I'm certainly not going to get into all of my feelings of panic and relief when he soothed me. He felt so good.

I gaze out into my room as my cheeks begin to flush. I'm pretty drunk. I hiccup and laugh a little.

"Really, Carly. You both looked so hot and bothered when we arrived. What do you have to say about that?" Manny's finger is in my face, practically poking out one of my eyes. I wrap my arms around him, rest my head against his chest, and squeeze tight as he returns the gesture.

I take a few deep breaths and look up into his eyes. "Manny, honey, I'm fine. He just made me feel good. That's it. He has a girlfriend. It meant nothing."

He rests his chin on the top of my head and huffs.

"Carly, what are we going to do with you? Wait, you did his laundry?" he asks incredulously. *Yeah, all six loads of it.*

I pull away from Manny and flop back onto my bed. Now I'm feeling super woozy. Damn this wine.

Becca scoots over next to me and grabs my hand. "Carly, we don't want you to get hurt. Please don't let him use you. Especially not to do laundry." She giggles a little.

"No. It's not like that either, Bec." I try to defend my situation. "I did his laundry as payment for keeping my secret from Professor Martin. I may have told a little white lie about the reason why I was missing her classes." *Am I even making sense?*

"Carly...," Callie chimes in, scolding me.

"I told her that I had the chicken pox." I hiccup again. This confession is not going well. "Kyle kept my secret and tutored me on my missed lectures. Now we're even." I look up, very pleased with myself and the deal that I made. I cross my arms over my chest.

Manny starts laughing loudly and eventually we all join in. Callie grabs the jug and hands it to Becca. "Bang it!" She demands. So Becca chugs.

"So, enough about me. What the hell is going on with all of you?" I point at each of them sweeping my finger through the air.

"Becca hooked up with that soccer player," Callie mentions, nonchalantly.

Becca swats at her arm. "Callie!" she yells.

"Oh, don't even try to deny it. He's so hot. Spill it!" Callie demands.

"It was nothing, guys. We kissed after the Delta Phi mixer. Just kissed. He's really sweet. I don't want to rush into anything, so it was perfect." She gazes past us and her smile is huge. She starts to blush.

"So it's okay for Becca to say 'it's nothing'? When I said it, you all jumped down my throat." I accuse the group of not treating our declarations equally.

Callie answers, "Carly, you need to take it slower. You need to heal. That's all; we just worry about you more."

Becca chimes in, happy to divert the attention back to me, "Exactly. We just want to be sure that you don't get in over your head with Kyle. You don't deserve the heartache, honey."

Manny hands me the jug, "Bang it!" I'm glad to continue to drink and not discuss this matter any further. I take my turn chugging.

A half hour later, the jug is empty and I'm curled up on my bed next to Manny. The room is spinning and I plant my foot against the concrete wall to make it stop. Callie and Becca are down by our feet leaning against a bunch of pillows. Becca is sound asleep and snoring softly.

"Carly, we only want to keep you safe," Callie slurs. "Safe from douchy-douche guys." She sounds profound in this declaration. "You know?" she finishes.

"Yes, I know." My eyes begin to close. "No douchy-douche guys for me."

I squeeze Manny and rest my head on his chest.

"I love you guys," I say through a huge drunken grin. I yawn and press my foot into the wall harder. The room is still spinning, but not as bad.

"I love you guys, too," Callie says.

Becca sighs deeply and mumbles something as she drools into the pillow.

"Bitch, if you puke on me, I'm going to throttle you." Manny says to me as he hugs me tighter.

Ah… the love.

"I love you guys and Wine Wednesdays," I slur as I drift off to sleep.

I really do.

I. Love. Them.

# Chapter 22

## Carly

*New Brunswick, New Jersey*
**Past**
*Age 18*

THIS SEMESTER IS flying by. I'm finally caught up in Biology and Professor Martin is none the wiser about my little white lie. I still feel guilty about it, but relieved that nobody knew what was really going on. It's been a few weeks since I was alone with Kyle and I miss the closeness that we shared that day. He was so genuine and tender.

It's time for me to focus on my finals and then I go home for winter break. I'm actually looking forward to ending this semester and enjoying some time off.

I love the holidays. There are no bigger Christmas geeks than my family. Our Christmas tree is always up the day after Thanksgiving. Some of my favorite memories of the holidays revolve around my family and decorating our house. My father is a stickler for traditions and keeps us to them religiously.

Our tree is artificial, so it's okay that it goes up so early. This is an embarrassing fact, but our tree is on a rotating stand. My father has had it since the Seventies and the thing still works. You can hear the motor churning as it spins and every year we expect sparks to shoot out of it. But it still keeps turning. It spins the Christmas tree in our living room window for all of the neighbors to admire. To laugh at. It even plays a tinny sounding "Jingle Bells" that's always on a constant loop.

So yes, we are Christmas nerds. And I'm so proud.

So proud, in fact, that I decorated my dorm room as soon as I returned from Thanksgiving break. Lights are strung throughout and a small twinkling tree sits on the windowsill. All of these decorations are mine since I haven't seen Ginger in what seems like weeks. I know she's been in and out because some of her things have moved. I'm not sure if she's avoiding me deliberately, but I try not to let it bother me.

I have my Biology final today and I'm so glad to put this class behind me. I grab my backpack and head out.

After a brisk five-minute walk, I reach the lecture hall. It's already full and I make my way to my usual seat. I look up and see Kyle at the front of the room. He seems to be collating tests. He looks up at me and I immediately flush. *I've missed him.* His eyes. His dimple. His smile.

He flashes that famous smile and winks at me.

Now I'm never going to be able to concentrate. I've come undone with one look.

He starts passing out the exams and when he reaches me he says, "Carly. You look good. Are you ready for winter break?"

I take the packet of papers from him and our fingers brush against each other. The familiar tingling starts in the tips of my fingers, moves up my arm, and radiates throughout my chest.

"Yes, I'm ready," I answer breathlessly.

He nods and moves on. "Have a Merry Christmas."

He passes me to hand out exams to other students.

"Merry Christmas," I whisper, unsure if he can hear me.

I take out my pen and open the exam. I read the first question and I immediately draw a blank.

*Oh no.*

I take some deep breaths and try to focus. *How can he affect me so much?*

I finally start to answer the exam questions and I think I'm doing okay. I have to write an essay describing the blood type lab and how results are determined. As soon as I start to write, I picture Kyle stabbing my fingertip with a needle. I laugh out loud and Kyle looks up from the proctor's seat. Our eyes meet and I hold his gaze for several moments. I smile at him and lower my eyes back down to my paper. I can still feel him looking at me as I remember that day. *If only he didn't have a girlfriend.*

I complete my answer to the essay and realize I've finished the exam. I look around the room and at least half of the students have left. I'm so glad to be done with this class. *But I'm going to miss him.*

I stand up and practically skip down to the front and place my exam in the pile of completed tests.

"Bye, Kyle. Merry Christmas," I say softly, turn and leave the room.

I don't want to linger. There's really nothing more to say to each other. We're acquaintances at best. He helped me through a jam and I'm grateful but there isn't anything more. *There can't be.*

I walk out of the building toward the library. I have another exam tonight and I need to spend the rest of the day in my secluded corner on the third floor. I need to nail this last test before I can be comfortable that I'm home free.

I find that my 'secret' area in the library is deserted, as usual. I pull two chairs together so I can stretch out my legs. I settle in, take out my Sociology book and notes, and commence studying. The test is five hours away and I confidently think I'm going to ace it.

After several minutes of perusing my notes, my eyes start to feel heavy and I'm suddenly so tired. I look at my watch; it's twelve-thirty. If I take a little nap now, I can wake up with plenty of time to spare. I'll finish reviewing my notes and go ace the test.

I drift off to sleep as I continue to rationalize this.

～

I'm mostly groggy as I start to wake up from my impromptu nap. My wrists feel tight and they're pinned on either side of me. I feel pressure on my pelvis and hot breath in my face. My eyes jolt open and I'm face to face with my worst fears. I start to panic as I stare into Todd's cold, dark eyes.

He smirks as his nose is touching mine, "Hey, Pussycat." He doesn't give me the chance to say anything. He crushes his lips onto mine, forcing his rigid tongue into my mouth. I'm gasping, trying to breathe. His weight is heavy on me and I'm completely immobile. I feel how hard he is as he grinds his hips into me and he's pressing into my gut as he moves lower to grind against me. I'm wearing thin jogging pants and I can feel *everything*.

I struggle but he has me completely pinned. His open mouth is absorbing my muffled cries. He won't stop. I try to bite his tongue and his lip, but he's too quick. He's suffocating me with his mouth. My panic takes complete hold of my body and I thrash beneath him. I can't let this happen again. *I need to fight.*

My wrists are burning and I feel so weak. I can't get him off of me. My body weakens, betraying me as he's grinding up against my most sensitive area.

He's now holding both of my wrists with one hand as he grabs my breast and squeezes my nipple. He doesn't remove his mouth from mine as he continues to absorb my grunts and pleas. His hand travels down over my belly, pulls down my loose pants, and dips into my panties. His finger finds my sensitive area and starts to rub vigorously. I'm having trouble breathing because I'm gagging on my own saliva.

I buck my hips, trying to push him off of me.

"Pussycat, you know you want me. I can feel it," he says as he plunges his fingers into me. I immediately tense up as his fingernails scrape against my walls. The pain I feel flips a switch and my panic is spiraling out of control. He's pumping his fingers into me, "Come for me, Pussycat." No! He's fucking demonic. How can he think he can get me aroused?

I'm gagging on his tongue as it thrusts in and out of my mouth. I'd rather choke to death than allow my body to respond to his torture. I'm burning all over and feel immense pain between my legs. He's tearing up my most sensitive areas with his fingers. My insides are being shredded.

He covers my mouth with his hand, further muffling my cries, and bites the side of my neck. Pain shoots down my spine and I feel warmth on my neck.

Blood.

He then bites the top of my breast. The pain is excruciating. I feel more blood on my chest as he bites me in two more places. His hand closes tighter over my mouth and moves to cover my nose. He's going to suffocate me. I thrash, but it's useless. He's completely overpowered me and I begin to go limp. I can't pull any air into my lungs and whatever strength I had leaves me. He opens his jeans and begins to push himself inside of me. I feel a stabbing pain in my gut.

Everything fades into darkness.

~

I feel like I'm moving and I'm freezing. I'm laying down on something and it's bouncing a little. I'm shaking uncontrollably as I try to open my eyes. I feel someone's hand on my wrist and hear the words, "Pulse is weak. Her blood pressure is low. She's in shock." I hear sirens coming from somewhere.

*Who's talking? I'm freezing. Can someone give me a blanket?* I feel tremors rattle my entire body.

"Carly." I hear my name. I think I recognize the voice. It's a male voice and it seems so far away.

"Carly, please wake up." He is pleading with me now. I can barely hear him as my ears start to ring and blackness envelops me again.

~

I feel a warm, soft hand on my arm, slowly rubbing me. I hear a loud, steady beeping noise and I slowly open my eyes.

Everything is blurry, but I can make out a large figure sitting next to me. He has his head bent down and he appears to be sleeping while sitting up. His hand is moving on its own up and down my arm.

*Kyle.*

I try to speak but I have a mask over my face. I can feel the cool oxygen as I start to breathe rapidly.

My eyes are wide and I begin to panic. The last thing I remember is Todd forcing himself on me. Raping me. Again.

I gasp for air and sob. The moans coming from my throat sound almost guttural.

Kyle jolts awake.

"Carly, calm down." He stands over me and places both hands on my arm.

"You're safe." His soothing eyes center me and I begin to breathe more normally.

"Don't speak, just listen to me. Everything is going to be okay."

I close my eyes and nod. I'm trying to calm myself down. *Why is he here?*

"What happened?" I ask, closing my eyes. Bracing myself for the answer.

"I was looking for you after the Biology exam. I ran into your friend Becca and she said that I could find you in your 'secret' spot." He takes a deep breath and I squeeze my eyes shut tighter. I feel tears streaming down the sides of my face.

"When I got to the third floor, I could hear what sounded like muffled cries. I heard someone grunting." He squeezes my hand tight and rubs his thumb over the top of my hand gently.

"What I saw," he pauses and my eyes pop open. *What did he see?* "There was so much blood. Todd was on top of you and was about to rape you. If I didn't get there when I did…"

He's quiet for a few moments and then continues.

"I don't know what came over me, but I hurt him. Bad. He's here in the hospital, unconscious. The fucker deserves to die."

I try to focus on his face. There are scratches all over it. His lip is swollen and bruised. His left eye is practically swollen shut. I look down to his hands and the knuckles are torn with dried blood caked on them.

I gasp and sob again.

"I'm sorry," I cry. "I'm so sorry that you got involved in this."

He shakes his head, "Stop. I did what anyone would do. He was hurting you." His voice breaks and if I could see through my own tears, I would swear that he is also crying. "He hurt you so bad that you passed out, went into shock. He almost killed you."

"Oh my God," I say, turning my head to look away. *I can't believe I let this happen to me again.*

I feel his hand rest lightly on the top of my head as his thumb starts to massage my temple.

"You're going to be okay. I won't ever let this happen again. I *promise* you that I'm not leaving your side again." His declaration seems sincere. But I'm confused. *Why would he make this promise to me?*

He leans over and softly kisses the top of my head. His lips linger and for the first time in a long time, I feel safe. I'm not afraid of him. I'm in so much physical and emotional pain, but I'm happy that I'm finally not afraid.

I lean into his chest and wrap my arms around him. The tubes hanging from my arms get tangled, but I don't care. I just hold on tight and let out all of my sobs.

His shirt is wet from my tears and he sits on the bed with me as I curl into him.

The door opens and a doctor comes in.

"Miss Sloan? I see you're awake." She smiles softly and nods to Kyle.

"Mr. Finnegan, would you mind stepping outside for a few moments? I'd like to speak with Miss Sloan about her injuries."

Kyle kisses the top of my head one more time and stands up to leave.

"I'll be right outside. I am not going anywhere."

He walks slowly out the door.

"Miss Sloan, or can I call you Carly?" she asks.

"Carly is fine," I say quietly.

"How are you feeling?" she asks, pulling a chair next to my bed.

"I'm in pain," I say weakly, wincing as I hold my side. "Is it bad?" I ask, worried.

"Your injuries are serious, but not life-threatening. You went into shock after your ordeal. Your lacerations on your neck and your breasts were mostly superficial. However, the one on your abdomen was quite deep. You lost a considerable amount of blood from that area. We cleaned and closed up the wound. The knife missed all vital organs Carly, you are very lucky."

*Knife?*

"Knife?" I ask incredulously. "He didn't have a knife. He was *biting* me." As I say that out loud, my stomach lurches at the sheer violence of

Todd's act. I feel like I'm going to vomit.

"Yes Carly, the marks on your neck and breasts are indeed bite marks. But the wound to your abdomen was most definitely caused by a medium blade knife."

I close my eyes and try to regulate my breathing. Burning pain shoots down my side and through my gut. I swallow heavily as I feel the bile begin to rise.

"We examined you internally as well. Your friend, Kyle, arrived before Mr. Mitchell could penetrate you. Before he could rape you. However, you do have some internal lacerations along your vaginal walls. Presumably from his fingers or another blunt object."

I stare at her as tears continue to fall down my cheeks. I can't listen to this anymore.

"He didn't rape me?"

"No."

I don't know why that's important because he's already done so much physical damage to me. But I'm almost relieved. He didn't get the chance to rape me again and that is all that seems to matter.

"Is there anyone else we can call? The campus police have contacted your parents and they're on the way."

My parents. What am I going to say to them? How am I going to explain what happened to me? *Twice?*

"No," I say. I hesitate before I ask, "What happened to Todd?" *I need to know.*

"Your friend out there roughed him up pretty badly. He beat him senseless, actually. Mr. Mitchell should regain consciousness, and when he does, he'll find himself handcuffed to a hospital bed and a police officer outside his door. Mr. Finnegan has already given a detailed statement to both the campus and local police. This should be an open and shut case, Carly. They'll just need your statement."

I need this to be over. "I'll tell them everything."

Kyle peeks his head in the door. "Is it okay for me to come back in?" He looks worried.

The doctor stands to leave; she touches my hand softly and says, "Carly, you're a survivor. You're very lucky. Make it count and put him away for a long time."

She leaves the room and Kyle is back at my side.

I look at him and I'm about to lose my composure. "I don't know what to say."

He takes my hand and squeezes, "Nothing. Say nothing. Just get better. Please." His eyes are glassy as he pleads with me then he lowers his head.

I hold his hand tightly and say, "I'll try."

I hear commotion in the hallway as Becca, Callie, and Manny storm into the room.

A collective gasp sounds and they rush to the sides of my bed. None of them pushes Kyle out of the way and they don't seem surprised that he's holding my hand.

"That fucking asshole," Manny states coldly as he takes my free hand in his. He looks up and makes eye contact with Kyle, "Please tell me you fucked him up so bad he will never be able to do this to anyone ever again?"

"Yes, he's incapacitated. If I had seen the knife that he used on Carly, he also would be castrated. I guess he's lucky that way." Kyle shrugs his shoulders and shakes his head.

"Carly, the police are all over this place. Apparently, they're waiting for Todd to regain consciousness so they can arrest him and throw the book at him." Becca exclaims.

"How are you, honey?" Callie asks quietly.

"Oh, you know, I've been better," I state and look at Callie. "It's over."

She nods and squeezes my ankle.

I hear both of my sisters as they loudly approach and I see my parents walk into the room.

My family is here. *All of them.*

My parents, sisters, and brother.

Callie, Becca, and Manny.

*And Kyle.*

My entire family.

I close my eyes and try to feel safe again.

# Chapter 23

## Tabitha

*Philadelphia, Pennsylvania*
### Past
*Age 19*

I FEEL WARMTH and a soft touch on my ankle. I slowly wake up and realize that I'm in the back room of the bar, alone with Alex. *What happened?*

I open my eyes and see him sitting at my feet. He looks at me and he's wearing so much pain on his face.

I've had about a dozen panic attacks over the past few years. The one that I had tonight was bad. Although I've come close, I've never actually passed out from one.

I'm embarrassed as I start to sit up and Alex quickly jumps to his feet.

"Whoa, Tabs. Stay put. You fainted before and need to get up slowly."

"I'm fine, Alex." I sit up quickly and immediately get woozy.

"Well, maybe not so much." I lean against the back of the couch and rest my head on the cushion. "Fuck," I groan.

I recall what caused me to panic in the first place. "What was that?" I ask, touching my lips, remembering his crushing kiss. A kiss that I felt all over my body. A kiss that I now miss. *What the hell?*

Alex sighs, takes a deep breath, and looks at me.

"I think that was us crashing into each other and bursting into flames," he says softly, shaking his head. *He feels guilty.*

"Oh," I say. I feel tears form in my eyes and if I blink, they'll spill down my cheeks. I inhale deeply trying to stop that from happening.

"I shouldn't have done that, kissed you. You clearly panicked and tried to get away. I should have realized…, I'm so sorry, Tabs."

He looks away from me and runs his hand along the arm of the couch. His fingers are barely touching the fabric and they look as if they're walking. I wonder if he's creating a soundtrack for this moment as his fingers continue to travel up and down.

"Alex, it's not that I didn't want you to, um, kiss me. It's just that my past is so fucked up. I don't know if I can do this with you. With anyone." I look away and continue. "Timing is everything, right? Well, at this exact time, right now, I just can't. I want to tell you why, but I'm afraid that you'll run. I'm really messed up, Alex. I've done some terrible things and allowed terrible things to happen to me. I'm damaged. Broken. Used." My voice trails off and I close my eyes.

The tears that were on the brink finally spill down my cheeks.

"Tabs, nothing you can say will scare me away." He lifts my chin up and wipes the tears from my cheeks with his thumbs. He's cradling my face in his hands and staring into my eyes. *Comforting me.*

His gesture is so tender that it catches me off guard.

"I've been through my share of shit. Trust me," he continues. "I'm not asking you to share with me now, but please consider talking to me soon. Whatever you're dealing with is clearly affecting you in ways you can't even cope with or process. For fuck's sake, you fainted. You need to face head-on whatever is haunting you. Please."

He slowly removes his hands from my face and backs away.

"I'll go get you some water. Don't go anywhere. Understand?"

"Yes," I reply. I'm still too dizzy to stand up. I won't be going anywhere yet.

He returns a few minutes later with two empty cups and a large pitcher of ice water. After filling our cups, he hands me one and sits down on the couch next to me.

I take a long, cool sip and lean into the back of the couch.

"How are you feeling?" Alex asks.

"Better."

"Has this ever happened to you before? Shit, Tabs, you scared the crap out of me."

"Yes, I'm prone to panic attacks. I've been having them since Trina died when I was about seven. I don't know what happened, Alex. I guess I just kind of freaked out."

In all honesty, I have never been kissed like that. Tony was brutal, never tender. Alex was my first real kiss and I completely panicked.

"Hey, it's okay. I just need to know what I did to trigger it. I'm so sorry." He looks away, ashamed.

"I can't even begin to tell you what brings it on. Certain situations, maybe? I just don't know." I lie. Tony was the last man I'd been with and, well, that wasn't so consensual. Hell, the last time a man had his hands on me like that, the fucker tried to kill me. So yeah, I lied.

"I'm sorry for whatever you went through. I think I understand, though. I know I told you about my pops and how he couldn't cope with my mom's death. He used to take tons of shit out on me." He lifts up his black t-shirt to reveal a long scar on his side. It's somewhat camouflaged with a tattoo of a rope tied into a noose.

"Alex," I whisper as I reach out to touch the scar. He flinches, sucks in a breath, but doesn't back away. "What did he do?"

"This time? He didn't enjoy the dinner I made for him that night. It happened when I was fourteen. He came home from work drunk off his ass, which was almost a daily occurrence. I made pancakes." He huffs and continues. "He dragged me out of the kitchen into the garage and started kicking me around. He took a swing at me with a metal garden rake that tore into my side."

I gasp, drop my hand to his, and squeeze. Our fingers become entwined. We are somehow united through the abuse that we've both endured.

"Why the noose?" I ask hesitantly.

"It's what Pops used to kill himself."

*Holy shit.*

*Dear Emily*

"Alex." I start sobbing as I wrap my arms around his waist, resting my cheek on his abdomen. With all that I have endured and lost, I can't believe that I've found someone who has lost more.

He places his hand on the back of my head, holding me against him.

"I'm so sorry."

He releases me and grabs my shoulders, pulling me onto my feet.

We're standing eye-to-eye as he wipes my tears from my cheeks.

"Please don't cry for me."

I suck in a deep breath. "I'm crying for both of us. For all that we've lost."

He pulls me into an embrace and kisses my forehead.

"I don't know what has caused you to withdraw into yourself, but you have to know that I'm here for you. I'm drawn to you and can practically feel your pain. And I can tell that we need each other."

He's right. We need each other.

*I need him.*

To heal.

"So my last boyfriend tried to kill me." I blurt out, surprised that those words just came out of my mouth.

He places his hands firmly on my shoulders, pushing me slightly away from him so he can look into my eyes. "You don't have to say anything else."

Yes I do. I really do. I suddenly feel the need to tell him everything.

"He was horrible. Tony. He was vile. He took advantage of me." I move my hair away from my face to expose my cheek and the scar. "He sliced my face when I refused to give one of his club patrons a blow job. Then he tried to strangle me." I pause as I look into Alex's eyes. They're full of concern as he lightly touches my scar.

"I was able to get away, to start over. I'm constantly looking over my shoulder because I know that if he ever finds me, he'll make sure he completes the job and kill me."

My eyes fill with tears.

"He took everything from me. Everything. He took my baby."

*Why did I say that?*

He squeezes my shoulders tighter. "What?"

I begin to tremble as sobs wrack my body.

He pulls me against him, tucking my face into his chest. My tears are soaking through his t-shirt.

"He got me pregnant and forced me to give her away. Her name was... is... Sara."

"Oh my God. When?"

"Two months ago."

"Jesus."

He's squeezing me so hard as he rubs his hands down my back. "Tabs, I just don't know what to say."

I sniffle. "Don't say anything. It's too painful." I sob loudly again as I wrap my arms tighter around his body. I can't believe I'm coming apart at the seams as I tell Alex everything.

Suddenly, the door swings open as Dax walks in.

"Hey, oh, uh, sorry," he says, stammering.

I quickly pull away from Alex and turn to face the wall. This is just perfect.

"Wow, Tabby, you don't look so good," he comments.

"Dude, seriously, what do you want?" Alex demands.

"Show's about to start and you've been M.I.A for the past half hour. We need you now."

Alex turns to me and gently caresses my face, angling it toward him. "Are you going to be okay? I have a show to do."

I nod slowly, "Yeah, just go do what you need to. I'm not going to watch the show tonight if that's all right with you. I'm just not up to it."

"Of course, but please stay back here. I'll make sure you get home after the show."

"Um, okay." I don't think I have it in me to leave just yet.

He runs his knuckle over my cheek, wiping away my tears. I close my eyes as I lean my head into his hand. "You'll be safe back here. Get comfortable and I'll see you after the show."

He turns to leave and I notice Dax staring at me with a furrowed brow. Concern and sympathy sweep over his face.

Alex walks past him out the door and Dax follows.

I throw myself back onto the couch and pull my knees up to my chest. I can't believe that I just told Alex about Sara. *What was I thinking?* How could I have just blurted that out? How could I have shared something so deep and personal? I've exposed myself and I begin to panic once again.

The door swings open as Garrett saunters in.

"Oh, hey, Tabby," he smirks.

"Why aren't you in the bar with the rest of the groupies?" he asks.

*What a jerk... seriously?*

I sniffle a little and say, "I'm just not up for it, Garrett. Why don't you go back out there and entertain your faithful minions." I huff and look away from him.

"Get used to the crying, Tabs. Alex will break your heart over and over. You're no different than the rest of them."

*What. The. Hell?*

Before I can respond, he turns around and walks out of the room. What a douchebag.

Why do I subject myself to this? And why does Garrett feel the need to make me feel like such crap? *Maybe I deserve it.*

I shake my head. I should just leave. I suddenly don't want to be here anymore. But then I hear the low strum of a guitar. Epic Fail must be starting their set.

I sit back down on the couch and stretch out my legs. The low hum of Alex's voice begins to soothe me.

I'm asleep before he reaches the end of the first song.

~

I hear soft whispers.

"What are you going to do with her, Alex?" a voice says quietly.

"I'm going to let her sleep. She's obviously exhausted," Alex says.

"That's not what I mean and you know it."

"What do you mean, Dax? I'd like to know." Alex is no longer whispering.

"You don't do relationships, especially with a chick like this. She's a mess," Dax says.

163

I decide that I've eavesdropped enough. Alex turns to me as I stretch my legs out and open my eyes. "I should be going…," I stand up and walk to the door.

"Dax, will you give us a minute?" Alex asks.

Dax huffs. "Fine. Good to meet you, Tabitha," he says through tight lips. "See you around." He turns and leaves the room.

"How much of that did you hear?" Alex asks.

"Enough. I heard enough, Alex, and what did Dax mean?"

"He didn't mean anything malicious by it. He's just worried about me. He's like my brother and knows that I have a history of bad relationships."

"Oh," I say weakly.

"I don't know what's going on here, but I feel something strong. Do you? Feel it?" He places his hands on the outside of my arms as if to keep me steady and looks into my eyes.

My heart is pounding in my chest as I return his gaze. "Yes," I say. Goddamn it, I can't deny this attraction. *I feel it*. I feel the magnetic pull, the energy that's between us, enveloping us.

He slowly pulls me closer to him so our chests are touching and slides his hands up my arms to my face. He brushes the tears from my cheeks and places his lips chastely on mine. Leaning his forehead into mine he says, "I've needed this since I walked into your bookstore and saw you for the first time. I've never felt this kind of pull before, with anyone. I just can't explain it."

He wraps his arms around me, pulls me into a tight embrace, and rests his chin on the top of my head.

I tremble slightly and squeeze him tight. "I don't know what I can be to you, for you. But somehow, I know that I need this right now too. I need a friend. I need you."

"Let's get you home, okay?" He takes my hand and walks toward the door.

We walk through the hallway, passing Dax and Garrett. Neither says a word but they look almost disapprovingly at us as we walk by.

I can't bother myself with what others think about Alex and me. I'm hard enough on myself as it is.

*Dear Emily*

Maybe he is exactly what I need to heal.

To move past what Tony did to me. What he took from me.

I squeeze his hand tightly as I follow him through the club.

For the first time in as long as I can remember, I have hope.

Hope that the crushing pain that I feel in my chest every day will begin to fade.

My youth is gone.

My innocence is gone.

My baby, Sara, is gone.

But Alex is here.

I have hope.

# Chapter 24

## Carly

Spring Lake, New Jersey
**Present**
Age 29

Dear Emily,

Your room is now completely ready for you. I'm sitting in the comfy rocking chair looking out your window, peering into the backyard where your swing set, sandbox, and princess castle will be.

I imagine you playing with your future girlfriends, frolicking in pink dresses and tutus. I also imagine your Daddy outside playing with you, wearing the princess crown that you give to him. He's laughing and twirling you around while the pink boa decorating your princess ensemble trails behind you.

Your giggles are making my heart race with excitement. This is your future, Emily.

This is our future.

We will be a Forever Family.

My heart is bursting with Love,

Mama

*Dear Emily*

I close my journal as I stand up from the chair in Emily's room. I walk over to her dresser and place the journal in the top drawer next to the little booties and socks that I purchased last week. I smile as I run my fingers over the frilly pieces of infant clothes. She'll be here. *Soon*.

It's well after one in the morning as I make my way back to our bedroom. Kyle is sound asleep – passed out, actually. He drank more wine than all of us combined during this edition of Wine Wednesday. I laugh quietly and hope that I don't wake up the others. Callie and Becca are sharing our guest bedroom while Manny stayed downstairs on the couch to sleep.

It felt wonderful to kick back with my best friends tonight. We all had the chance to blow off some steam and just relax.

I'm so excited for Emily to become part of our extended family. Callie, Becca, and Manny are going to be such great influences on her life. She's going to love them as much as she will her other aunts and uncles.

I slide into bed next to Kyle, wishing we didn't have a house full of guests and he wasn't passed out. *I need him*.

I cuddle into his side, nuzzling my chin into his neck. I place a soft kiss there and he pulls me close.

"I love you Carly," he whispers. He turns us so we're spooning and he wraps his arm tightly around my waist. "I love you so much."

I smile and sigh. "I love you, too, Kyle. With all that I am." I lightly touch his arm.

"Goodnight."

He squeezes me tighter and places his lips on my ear.

"Goodnight, Carly."

He kisses me where his lips were and I drift off into dreamland.

# Chapter 25

## Carly

*New Brunswick, New Jersey*
### Past
*Age 18*

I'M BEING RELEASED from the hospital today and I don't want to leave. I know that's weird, but if I leave here that means I have to go home for Christmas. And this year, I just can't get excited about it. With everything that has happened to me over the past few months, I can't see myself enjoying the usual Sloan family holiday activities.

"Hey," Kyle says as he walks into my hospital room.

I look up and smile softly. "Hi Kyle." Warmth spreads into my cheeks, his presence comforting me.

He's spent the last few days with me. He's kept me company, helped communicate with my professors and plays a great game of Scrabble. Although I missed my Sociology final exam, Kyle was able to get the professor to excuse my absence and I still earned an 'A' in the class. She was more than understanding of my situation and used all of my prior assignments and tests as a basis for my final grade. For that, I'm so thankful.

The nurses look the other way when visiting hours end and he sleeps in the chair in my room every single night. He refuses to leave me alone. We haven't talked about what happened to me and he doesn't want to pry. Just having him here keeps me calm and I'm able to sleep at night. *I feel safe. Protected.*

"Are you about ready to go? I saw your parents out by the nurses' station taking care of your discharge paperwork."

I shrug. "I guess I'm ready."

"What's wrong?"

I look down at my hands as I rub them along my legs. "I don't want to go home."

He sits at the end of my bed and places his hand on my ankle. His touch is soothing.

"I'm sorry." He softly traces my ankle with his thumb as he continues. "I wish I could take away all of your pain. Tell me what I can do." *Stay with me.*

I look up and meet his gaze. I see the pain and worry in his eyes, and immediately feel terrible that I'm causing him to feel this way.

"Kyle, you being here with me over the past four days is above and beyond what I could ask for. You've made me feel safe for the first time in months since... since Halloween." I can't believe it's been almost two months since Todd first raped me. I wish I had done something. Said something. I wouldn't be in this hospital room recovering from another attack.

I close my eyes and shiver as Kyle softly rubs my leg.

Todd regained consciousness three days ago, was promptly arrested, and is currently in jail and being held without bail. Detective Patricia Meyers has been to see me several times since and I've given a full statement of both attacks. Kyle stayed with me and quietly listened each and every time I told my story. As hard as it's been to recount my ordeal, it's been equally hard watching his reaction. I feel terrible that he's been reliving my rape and attack. It's not fair that someone else should continue to live through the pain and anguish that I'm feeling.

Detective Meyers told me this morning that the prosecutor of the case believes this is going to be one of the easiest convictions she's ever worked on. In addition to my testimony and physical evidence from my brutal attack, several other victims have stepped forward. While my attack was the most violent, three of the other girls were also brutally raped. It seemed that his attacks continued to escalate in severity. I blame myself. I should have reported him after the Halloween party. If I had, others wouldn't have fallen prey to his demented attacks. I'm crushed with guilt over this and I don't know what to do about it.

Kyle's soft voice brings me back to reality. "Carly, you're going to be okay."

I choke on a light sob. "Am I? I just don't know, Kyle." I slowly shake my head as a tear rolls down my cheek. *I don't believe that I am.*

He gets up, moves closer, and I recoil slightly as he lightly touches my cheek. "You are, Carly. I just know it." He wipes the lone tear from my cheek and tilts my chin so I'm looking into his eyes. "I'm here and I'm not going anywhere."

"Hey guys." My sister, Lyn, prances into the room. She's always so bubbly and positive, even when something unimaginable happens. "Are you ready to leave?"

Kyle's hand drops from my cheek to my shoulder and he lightly squeezes.

I look up and see Lyn's warm smile. "I guess so."

My parents enter the room next. "Carly, you're all set to leave," my mother says. Even though they've spent many hours in this room with Kyle and me, my father still looks uncomfortable with him. He frowns when he sees that Kyle is touching my shoulder and crosses his arms over his chest.

"Hi Mom, Dad," I say softly. "I'm ready."

I swing my legs over the side of the bed as Kyle bends down to get my flip-flops. A pain shoots across my abdomen and I wince.

"Carly, it's December. Can't you put socks and shoes on?" my mother asks, scoffing at my bare feet.

"Mom, will you leave her alone? Do you remember last year when it snowed on Christmas and she went outside to help shovel in those?" Lyn chuckles.

Kyle helps me stand and places his hand on my lower back. His touch is so soothing that I just want to lean into him and let him cradle me in his arms.

My father huffs, grabs my bags, and walks out of the room.

Lyn smiles and says, "Kyle, don't take it personally. Our father isn't dealing with Carly's situation very well. Right now he doesn't want men around any of his daughters."

"It's okay. I totally get it," Kyle states.

My nurse, Lauren, enters the room. "Carly, it looks like you are all set." She smiles warmly and continues. "Your parents have all of your discharge instructions. Please make sure you follow up with your family doctor to have your stitches removed in ten days. In addition, we've provided you with names of several therapists. Contact one of them when you're ready."

Of course, I know I need to talk to someone who can help me sort out my feelings over all of this. Kyle actually took the initiative and already made an appointment for me with Dr. James during the week that I return from winter break.

"Thanks, Lauren. I actually already have that taken care of." I look at Kyle and smile softly.

"Good. Please take care of yourself." She turns and leaves the room.

"Ready?" Lyn asks.

I look around the hospital room and then at Kyle. He smiles at me as he takes my hand.

"Yes," I say as I let him lead me out of the room.

A pit forms in my stomach as I realize that I'm heading home where Christmas has surely exploded all over my house.

It's supposed to be a happy and joyous time of year.

But I don't feel festive.

I feel empty.

Guilty.

Regretful.

*Ashamed.*

# Chapter 26

## Tabitha

*Philadelphia, Pennsylvania*
### *Past*
*Age 20*

I'M SITTING AT the counter in the diner while on my break, scarfing down a grilled cheese and tomato sandwich. I chew slowly, savoring it as if it were my last meal. It's the first thing I've eaten all day.

"Hey Tabby." Seth's familiar voice is behind me.

I stand up and throw my arms around him, swallowing the last bite. "Hey Seth." He gives me a kiss on my cheek and sits on the stool next to me.

"What time are you off work today? We're still on for the zoo today, right?" His smile is huge as he pokes my shoulder gently.

Over the past year and a half, Seth has become one of my best friends. I feel so accomplished to actually have friends. Seth and Kirsten provide me with such support and for the first time I value others. I smile as I remember his persistence that day last year when he came to visit me in the bookstore for the first time.

*I'm flipping through a magazine while sitting on the leather couch with my feet planted on the coffee table in front of me. I'm so bored today. I've unpacked all of the boxes that were delivered this morning, dusted the bookshelves, and even rearranged the bookmarks. I stretch and yawn* as the door chimes jingle and am surprised to see Seth walk in.

He smiles softly as he walks toward me. "Hi Tabby." His teeth are so white I swear I can see my reflection in them. "I hope I didn't wake you," he chuckles.

"Oh hey, Seth. And no, you didn't wake me. I'm just catching up on the latest 'Brangalina' gossip." I look away, embarrassed that I'm even reading this drab.

"So this is your bookstore?" Seth looks around.

"Well, not my bookstore. I don't own it. But yes, this is where I spend the other half of my time, working."

"It's quaint," he says. "It suits you."

"Thanks for inviting me here. I've been looking forward to it since we talked at the diner. And I've been looking forward to making a new friend. We can learn the ins and outs of Philly together."

He sits down on the couch next to me and places his hand on my knee. I flinch a little but I'm surprisingly not uncomfortable by his touch. I shimmy my knee from under his hand and scoot to the side of the couch. I don't want to give him the wrong impression, after all. We're only friends.

"I'm not usually one to make new friends, but I guess it can't hurt to try, right?" I ask.

"It never hurts to try new things," he says. "Today's going to be great. Our first order of business is to enjoy ourselves. What time do you get off work?"

"Kirsten should be here in about an hour." I'm not sure when I'm going to see Alex again. When he took me home the other night, we didn't really discuss it. He placed a chaste kiss on my lips and left without saying another word. I wonder if he's second-guessing wanting to be with me. My panic attack at the club may have caused him to take a pause on where he wants to take things.

I shake my head, thinking that I shouldn't be worrying about when I'm going to see Alex again. I'm here with Seth and he's my new friend. Alex shouldn't matter or weigh in to how I proceed. I've just never been in the driver's seat in any relationship before. I've always been controlled, contained, and restricted. This actually feels good.

"Let's go do the Philly tourist thing. I want to see the Liberty Bell and *go to Penn's Landing. Are you up for that?"*

"Sure." *I'm actually excited about this. I've been here for a little over two months and I haven't ventured away from this area. While I grew up in Philadelphia, I never got to see much of the city when I was younger.*

*"If we have time, let's go to The Franklin Institute." I say enthusiastically.*

*I'm so happy to finally experience what makes this city so unique and I'm happy to be doing this with my new friend Seth.*

"Hey… Snap out of it, Tabby." Seth shakes my shoulders gently. "Are you here with me?"

"Oh. Sorry, I was just remembering the first time we did geeky tourist stuff together. You know, Liberty Bell, Penn's Landing, and The Franklin Institute. I can't believe over a year has passed since we first became friends, Seth." I smile, grab his hand, and squeeze.

"You know I think about that day a lot." He pauses and looks into my eyes. "You're so special to me." I smile and want to squeeze myself. *I'm lucky to have him in my life.*

"Are you ready for the zoo?" he asks, excitedly pulling me into an embrace. His hugs are always comforting. I hear someone come into the diner and feel Seth's arms around me stiffen.

"What the fuck are you doing with my girl, Tyson?"

*Alex.*

He despises Seth. He refuses to call him by his first name.

Seth lets me go and I turn to face my boyfriend.

"Hey Alex." I smile and lean in to kiss him lightly on the lips.

"We're getting ready to go to the zoo. I'm off work in about fifteen minutes."

I can see Alex's irritation grow as he looks back and forth between Seth and me.

"Did you forget, Tabs? We have plans this afternoon. Me and you."

*Dammit!*

I did forget.

We're supposed to be going to see a couple of bands play at The High Note. Epic Fail is touring soon and this afternoon they're auditioning opening acts to join them on the road. He really wanted me to be there so I could be a part of the decision.

"Oh. Sorry, Alex. I forgot."

I turn toward Seth. "Seth, I'm sooo sorry! I had this planned with Alex. I must have gotten my days screwed up. I'm so sorry. Can we do this next week? I'm free on Tuesday after my shift here."

Seth reaches out and grabs my hand. I see Alex flinch out of the corner of my eye.

"It's okay, Tabs," Seth says, using the nickname that Alex owns. He's now just doing things to get Alex even more agitated.

"Next Tuesday it is. I'll pick you up here when you're done with work." He leans in, kisses me on the cheek, and walks past Alex. I notice the intense stare between them.

"What the fuck, Tabs?" Alex is very distressed and I need to calm him down, fast.

I quickly throw my arms around his neck and press our lips together. "Alex, I don't know why you get so bothered when Seth is around." I kiss him again and lean back to look into his eyes.

"In case you haven't noticed, he's been trying to get into your pants for over a year. I can't believe it's not at all obvious to you." Alex's irritation is growing.

"Alex, I love YOU. Only you. We've been through so much together over the past year. You should know by now that it's just you and me. Seth is my *friend*. That's all. Period. I love you with my everything. You own me, Alex. I'm only yours. Do you understand?"

"I know you love me. And you know that I love you so fucking much. It just bothers me how much time Seth spends with you when I can't. I'm getting stressed about going on the road and being away from you for several months. I just don't want to lose what we have. It's too perfect. And I don't want Seth to feel like the door is open after I leave. He's just waiting to pounce, I can feel it."

"Alex..."

"What do you want me to do? I don't know how to deal with this. Do you want me to just look the other way every time he looks at you? I know he wants you. I just can't help how I feel."

He's so insecure about us; I just don't know how to make it better. He's the one that's leaving. I should be the one fretting day and night about groupies, booze, and the band. For once in my life, I feel secure in a relationship and he's stressing out about my friend. *This sucks.*

"Let's drop this please. You're being ridiculous. We need to get to The High Note and we need to find your opening band." I squeeze his hand and pull him out the door.

He pulls me against his body and drops his lips onto mine, kissing me fiercely. I barely have time to react, but the familiar warmth of his touch begins to spread throughout my body. I part my lips and kiss him back.

"I just don't know what to say. I can't stand the thought of not being around you." He moves his lips across my cheek, over to that spot behind my ear that sends shockwaves between my legs. "I love you, Tabs," he whispers in my ear as he takes my lobe gently between his teeth.

I whimper and say, "Alex, if you keep that up we'll never make it to the club." I don't want him to stop but we're in the middle of a busy sidewalk.

He nips my earlobe again and his lips softly trail down my neck. He pulls away and smiles at me. "I'm sorry. I'll figure out how to keep my jealousy and worry in check. I promise." He leans back in and kisses me quickly before taking my hand and leading me toward The High Note.

He puts his arm around my shoulders and tucks me into his side as we walk. He makes me feel protected and safe. I love him with all that I am.

And suddenly I'm afraid that it's all going to come crashing to an end.

# Chapter 27

## Carly

*Colts Neck, New Jersey*
**Past**
*Age 18*

My PILLOW IS vibrating. Buzzing. My eyes pop open and I see the sun streaming through my bedroom window.

I reach my hand underneath my pillow and grab my phone where I left it after I said goodnight to Kyle last night.

I flip it open and groggily say, "Hello?" I rub my hand over my face.

"Merry Christmas, Carly."

Kyle's soft voice soothes me and I smile. He has called me every day, at least twice a day, since I came home from the hospital. Last night, we spent hours on the phone together as he told me his favorite Christmas memories with his family. I can tell that it's hard for him to try to remember the days when his mother was alive. She passed away when he was just seven years old. He recounted cheerful times when he and his sister enjoyed the holidays. I laughed last night for the first time in weeks when he told me a story about their Siamese cat, Mo. Apparently, he used to climb their Christmas tree, and he would swat ornaments to the floor. His father used to constantly grumble about the cat, as he had to redecorate the tree on a daily basis. Just picturing a crazy cat climbing a Christmas tree made me laugh out loud. It felt good and I'm so grateful that Kyle is going out of his way to cheer me up.

"Merry Christmas, Kyle," I say as I yawn into the phone. I stretch and my side aches.

"Still asleep?" He chuckles.

"I'm not anymore. Gosh, what time is it?" I ask.

"Nine o'clock," he answers.

I sit up. "Shit, my family is probably sitting outside my door. You know, it's a rule in our house that no one can go downstairs on Christmas morning until we're all awake."

He laughs. "You shouldn't keep them waiting. I just wanted to call to see how you slept last night and to say Merry Christmas."

"I slept great," I answer. And I did. It was after midnight when I got off the phone with him and for the first time in weeks, I drifted off to sleep immediately and dreamlessly. *Peacefully.*

"I'm glad, Carly. Now go before your brother and sisters knock down your door."

"Okay." I smile.

"Kyle?"

"Yes, Carly?"

I pause and breathe deeply.

"Thank you. I really don't know what else to say."

"Say yes when I ask you to join me for breakfast tomorrow," he says and I can hear him smiling.

"What?" I ask.

"Just say yes."

I want nothing more than to say yes to his invitation and I don't know why I'm hesitating. I don't say anything and remain silent for what seems like hours.

"Carly, are you okay? I'm sorry, I just thought. I mean...," he's stumbling over his words. "I just want to see you. To be sure that you're all right. I need to see you."

It's been over a week since he drove me home from the hospital and I feel the same exact way. I want to see him so badly. I'm just nervous. Worried that I can't possibly be who he's looking for right now.

"Okay." I finally answer.

"Are you sure? If you're not that's completely fine. I don't want to push, make you do something you may not be ready to do."

"Kyle, I'll go to breakfast with you." I smile. "But I have to warn you that I eat pancakes like a seven foot lumberjack. I have no restraint."

He laughs. "Great! I'll call you later. In the meantime, have a wonderful day, Carly."

"Thanks. Hey, what are you doing today?" I ask hesitantly, knowing that it's just him and his sister.

"Oh, nothing really. Patrice is spending the day with her boyfriend's family."

Oh no… he's going to be alone.

"Kyle, please come here for dinner. My mother will be happy to set another place at our table. You shouldn't be alone on Christmas."

"Are you sure?" he asks.

"Yes, please come."

"Okay, I will. What time should I be there?"

"Dinner will be around four, so come any time before then."

"Great, see you later."

"Bye," I say softly.

I hang up the phone and wonder if I just made a mistake inviting him here. I'm so grateful for his constant support and presence, but I don't want him to get the wrong idea. I can't be with him right now and I'm not sure if I can any time in the near future.

I open my door and my youngest sister Renee is sitting on the floor outside my room and leaning up against the wall. I have to step over her candy cane striped pajama legs to get into the hall.

"It's about time you're up, Carly. Lyn is about to go back to sleep and Jimmy is in the bathroom. This is the latest any of us has ever slept on Christmas so get a move on!" She finishes scolding me and stands up to give me a hug. "Merry Christmas."

Lyn and Jimmy meet us in the hallway as Renee turns to race down the stairs. Jimmy grabs her and pushes her behind him as he makes it down the stairs first. Typical Sloan family Christmas morning antics. I smile as I follow my siblings into the living room.

Mom and Dad are drinking coffee and watching the Christmas tree spin. "Good morning," my mother says, smiling. Her eyes meet mine and her smile softens slightly. "Merry Christmas."

We all have our own places around the tree and we settle onto the floor in front of our piles of gifts. We take turns opening our gifts and act like this Christmas is like every other. Even though my family is trying to maintain a sense of normalcy, Christmas just isn't the same for me this year and I'm not sure it ever will be again.

~

"Kyle's here!" Renee yells up the stairs. After opening all of our presents, my mother made a huge breakfast that we devoured. After my shower, I closed my door and lay down on my bed. I didn't feel like bringing everyone down with my mood, so I thought it would be best to stay upstairs, alone.

My heart jumps a bit in my chest as I walk downstairs.

Kyle is standing in our foyer. He looks up and smiles at me.

I melt.

"Merry Christmas," he says.

"Hi, Kyle. Merry Christmas."

Lyn takes his jacket into the other room as he hands my mother a package that looks like it came from a bakery. "Thank you for having me, Mrs. Sloan. I didn't want to come empty handed."

Mom takes the package and says, "Of course, Kyle. We're very happy that you could join us for Christmas dinner." Her eyes glisten and she looks away. She's more than happy, she's thankful. She knows how much time Kyle has spent with me and she loves him already.

My father joins us in the foyer and extends his hand to Kyle. "Merry Christmas. We're glad you could be here." Wow. I'm stunned that my dad just made this effort to welcome him into our home. I smile and think that today may just turn out to be okay after all.

"Thank you, Mr. Sloan. Are you ready for the game?" He knows the way to my dad's heart is basketball.

"The pre-game show is on right now so let's go get comfortable while the girls get dinner ready."

*Dear Emily*

Renee huffs. "Dad, you could stand to help Mom out in the kitchen every once in a while, you know."

"Not a chance, Renee." My father chuckles. "Jimmy, can you get Kyle a drink?"

My brother yells from the other room. "Sure Dad. Kyle, what do you want?"

"Water is fine, thanks," Kyle answers back.

We all settle into our Christmas routine. Kyle fits in perfectly as he, Jimmy, and my father are constantly yelling at the television and high-fiving while watching the NBA game. It's a good thing they all agree on their favorite team.

Dinner is over and we're able to avoid any awkward conversations. Kyle is happy to retell the story about his tree-climbing cat and he had my entire family laughing through dinner.

As my sisters and mother get up to start clearing the table, Kyle leans over and whispers into my ear, "I'd like to see your revolving Christmas tree, please." I shiver a little as his lips brush my hair.

"Okay," I answer, hesitantly.

We get up and go into the living room. I immediately spot a wrapped gift placed close to my spot by the tree.

"What is that?" I ask, pointing to the gift.

He smiles slyly at me and says, "Santa left something for you at my house." He then grabs my hand and pulls me over to the tree.

We sit on the floor next to each other as he leans over, picks up the present, and places it into my lap. "Merry Christmas."

"Kyle, you shouldn't have. I don't have anything for you." I'm suddenly embarrassed that I didn't even think to get him anything. Shit, he's been by my side for weeks and I didn't do anything. I feel absolutely terrible. I was able to get all of my Christmas shopping for my family done when I was home for Thanksgiving break. But I haven't done anything since, and I certainly didn't take the time to get anything for Kyle.

"Carly, just open it, please." He smiles at me and nudges the gift.

"I feel terrible. I don't want to open this because I have nothing for you. This is so embarrassing." I shake my head as I look away.

181

"Carly." Kyle insists.

I slowly tear open the paper and gasp as I see my gift. It's a beautiful journal, wrapped in light brown leather with my initials stitched into it. "Kyle…," I can't get out the words. *It's amazing.*

"I hope you like it," he says. "I thought you'd like to have a journal, you know, to write down everything that you can't say out loud."

I don't know what to say to him. This is such a thoughtful gift and it's as if he's known me for years. I have a dozen journals tucked away in my closet upstairs that contain my private thoughts and musings for as long as I can remember. But I've never had one as beautiful as this.

"I love it," I say as tears threaten to spill down my cheeks.

I slowly turn toward him, lean close and wrap my arms around his neck, hugging him. He hesitantly puts his arms around me, pulling me closer to him. "You're welcome," he whispers into my ear, causing me to tremble. I'm lost in his arms and my heart is beating wildly in my chest. I panic a little as I realize how close we are and pull away. He easily releases me from our embrace and smiles.

"And I'm glad you like it," he says as he squeezes my hand.

"I just wish I'd gotten something for you," I say as he quickly puts his finger against my lips to quiet me.

"No need to say anything more. Your gift to me was this incredible Christmas dinner. I'm thankful to have a place to be today."

He removes his finger from my lips as he smiles.

So I don't say anything more. I lean over to the control box underneath our tree and switch it on.

I lean into him and place my head on his shoulder as he takes my hand in his again.

"Jingle Bells" plays as we watch the lights twinkle and the Christmas tree slowly spin around.

# Chapter 28

## Tabitha

*Philadelphia, Pennsylvania*
**Past**
*Age 20*

WHEN WE ARRIVE at the club, the entire band is there. Tristan and Dax wave to us as Garrett smirks. Since Alex and I became 'official' almost a year ago, Dax has accepted our relationship. Tristan never really cared. But Garrett is still a douche. He's like that with everyone, so I've learned to shrug it off.

Alex and I barely spoke another word as we walked to the club. Our silence was tangible. I'm sick to death of arguing with him over his unfounded jealousy. Seth has never crossed any boundaries. *And neither have I.* He's just my friend and Alex needs to learn how to accept this.

"Alex, are you ready to find our support act?" Tristan asks.

Alex smiles, lets go of my hand, and smacks his hands together. "Yes! Let's get this party started!"

His mood changes immediately and he's like a kid in a candy shop. He's usually so hot and cold with his music, but this last album has really done well and has started to gain a more mainstream audience. In just under a year, Epic Fail has gained such momentum that they've been signed to a major indie label. The band has handled their rise to stardom fairly well. All except for Garrett. He's taken to whoring around with as many groupies as he can get his hands on. Sometimes several at a time. His behavior disgusts me and, quite frankly, worries me about what's going to happen on the road. Temptation will be all over the place and I pray that Alex doesn't get caught up in it.

We settle into our favorite booth and Darcy brings ice water to our table right away.

"Hi-ya kids. Any appetizers tonight?"

"Sure, Tabs will have hot pretzels with spicy mustard and I'll have chicken wings."

Alex ordered exactly what I wanted. *He always does.*

Dax and Tristan slide in on either side of us, and Darcy is immediately back at the table with a pitcher of beer and two frosted mugs.

"Our Darcy knows how to take care of us," Tristan says as he fills up the glasses.

She smiles back at him. "Anything for you guys, you know that."

She walks away to help another table.

"I'm excited to hear these three bands tonight. They all have such potential," Tristan exclaims. He really is excited.

"What bands are auditioning tonight?" I ask.

"Punch Drunk, Bitter Pill, and Young Captives," Dax answers. "I think Bitter Pill have the best chance. Plus their lead singer is HOT!" He elbows Alex and winks.

"Dude, shut up," Alex replies. He nudges close to me and puts his arm around my shoulder. He kisses me and whispers, "Don't listen to that jerk."

Darcy brings back our appetizers and Tristan quickly grabs the nub from the end of one of my hot pretzels. "Tristan…," I try to grab his hand before he puts the piece into his mouth.

"Sorry, I couldn't resist, Tabby." He winks and chases the pretzel with a large gulp of beer.

The first band, Punch Drunk, takes the stage. They begin their first song and the lead singer starts thrashing around the stage. *Whoa.* Way too punk rock for this tour. He's got a great voice, but he's singing so fast and he's screeching so many of the lyrics that it's hard to appreciate or even understand. I can tell that Dax and Alex have lost interest rather quickly. Tristan finds this band amusing; I can tell by the way that he's intently watching the lead singer and the drummer.

"Their rhythm is all off," Dax yells toward Alex.

Alex nods and indicates that their audition is over.

"Hey guys, thanks for coming out. We'll be in touch." Dax is short and to the point.

As the next band, Young Captives, starts to play, I see Kirsten walk into the club. I completely forgot that I told her to meet me today.

I squeal. "Kirsten is here! Alex, let me out so I can go get her."

"Sure, Tabs, ask her to join us." Alex slides out of the booth.

I give him a quick kiss on the cheek as I walk toward Kirsten.

Tristan comes out of nowhere, lightly grabs my arm, and says, "Who's your friend, Tabby? She's so hot."

I chuckle. "That's Kirsten; she'll be joining us if you want to meet her. And be nice."

She's waiting for me by the bar and reaches out to give me a big hug and kiss on the cheek. "Hey Tabby! I can't believe you and Alex have been together for a year and I haven't yet met the band." She peers over my shoulder, looking nervous.

"Well now is your chance, sister! C'mon, let's go sit in our booth."

Tristan watches as we walk over to meet Alex and Dax.

Shit, Tristan is such a flirt. He better keep his paws off Kirsten.

We slide into the booth and Tristan is there almost immediately.

"Guys, this is my boss, Kirsten."

"Your friend first, boss second," Kirsten chimes in.

Dax reaches across the table to shake her hand and smiles huge. She seems nervous. Tristan scoots closer to her and takes her hand from Dax. "Hello, gorgeous. How have we not met before?"

Kirsten is so not used to all of this attention.

"I know, right?" she says nervously. "When will I get to see Epic Fail perform?"

"How about next Friday?" Tristan offers.

Dax shakes his head and Alex smirks. They both know that Tristan is the love-em-and-leave-em type and this can only turn out poorly.

*Shit.*

"Guys, shouldn't we be watching the band?" I ask.

We've pretty much missed the entire set of the second band. I guess they didn't really cut it because none of the guys seemed engaged.

Dax states, "Boring. Bitter Pill is next. If they don't fuck it up, I'd say they're going to be our opening act."

Alex nods, looking uncomfortable. *Strange reaction.*

Bitter Pill finally takes the stage. There are four band members. Three guys and one girl. She's the lead singer.

She struts onto the stage and immediately takes command of the room. She's stunning. Her voice is brilliant and I'm suddenly jealous. Tremendously jealous.

Looking at her and realizing how strong she is, I'm suddenly insecure with my relationship. I don't know if I can handle knowing that she's on the road with Alex. She's everything that I'm not. Gorgeous, confident, and sure. I picture her seducing Alex, causing him to forget about me. Her eyes find us and she's singing to him, as if he's the only one in the room. *What the hell?*

I immediately start to tense up while jealousy takes over my body.

Alex notices my insecurities immediately and he pushes me out of the booth. He leans over to Dax. "Hey, keep an eye on Kirsten for us. We'll be right back." He firmly grabs my hand, pulling me into the back room.

He doesn't say a word as he shuts the door and pushes me toward the couch. He backs me up until the backs of my knees hit the edge of the couch. He then slams his mouth into mine, barely breathing as he devours my mouth.

Our tongues entwine as he pushes me onto the couch. My black skirt is already around my hips as he plunges his fingers into my panties, finds wetness, and parts my lips.

"Tabs, never forget that I love you. That I want only you. " He knows exactly what I want to hear. What I need to hear right at this moment. This is his way of making things right. Trying to settle my insecurities. Erasing his anger over Seth.

He continues to swirl his fingers in my cleft as I fumble with the button and zipper of his jeans.

"Alex," I moan softly.

He bites my ear lightly, then his teeth drag down my neck. He nibbles a trail to my collarbone, licking and sucking.

His tight black jeans are now pushed down, freeing him. I gasp and moan, and gaze into his eyes. He crashes his lips back onto mine, and plunges into me with one thrust. "Alex!" Oh, God, he feels so good inside me.

My heart is thumping to the drumbeats of the band and I'm moaning while yelling his name. "Alex!" He's pounding into me and my walls start to convulse around him. I'm already starting to tip over the edge. We're sweating and moaning each other's names.

"Tabs, tell me that I'm the only one for you."

"Yes, Alex, yes!"

He quickens his pace and pushes me over the edge. My entire body shudders as a mind-numbing orgasm ravages my body. His release comes seconds after mine and he collapses in a sweaty mess on top of me.

He continues to twitch inside of me as we both come down from that session.

"Tabs. What you do to me. I have no words." He's stroking my hair as his lips brush my neck. "I love you."

"I love you, too. So much. I'm going to miss you."

A single tear slides down my cheek and he immediately covers it with his lips, drinking my tear.

We separate ourselves and clean up. He suddenly freezes and looks into my eyes.

"Shit, Tabs, I didn't use a condom."

We've always used one before. I'm not on birth control because I can't handle the mood swings that it causes. I'm already bipolar and why make it worse? We're usually so careful.

"I'm sure it's fine," I say nervously. "I'm not worried." I try to make light of it. It's just one time.

That wouldn't happen, right?

# Chapter 29

## Carly

*New Brunswick, New Jersey*
**Past**
Age 18

THE HOLIDAYS HAVE come and gone and I've been settled back in my dorm for the past week.

Even though my family tried their hardest, the holidays were just not the same this year. Our home was somber and reflective. The cheerfulness that is the Sloan Family Christmas just didn't exist. We didn't talk about what happened to me and I'm glad, but it hung over our home like a black cloud. This isn't a subject that I want to discuss with my parents. I did, however, write about it. A lot. My new journal is now broken in and has been put to good use.

Over break, Kyle still called me twice a day and we saw each other several more times. While I'm not ready to admit it to him or myself, I feel like we're moving toward something more. I care about him so much it hurts. He's so patient and gentle with me and is a constant pillar of support.

Before I left the hospital, I agreed to finally speak with Dr. James, the school psychologist. Kyle was nice enough to take the initiative and set it up for me. Today is my first appointment with her. I walk across the commons to her office in the Sociology building. I shiver and my stomach clenches as I walk past the library. Bile begins to rise in my throat as I start to panic and my pace quickens. I can't imagine ever stepping foot in that building again, especially my super-secret nook on the third floor. That special place was mine and now it will be forever tarnished by a vile presence. I shudder as I think about my attack.

I reach Dr. James's office, write my name on the sign-in sheet, and take a seat. My hands are sweaty and clammy as I wring them together. I'm so nervous.

The office door opens and a middle-aged woman with vibrant red hair peers out into the waiting room. She's very distinguished-looking with an edge to her.

"Carly Sloan?" she asks. I'm the only person in the waiting room.

"Yes, that's me," I answer.

"Follow me, please."

I follow her into her office. The furniture is dark and there's a leather couch you would expect to find in any psychologist's office. There are pictures of her dressed much more casually, posing with various bands and musicians. *She doesn't strike me as the groupie-type.*

She smiles warmly as I cross my legs, trying to get comfortable. This is going to be weird.

"Carly, I want to start out by saying that everything you say to me is completely confidential. I'm here to listen, not to judge. I hope that I can help you cope with what happened to you and help you move on."

I silently stare out the window, watching several students rush to class. My eyes slowly move back toward Dr. James. I nod and I speak.

I tell her everything about Todd raping me last Halloween. About ripping my virginity from me. I relive all of the pain as I describe in detail what happened.

She's silent throughout. Her eyes remain soft and comforting.

I tell her all about the run-in that I had with Todd the day that Kyle and I worked in the Bio lab. About how I felt when he grabbed me, bruising my arm.

I finally tell her what I remember of the last vicious attack. I start to feel the same terror and my heart begins to race, my palms sweat and I feel bile rise in my throat.

I swallow hard and place my hand over my chest. I try to slow my breathing so that my heart rate slows.

"Carly, what you've been through is utterly vile. Your ordeal is far from ordinary and I'm so proud of you for coming here and sharing this story with me. First, you need to know that you are not at fault. Understand? You're a victim and did nothing to bring this on."

I nod slowly as tears pool in my eyes. "I understand, but I could have done something to prevent him from attacking the others. I didn't say anything until it was too late." I blink and tears stream down my cheeks. My guilt is overwhelming.

"You have to remember that you don't own what he did to you. Those were his actions, not yours. He's a predator, plain and simple. You weren't his only prey. He targeted you at that party, just as he targeted his other victims. I'll say it again; you did nothing to bring this on yourself."

"Okay." I try to believe her as I let her words sink in.

"You could have done nothing to stop him from doing this to others. Remember, some of the other victims were assaulted before you."

She's right. Two of the girls were attacked over a year ago. They're probably carrying the same guilt that I am.

"How else is this affecting you, Carly? I mean, are your feelings and anxieties spilling over into your personal life, preventing you from functioning at normal levels?" *What's normal?*

I pause to think before I answer. "Well, my friends have been great. They provided my first therapy after the rape. They did encourage me to seek help and report my attack. I wouldn't do it and yet they still supported me and stood by me. They provide me with the comfort and support that I need. They're truly wonderful." I smile as I think of them and the many jugs of pink wine we've consumed over the past few months.

As if she's reading my mind, she says, "Carly, you need to be especially careful with what you choose to do to numb the pain. I'm not making any accusations, but please stay away from drugs and alcohol during this time as you learn to cope. I'm glad that your friends are so supportive and I think it's great that you're surrounded by people who can lend a shoulder."

"They're great, Dr. James, and I trust them completely."

"Are you in a relationship with anyone?" she asks.

"Like a boyfriend?" I reply.

"Well, yes. I'd like to know if you're able to open up to someone in that way."

"Um… well, he's not my boyfriend. I mean we've known each other since last fall. He helped me catch up on schoolwork after I blew off classes after the first attack. He was the one that found me as Todd tried to rape me again. He saved my life. He promised me that he would protect me and he's been there ever since."

"He promised?" Dr. James asks.

"Yes, he made a promise to me after I had been injured. He swore that he would never let something like this happen again. After my attack, he spent every day with me in the hospital. He visited me at home during winter break. He even broke up with his girlfriend for me." As I say all of this out loud, I realize how much Kyle has given up for me. *Shit. I've taken away his life.*

I start to panic a little bit.

As if she can sense my mood changing, Dr. James interjects. "Carly, it sounds like Kyle really cares about you. I wouldn't dwell on what he did or gave up to help you. Just know that he did it on his own, not out of guilt or obligation. While ending a romantic relationship might seem abrupt, you may not know the reasons behind it."

I nod slowly. I do know that he actually ended things with Courtney the morning that I was doing his laundry. I walked in on him breaking up with her and the emotions that I witnessed were all about her. She was upset and didn't understand the whys or the hows. Kyle was explaining this to her when I stormed into his room.

"Kyle broke up with her because he had already developed feelings for me," I admit. "He didn't want to string her along when their relationship was going nowhere. He knew there was something worth pursuing with me the moment he met me. So to be fair to her, he broke it off."

I smile as Dr. James speaks.

"See, Carly, this is definitely something to consider when you're giving yourself a hard time over why Kyle has made the choices that he has. He did it for you, without even knowing what you'd been through."

"Are you intimate with him?" she asks.

*Geez.* I am not ready for this question. "Umm, no. We haven't even defined what we are really. It's too soon. Even though I feel something, like maybe I want to be something more. But I can't just yet. I feel dirty. Tainted. Is that wrong? Should I even want to be with him? After what Todd did to me?"

I'm being as honest as I can. Because I do feel dirty. *Contaminated.*

"Carly, your feelings are completely normal and natural. As your relationship grows with Kyle, you may want to explore other things. But I'm happy to see that you aren't rushing into anything. He's certainly giving you the space you need to continue to heal. And you are NOT dirty or tainted. Remember, you did not freely give your body to Todd. He TOOK it. While you may have physical scars from your attack, they're not badges that you wear to broadcast what you went through for others to judge. They make you stronger, Carly. Not weak and certainly not tainted."

Hearing these words coming from Dr. James lends credibility to these thoughts.

"I will try to remember that, Dr. James. It's just hard. My friends. Kyle. They all make me feel whole and give me hope that I can be normal again."

She laughs. "Normal. What's normal, Carly?" She pauses briefly. "Don't answer, that's rhetorical. Only you define that for yourself, not anyone else. What happened to you was NOT normal, but the feelings and the stress that you are going through while you try to cope ARE."

I sit silently for a few moments as she continues. "It seems to me as if you've already opened yourself up to emotional intimacy with your friends and even with Kyle. You will know when you're ready for physical intimacy. And it's OK to battle the constant emotions that it brings. It's normal, Carly. And you are normal. You are also beautiful and strong. You should be very proud of yourself the way you have come out stronger. I applaud you."

*WOW.* Not at all what I was expecting.

"Thank you, Dr. James. I feel a bit better." I smile.

"You're welcome. Let's continue to meet every two weeks. I think you've made significant progress in coping with your emotions and I'd like to keep this up. Same time in two weeks?" She takes her date book out of the top drawer of her desk.

"Yes, that works for me." I take a deep breath and stand up.

"Thank you." She smiles and nods at me.

I leave her office and make my way back to the dorm.

When I walked into her office a little more than an hour ago, I was expecting the floodgates to open. But the opposite happened. Dr. James was able to make me believe her words.

I'm normal.

Go figure.

# Chapter 30

## Tabitha

*Philadelphia, Pennsylvania*
**Past**
*Age 20*

KIRSTEN AND I are at the bookstore getting ready to transition between shifts. I'm in a total funk and I'm just going through the motions of this day. I can't get *her eyes* out of my head and the way that *she* was staring at Alex. She wants him and she looked like she would do anything to get him. Despite what he said to me last night, I know what I saw and I just can't shake it. I don't know how I'm going to handle him on the road for so long, *with her.*

"Tabby, what am I going to wear Friday night? Wasn't it so cool that Tristan invited me to their show?"

"Kirsten, don't overthink it. Just be casual," I say to her, trying to shake off my stress.

She giggles as she grabs her purse. "I'm going shopping now to find something perfect. Thanks for closing tonight!" She kisses my cheek and leaves.

Kirsten is already caught in the Tristan trap. *Shit.*

Seth passes her as he comes into the store.

"Where is she skipping off to?" he asks.

"Shopping. She needs to find the perfect outfit for Friday night."

He chuckles. "I guess she's looking to impress someone?"

"Hmph, unfortunately. Tristan. This won't end well."

He shakes his head and sits down on the couch.

"So what's up, Tabby? Your message sounded urgent."

I called Seth this morning because I needed to talk to *someone* about my fears, irrational or not. He always has a level head and is very good at talking me off of the ledge that I always seem to be on.

"They selected Bitter Pill to open for them on tour." I plop down on the couch next to him.

"So?" He doesn't understand what I'm getting at.

"Their lead singer is so incredible. Gorgeous. Perfect. Mysterious even. She's everything that I'm not. Alex is going to be drawn to her, I can feel it. And she has a thing for him." *She's a predator and Alex her prey.*

I can't believe this is coming out of my mouth. Where is this jealousy coming from? I've never been in a real relationship before, but still, I don't like this feeling.

"Tabby, I think you're overreacting. Alex would never. Would he?" Now Seth is starting to sound unsure.

I immediately gasp and cover my face with my hands. "Seth, I don't know. How could he want me if someone like her exists?" I start to cry into my hands. I can't believe I'm coming apart at the seams over unfounded jealousy. I rub the faded scar on my cheek and begin to tremble.

Seth turns to me and takes my hands from my face. He slowly wipes the tears from my cheeks and pushes my chin up so I'm looking at him.

"Tabby, you are the most perfect, beautiful person that I've ever known. There is no way any sane person would ever do anything to jeopardize that. Not even Alex."

He rubs his thumb on my cheek, swiping my falling tears.

"Seth." I'm touched by his tenderness and sincerity. He always knows what to say to me. I place my hands on his knees, and lean into his hand.

His eyes suddenly change and his stare becomes more intense. He licks his lips, takes a quick breath and suddenly his lips are on mine. He pulls my face into his and devours my lips. His kiss is frantic and tender at the same time.

I don't know what comes over me, but I begin to return his kiss. I bring my hands to his face and feel dampness on his cheeks. I don't know if it's from my tears or his own. He deepens our kiss and our tongues entwine together. His hands move from my face to my shoulders, down my arms and back to my face again.

Then suddenly he's not there. I feel a whoosh of air between us as he's pulled away from me.

I open my eyes and see that Alex has Seth by the neck and has thrown him up against the wall.

"Alex! Stop! Don't hurt him!" I yell. Alex doesn't seem to hear me as he begins pummeling Seth's face with his fists. Seth is doing nothing to fight back or protect himself.

I jump up and try to pull Alex away.

"Stop this!"

Seth sinks to the floor in a daze as Alex turns to me. He has a wild look in his eyes and I'm suddenly afraid of him. I haven't seen a look like that since Tony and he's glaring at me with his fist still in the air.

Sobbing, I back away.

"Alex." I bring my hand to my lips and realize what I have done.

Seth sees the terror in my eyes and jumps up to get between Alex and me. "Alex, leave," he says.

Alex suddenly realizes his threatening stance toward me and immediately drops his bloody fist to his side. He glares at me as he turns and leaves the store.

"What have I done?" I wail as I fall to my knees on the floor and my body starts trembling.

He joins me on the floor and wraps his body around mine, absorbing my cries. He whispers something softly into my hair as my cries get louder.

We remain huddled on the floor together, afraid to say another word.

After a while, he helps me close up the shop and walks me home in silence. He touches my face as he leaves and says, "I'm here for you, Tabby. Just say the word."

Once inside, I curl up on my couch and cry myself to sleep.

~

A knocking sound startles me awake and I jump up from my couch. It's after ten o'clock at night. I tense up as I wonder who it could be.

I look through the peephole and start to tremble.

Alex.

"Tabs, open up. We need to talk."

I slowly open the door and step aside so he can come in.

"Is he here?" he asks angrily.

"No," I whisper.

He strides past me into the living room. "I don't know what to say to you. I can't fucking believe what I saw today. What you did with him!" He's beginning to yell and I back away.

I know what I did. I ruined us. I deserve whatever consequences he is about to lay on me.

"I'm sorry, Alex" is all I can say. I begin to sob as I look into his eyes. He looks destroyed. I've done this to him. Taken away the love that he had for me. *All because of my crazy jealousy.*

"You're sorry? Seriously? What would have happened if I hadn't walked in? Would you have fucked him? Wait, don't answer that. I. Don't. Want. To. Know."

He starts pacing through my living room.

"What? No, Alex! That's not what that was!" I choke on my cries.

"Then tell me, Tabitha, what was that? Because it sure looked intense to me."

"I don't know," I say.

He walks over to me and grabs my wrists, pulling me against his chest. "Tell me, Tabby. Have you fucked him?" His tone is demanding.

"No, Alex, no," I whimper. I want him to hurt me, punish me for what I've done to us.

He abruptly releases my wrists as he pushes me away from him.

"I'm done. We. Are. Done." He turns toward the door to leave.

"Alex, no!" I cry.

He turns to me and his eyes have nothing but hatred in them. I can't believe what I've done to us. I'm deserving of his hateful stare.

"Don't, Tabitha. I trusted you. I promised you that I would get over my issue with Seth. You swore to me *yesterday* that you only loved me. That you only wanted *me*. We made love. What the fuck?"

He pauses and shakes his head. "Did you do this on purpose? Sabotage what we had?"

"What? No…," I say. *Or did I?*

"It's over," he says, his eyes burning holes through my heart.

I'm silent. *I deserve this.*

"You did this to us, Tabitha. I would have given you everything. Gone to the end of the earth for you. Never. Again."

He turns toward the door and leaves.

*I did this. And I can't take it back.*

And now I've lost the only man I've ever loved.

# Chapter 31

## Carly
*New Brunswick, New Jersey*
### Past
*Age 18*

THE SEMESTER HAS been flying by. It's spring and time for new beginnings. But today I'm not feeling hopeful or happy. I'm feeling dread and panic as I vomit for the second time in ten minutes. I'm in the bathroom stall as I hear Callie's voice outside. "Carly, honey, are you all right?"

I wretch one more time and flush the toilet. I'm not fucking okay.

Today I'm testifying at Todd's trial.

I slowly stand up and open the stall. Callie's eyes are wide and comforting as she pulls me into her arms and whispers into my hair, "Honey, you're going to get through this. Remember what the prosecutor said. She's going to make this as quick and painless for you as possible." *How can she? I'll be on display for all to see.*

I walk over to the sink and splash water on my face.

"Callie, I don't know if I can do this. I don't want to see him." I begin to shake as I grasp the sides of the sink.

"Carly, it's going to be okay. We'll all be there with you."

We walk into the hallway and see Becca, Manny, and Kyle waiting outside my dorm room.

They all turn to me at the same time as Callie opens my door.

Everyone enters my room slowly without saying a word.

Ginger is in the room and I honestly haven't seen her in what seems like months.

"Hi Carly," she says softly. "Good luck today. I'll be thinking good thoughts for you."

I don't think anyone could have surprised me more than Ginger just did. I can't believe she actually cares. Of course, she knows about what happened because Todd's attacks have been widely publicized on local news channels as well as around campus.

"Thanks, Ginger, that means a lot." It does mean a lot, considering Ginger hasn't spoken to me since last semester. She picks up her backpack and leaves the room.

Manny's eyes follow her as she leaves. "All of a sudden she has a heart and treats you with respect. Go figure." He huffs through his apparent sarcasm.

"Manny, Ginger seems like she's trying." Becca scolds him gently.

"Car, is that what you're wearing?" Manny turns back to me as he eyes me up and down.

"Um, yes," I answer. I'm wearing a pair of dark corduroy pants and a sweater set that I received from my sister for Christmas.

"Your clothes are too dark, Carly. I think you should change into something lighter, more freeing. You don't want to look like the victim. You want to look confident and happy. You can't give Todd any more of your anguish."

He's right.

"Alright, can you guys wait in the hall while I find something 'less victim' to wear?"

Everyone leaves as I fumble through my closet and find something more appropriate to wear. I finish getting dressed and open my door.

Kyle immediately reaches out his hand and grabs mine. "Let's go, killer." He smiles and winks at me as he pulls me into his side. I melt into him and reach out to grab Callie's hand.

I'm trembling slightly as she says, "He can't hurt you again, Carly. It's your turn to hurt him and send him away for a very long time." She squeezes tight and smiles softly.

Becca chokes on a light sob as Manny wraps his arm around her shoulder. "Let's do this." He says as we all step onto the elevator.

~

We arrive at the courthouse to a barrage of media and reporters. *I'm not ready for this.*

I can't believe how much coverage this story is getting. I see local and major news station vehicles parked in the street, each with huge satellite dishes. Kyle and I are riding in the back of Becca's car and he reaches over and slowly pulls my hood over my head. "Incognito," he whispers in my ear.

We find parking and quickly make our way inside the courthouse. Thankfully, no one recognizes me and we're able to enter uneventfully.

Once inside, the assistant prosecutor approaches me. "Carly, sorry to rush you, but we need to get you into the witness room. Your friends will have to find a seat inside the courtroom as we go over our final preparations for your testimony."

My eyes are wide and my stomach lurches again. Kyle is still holding my hand as he squeezes. "Carly, it's okay. I'll be right inside if you need me for anything." He smiles softly and reluctantly drops my hand.

I turn to the assistant prosecutor and say, "Okay."

Kyle, Manny, Callie, and Becca enter the courtroom. As the door opens, I can see my family already seated in one of the first rows. My father turns to my friends and waves them to the empty bench behind them. I find it ironic that my family has saved seats for my friends to witness me recounting one of the most horrific things that has ever happened to me.

I watch the door close and walk toward the witness room.

I'm prepped and quizzed by the assistant prosecutor for just a few minutes before we hear my name over the intercom.

"Carly Sloan, to the witness stand."

I feel faint as I stand up and slowly walk through the door and into the courtroom.

Silence follows me as I'm instructed to take the stand and I'm sworn in. I sit down and look over to my family and friends as my hands begin to tremble. Kyle's eyes are soft and glistening as he nods slowly and smiles.

*I can do this.* It's only going to take a few minutes.

I then scan the room as my eyes fall on Todd, who is seated at a table on the left-hand side of the room. He smirks at me and shakes his head back and forth. He's trying to intimidate me.

I shiver and move my unsteady hands into my lap.

"Carly Sloan, can you please tell the jury in your own words what Todd Mitchell did to you on the nights of October 31st and December 17th?"

Wow, way to jump right in.

So I tell them. Everything.

I'm sobbing as I finish telling the last thing that I remember of Todd attacking me in the library.

"I have nothing further, Your Honor," the prosecutor states as he looks to the defense attorney.

"I have no questions, Your Honor," Todd's defense attorney states.

*What? I'm finished?*

The prosecution team prepared me for a round of cross-examination questions from Todd's defense, but apparently that's not happening.

Thankful by this unexpected turn of events, I stand up on shaking legs and make my way out of the courtroom. Todd is looking down at his hands and Kyle immediately stands up and is at my side as he walks me the rest of the way out.

As the door closes behind us, he pulls me into his arms and kisses the top of my head. "It's over." He's stroking my hair and squeezing me tight.

I lose whatever composure I had maintained and start to quiver in his arms, sobbing hysterically.

"Shh, I'm here." He's reassuring me as he leads me out of the courthouse toward the parking garage. The media has moved inside the building and we avoid them once again.

We climb into the back of Becca's car as he pulls me tight into his side.

"Thank you, Kyle," I sob. "I don't know what I would do without you here."

He kisses the top of my head as he runs his hands along my long hair. "I'll always be here, Carly."

I believe him.

Everyone eventually files out of the courthouse and Becca drives us back to campus. Kyle quietly takes me to my room and we silently cuddle together on my bed.

We stay like this for what seems like hours.

I drift off to sleep while safely wrapped in his arms.

# Chapter 32

## Tabitha

*Philadelphia, Pennsylvania*
**Past**
*Age 20*

I'VE BEEN HOME for days, not able to leave my bed. Kirsten has covered all of my shifts at the bookstore and Dottie thankfully is covering the diner. *I hate myself for what I've done.*

I've destroyed everything I had with Alex, my love. He hates me now and I completely deserve it.

I curl up into my pillows and cry again. I don't know how many more tears I can shed. *I'm empty inside.*

I hear my bedroom door open slowly and I turn to see who's here.

"Seth," I say quietly.

He silently slips into bed behind me and wraps his arms around me, spooning me. "Shhh Tabby. Don't cry," he whispers in my ear. "I'm so sorry. This is my fault." I feel his lips next to my ear and his soft breath on my neck.

I don't speak as he continues. "I don't know what came over me, Tabby. You seemed so worried the other day about Alex and I just wanted to comfort you. When I saw your tears, I lost it. I hate it when you cry and I don't want you ever crying over him. He doesn't deserve you."

He kisses my head again and then trails soft kisses down my neck. "You deserve to be taken care of, cherished, loved." His lips are back on my neck more firmly. My body begins to respond to his tenderness and I start to lean my back into him.

"Seth," I whisper.

"Don't say anything, Tabby, just listen." His hand lightly travels down my arm as he entwines his fingers with mine. I can feel his arousal pressing lightly into my back. My breathing picks up as he says, "The very first day that I saw you, I just knew that you were made for me, Tabby. I made you smile, remember?" I nod as I remember his smile and his perfect teeth that first time I served him in the diner. I remember how soft and kind he was. Unthreatening. *Safe.* He wraps his arm around my waist and pulls me tighter against him. I'm breathing harder now as our bodies move against each other.

"You were my first friend here, Tabby. I broke through your shell and you let me in." His warm breath is now on the back of my neck as he places soft kisses there and on my shoulder.

I shudder as he slides the straps of my tank top down past my shoulder. He places his open mouth where his fingers were and swirls his tongue on my skin.

"Tabby, you are so beautiful. Inside and out."

He's whispering as he kisses his way down my arm. He rolls me onto my back and maneuvers himself on top of me so that he's resting with his elbows on either side of my head. His arousal is firmly pressed into my belly and I suddenly need him lower.

He locks his gaze on mine and says, "I love you, Tabby. I always have." Before I can react, he crashes his lips into mine.

Tears stream down my cheeks as I'm overwhelmed by his admission. His tenderness. I part my lips and our tongues become entwined. I arch my back and press hips into him. I need him.

He quickly frees himself from his pants, reaches between us, and pushes my panties aside. His fingers swirl between my legs as he positions himself above me.

"Seth!" I beg him. "Please." *I need this.*

Our lips collide as he thrusts into me. Filling me. I'm crying thinking about all that I have done and what I am doing. I'm betraying Alex. I'm doing exactly what he accused me of.

I'm overcome with emotion when Seth whispers in my ear, "I love you."

I come apart as I climax, sobbing into his shoulder. *What have I done?*

Seth continues to push inside me until he softly moans. "Tabby." I feel his release and he slowly lowers himself next to me.

He pulls out of me and pulls me back into a spooning position.

"Don't say anything, Tabby. I can't bear to hear that you aren't able to return my feelings," he whispers into my ear. "Just let me hold you. Please."

And I do.

Let him hold me.

# Chapter 33

## Carly

*New Brunswick, New Jersey*
**Past**
*Age 18*

TODD MITCHELL WAS sentenced to 25 years without the possibility of parole for each rape that he committed. He will never be free and for that, I'm thankful. The prosecutor was right. This was an open and shut case as all of his other victims came forward and testified. They had so much physical evidence against him and our testimonies just solidified the case.

Kyle and I are sitting on my bed, studying for our Biology II final. I took a second semester of Biology because Professor Martin encouraged it and, well, Kyle is her assistant.

"I'm done. I can't possibly retain any more of this stuff." I slam my book closed and flop onto my back.

He chuckles, closes his book, leans over me, and places his hands near my sides. I flinch a little but immediately relax knowing that Kyle is the one who is so close. "What am I going to do with you? You're always trying to weasel your way out of bio." He smirks and softly kisses the tip of my nose.

I suck in a quick breath as my heart begins to pound in my chest.

He pulls back a little so that he's staring into my eyes. "You're so beautiful, do you know that?"

I blink as tears spill down my cheeks. I certainly don't feel beautiful with the scars on my body that Todd left behind.

Kyle quickly swipes the tears from my cheeks as he places soft kisses on each one. His lips linger so close to my own. "Please don't cry. Please don't give him any more of your tears." He brushes his nose against mine and places a soft kiss on my lips.

My heart is racing as I wrap my arms around his neck and kiss him back. He deepens our kiss as I part my lips to allow his tongue to slowly enter. My belly clenches and I press my body into his.

I'm grateful with how slowly he has been taking things with me, but at this moment, my body is responding in a way that I've never felt before. "Kyle," I whisper against his lips.

"Carly, you're not ready for more. We're not ready for more. I just needed to kiss you." He leans in close, places a soft, chaste kiss on my lips, and moves next to me.

"But–," I begin to say as he places a finger over my lips.

"You have another session with Dr. James next week. Please talk through your thoughts with her. Convince her that you're ready, and I'll be waiting for you."

He nuzzles into the side of my neck and wraps his arms around my waist.

"Carly, open up!" Callie yells from the hallway.

Kyle chuckles into my neck and his warm breath causes my body to quiver.

"I'm coming."

I reluctantly pull away from Kyle to open the door for Callie.

"Hey chick. The gang's all here. Wine Wednesday!" She looks past me into my room and sees Kyle sitting up on my bed. Manny and Becca share a knowing look and smile.

"I think there's enough in this jug for everyone." Manny places the large jug of pink wine onto my desk.

"Wow. My first Wine Wednesday. I'm so honored." Kyle smiles.

For the first time in months, my best friends and Kyle surround me, and I feel okay. Actually, better than okay. I feel wonderful, protected, and loved. *Safe.*

I smile as I sit next to Kyle and grab his hand.

Becca looks at me with a puzzled expression on her face as she notices how close I am to Kyle, and how our hands are entwined.

"What is it, Becca?" Kyle asks innocently. "Am I not allowed to cuddle with my girlfriend?"

I immediately gasp as he says those words. He pulls me closer and whispers into my ear. "You've been my girlfriend for a while now; you just didn't know it. Why not make it official with your friends on Wine Wednesday to toast to us."

I smile and lean into him.

"So, yeah, everyone." I look around the room at all of the bright eyes and smiles. "Kyle. Well, he's my boyfriend," I say through the biggest grin that I've had in months.

"Well it's about damn time!" Manny exclaims. He passes out our red cups filled with pink wine. I hesitate as I hear Dr. James's voice in my head. I'll be sure not to mention this to her during my next session.

"To us! And to freshman year coming to an end." Manny starts to clink our cups together.

"Almost to an end." I correct. "I still have a Biology final to take."

"It doesn't matter. Your boyfriend is going to help grade your test so you're home free." Becca chimes in.

We all toast and drink to the end of a tumultuous year.

I'm thankful for these incredible people.

This is the first Wine Wednesday where we're actually celebrating something rather than holding a therapy session.

I raise my plastic cup and say, "Thank you guys for everything. You have no idea how much you all mean to me. The support that you've given me has been incredible. You've all stood by me through one of the worst times of my life and have helped me come out stronger. I love you guys."

Everyone raises their cups and clinks them together.

Kyle wraps his arms around me from behind and rests his head on my shoulder.

"I'm so proud of you, Carly," he whispers into my ear.
I close my eyes and smile.
I'm proud of me too.

# Chapter 34

## Tabitha

*Philadelphia, Pennsylvania*
**Past**
*Age 20*

ALEX HAS BEEN gone for two months. My life as I know it, ended the day that he walked out of my apartment. He's gone and I'm empty. I can't help it, but I've been following the band's blog, following their various successes. Looking at pictures of him performing his soulful and melancholy music. I don't have the right to do this, I know. I just need to see for myself, validate that he's truly moved on.

Seth and I have been together since the night he made love to me, after Alex left me. We haven't spoken about our status as a couple, but he's a constant calming presence. He tells me at least five times a day how much he loves me. I need to hear that, even if I can't say the words back. I don't even know how.

We've found a rhythm together, and it just works.

He comforts me and that's what I need.

Now more than ever.

Because this morning, I found out that I'm pregnant.

I have been so preoccupied with my sorrow that I failed to realize that I missed two periods. For the past few days, ever since I took four pregnancy tests confirming my worst fears, I've been shut in my apartment.

I need to tell someone what's going on. *But who?* When I think back to the times that I had unprotected sex, only two instances come to mind. Alex and Seth, just days apart. *Who do I tell?* This baby could be either of theirs. I'm terrified of their reactions. Terrified of the truth.

Without thinking, I grab my phone and dial Alex's number. I have to tell him in hopes that he'll forgive me and come home. To make things right. I need him right now more than anything. I'm desperate. I love him and want nothing more than to fix what I've done.

I rest my hand over my womb, close my eyes, and listen to the line ring.

"Hello?" says a raspy female voice. Did I dial the wrong number?

Startled, I respond. "Is… Alex there?"

She answers quickly. "No, um… he's incapacitated at the moment." I can almost hear her smile.

*Oh, no.* My heart beats out of my chest; my pulse races and I feel faint. I can't believe that he's moved on. *Who is this woman?* I stifle a cry and say, "Please tell him to call Tabitha. I need to talk to him."

"Sure, whatever." And the line goes dead.

Sobs overtake my body as I pull my knees to my chest. I have no right to feel this way but I'm so overcome with sadness.

He has moved on.

Hasn't looked back.

He doesn't love me anymore.

*I truly deserve this.*

I don't hear Seth enter the room, but I feel strong arms wrap around my body. "Tabby, baby, what's wrong?" he whispers in my ear.

What do I tell him? My body is shaking as I sit up.

I look down and softly say, "Seth, I'm pregnant."

He sits completely still next to me and doesn't utter a word. I hear his breathing hitch and he puts his head into his hands. We sit like this for what seems like hours.

He finally breaks our silence, panic in his voice. "I don't know what to say. I don't know what to do. I'm not ready for this. Are you?"

I gasp at his admission and realize that he's going to leave me too. I start to sob uncontrollably as he pulls me tight into his side. "I'm sorry."

Out of desperation, I cry, "Please, Seth, please don't leave me. Please. I can't go through this alone. I need you."

He continues to cradle me in his arms and kisses the top of my head. "I won't leave you. I love you." I hold onto him tight, hoping that what he says is true, but I don't trust that it is. He should get out of here while he can. I don't know that I'm ready for a baby yet either. There is an empty void in my chest that Alex left behind that a baby just couldn't fill. I'm a monster to think this way, but I just can't do this. Seth will take care of me. Love me. *If he stays.*

I already know what we need to do as I silently make the decision for all of us.

# Chapter 35

## Carly

*New Brunswick, New Jersey*
**Past**
*Age 18*

I JUST FINISHED my last final exam for the spring semester and I'm in my room, stretched out on my bed. I look at my favorite happy picture of my family and for the first time since Todd raped me, I feel content that they aren't judging me. I grab and hug my blanket as I curl up on my side. Kyle and I have been spending so much time together. We're officially together and in a relationship and I'm finally ready for so much more. He's been so patient and gentle with me for the past eight months, I'm eternally grateful.

I don't know if I'll ever get over what happened to me, but I finally feel as if I can allow him to get close to me, in more ways than one. Dr. James has helped me immensely in making sense of my anger, pain, and intimacy issues.

He's perfect in every way.

I hear a faint tap on my door. "Carly, are you here?"

*Kyle.*

I smile, stretch, and walk to the door to let him in.

"Hi," he says, grinning.

Every time I see him, my belly clenches and the butterflies come alive. His smile gets even bigger as the dimple in his chin is just begging me to put my thumb in it.

He walks toward me as the door closes behind him. There is intensity in his stare that I haven't seen before as his bright blue eyes turn to liquid. I inhale quickly and feel my cheeks flush. He reaches out and wraps one arm around my waist, pulling me tight against his body. Our chests are pressed into each other; I look up as our eyes lock. My breasts swell as my nipples brush against him. My heart is racing and Dr. James's words ring in my ears.

It's okay.

*I'm normal.*

I want this with Kyle, more than anything.

I abandon all restraint. I want this. I'm aching for this.

His mouth crushes into mine. Tender, soft lips. Soft kisses. *Whoa.* I take a breath in as he slowly starts to savor me. He's kissing me gently, his tongue softly tracing my lips. I melt into his embrace. My tense shoulders drop and relax. His other arm wraps tightly around my waist, pulling me even closer. The heat builds across my ribcage where his arms are resting. I push into him and part my lips to allow him full access. He traces my lips softly with his tongue before he plunges into my mouth.

Our breathing is in sync and our noses brush together. He moves his hands below my ass and lifts me up, wrapping my legs around his waist. He turns, pushes my back into the door, and continues to ravage my mouth. I'm positioned on his hips perfectly. I feel his arousal in all of the right places and I want more. I need more. I'm burning between my legs. Our lips are fused together as I start to grind my pelvis into him. I quiver in his arms as a tremor of white heat passes through me.

His lips leave mine and travel across my cheek to my ear. His breathing is heavy and hot on the side of my neck and I groan. "Mmm, Kyle." I feel his lips brush against the spot just behind my ear, he softly exhales, and the cool air from his mouth sends shockwaves through my body. I shiver all over, grab his neck tighter, and press my body harder into his.

"Carly," he pants as his lips are back on mine. He opens his eyes and holds my cheeks in his two palms. "Perfect," he whispers. His ocean blue eyes glisten and he breathes deeply, pulling me into him. "So, so beautiful." He places a soft kiss on each of my eyelids, and then kisses the tip of my nose.

His palms are burning into me as he pulls me tighter. My panties are wet and the friction from his jeans against me is sending shockwaves through every single part of me. My body is throbbing and I need more.

"Kyle," I whisper. His kisses wander back to my lips.

Our eyes are locked on each other again and mine plead with his to take me. Take all of me. He once again crushes his lips against mine.

We don't say a word as he turns and walks over to my bed. He places me gently on my back onto the mattress as he kisses the side of my neck.

He locks his arms on either side of my body and pushes himself up for a moment. I immediately feel the void and miss his lips on mine.

I tremble as he stares into my glistening eyes.

"Why did you stop?" I ask, confused.

"I don't want to stop, I just need you to be sure. I want you so bad." His eyelids become heavy as his gaze moves from my eyes to my lips. I lick them and grab my lower lip with my teeth. He immediately puts his mouth over mine, and I feel his own teeth softly pulling and sucking my lip into his mouth. I raise my hips so that I can feel his arousal against me.

"I want you, Kyle, please."

He pushes away from me again and looks into my eyes. "You need to be sure, Carly. Please tell me you're sure. I won't be able to stop and I don't want to rush you." His lips are back on my neck and he whispers, pleads, "Please, Carly, please be sure."

"I'm sure. Yes, I'm sure. Please make love to me."

And I am so very sure. I want him more than anything else. His tenderness is erasing my past. I'm renewed and feeling as if I haven't been with anyone else. *This* is going to be my first time.

It's going to be my first time *making love*. With someone that I love. I love him. Actually, I'm *in love* with him. We've known each other for eight months, and have been through so much together; this just *feels* right. Tears spill from the corners of my eyes. Kyle gasps and pulls away.

"Oh, no. I'm so sorry. I shouldn't have… God. Forgive me." His own eyes are glistening now and I panic. He's mistaking my tears for fear.

"No, Kyle. No! I'm not upset. I want this. More than anything." I reach for him and pull him close.

"Then why are you crying?"

"They're happy tears. I just… I just realized something, that's all."

He stares hard into my eyes and his brow tightens with a look of worry.

"What did you realize?" he asks softly.

I look away, blink, and allow more tears to cascade down my cheeks.

He softly brushes his knuckles against both of my cheeks, wiping away the tears. I smile into his eyes, "I realize that I love you, Kyle."

He inhales deeply and cradles my face in his palms.

"Say it again," he demands gently.

I exhale and look into his eyes.

"I love you."

He crushes his lips to mine, kissing me with passion, longing, and love. We are each gasping for air as our embrace intensifies. I reach for the bottom of his shirt and start to pull it up to his chest, my fingernails softly scraping his chiseled abdomen.

He sucks in a breath and leans back.

"Stop, Carly. I need you to know…"

The silence is unbearable.

"Please don't stop," I beg. I'm burning up; I need to feel his heat against me. Inside me.

"Carly, I love you. I love you so much. I've never felt like this before. I've never needed to feel like this before. You've turned me upside down, inside out."

He's silent for a moment as he leans closer to me.

He kisses my cheek, and then my neck, and whispers, "I love you."

I throw my arms around his neck and pull him against my body. His weight pins me onto the bed, and I let him. It's okay. I'm not panicking.

Instead, my senses are heightened and my entire body is pulsating.

His hands slowly leave my face as his knuckles gently begin caressing my breasts. His fingers lightly pass over my already hardened nipples and I suck in a breath. His lips are back on mine instantly. Our kisses become more urgent and feverish.

He pushes off of me, onto his knees and reaches over his shoulder with one hand to pull his t-shirt off. My belly clenches at the sight of him. He's perfect. I softly bite my lower lip while allowing my gaze to go lower.

He leans back on his knees as I feel his eyes burning into me. He sucks in a breath as I slowly pull my sweater over my head. I immediately regret taking my shirt off with the light on. I don't want him to see the scars on my breasts and belly. I stiffen a little, thinking about the vicious marks that Todd left on my body. I feel ugly and scarred.

Kyle senses my discomfort. "Carly, don't." He reaches down and pulls my hands away from my body so he can look at me. His eyes travel from my neck to my breasts. He inhales again, lowers his head, and softly places his lips on the faded scar above my left breast. I melt as his tongue slowly traces the ridges of the scar. He's transformed the gruesome aftermath of my attack into a tender, loving moment. He savors my scars, softly kissing each one until they burn. A wonderful burn that radiates throughout my chest and into my belly.

My breasts spring free as he gently removes my bra; the cool air causes my nipples to harden.

His warm mouth immediately covers one of my exposed nipples as his tongue softly teases the tip. My breathing turns to gasps. I need more. His mouth is savoring both of my breasts as his hands push down my sweatpants. I wiggle my hips to help him remove them. I'm now only wearing my panties as I realize that Kyle still has way too much clothing on.

I reach down between us and undo the button on his jeans. He reaches down and places his hand over mine, stopping me.

"Wait," he whispers.

"What?"

"Are you absolutely sure?" he asks, his eyes pleading with mine.

"Yes," I say softly, nodding.

He immediately jumps off of me, removes his jeans, and slowly lowers himself back on top of me.

I feel *everything* against me. His full erection is pressing into my belly and his mouth has found my breast again. I arch my back into him, allowing him full access. My nipples are cool again as he removes his mouth and lightly traces his tongue down my belly.

I feel his fingers on my panties, sliding them down my hips. He stops, looks up at me with his liquid blue eyes, and says, "I want you so much." I nod my head, giving him permission to go further.

His tongue lightly travels over my belly button and above my panty line. As he rolls my panties down my hips and legs, his mouth and tongue follow. My hips buck up involuntarily as he places his mouth over me. White heat radiates throughout as his teeth and tongue make contact with my most intimate areas.

I need more.

"Mmm, Kyle," I moan.

His tongue parts my sensitive lips as I feel a finger slowly slip through my wetness. He guides his finger in and out so slowly as if he's worried about hurting me. Tears build in my eyes and I sob softly. I'm so profoundly moved by his tender gestures. He's erasing all of the violence of my last sexual experience with his gentle touches.

He slowly swirls his tongue around my nub, barely making contact. My hips are moving in motion with his mouth as intense pressure builds. My walls clench around his finger as I come apart completely. *Oh. My. God.* My moans become raspy as Kyle continues to ride the waves of my orgasm with his mouth and finger.

My chest is heaving as I try to catch my breath. Kyle slowly removes his finger and moves back up my body. He leans on his elbows on either side of my head as he cradles my face in his hands. "Carly, that was beautiful. You. Are. Amazing." He kisses me tenderly and passionately.

I reach down between our bodies and into his boxer briefs. I slowly place my hand around his length. It's engorged and scorching hot. The tip is wet with his excitement. He sucks in his breath and moans into my mouth, "Carly."

I push his boxer briefs lower and he takes over. He pushes them completely off as he leans back to grab something from the pocket of his jeans. I see a shiny foil of a condom package as he tears it open quickly. He rolls it down his length and I clench in anticipation.

He lowers himself back on top of me, softly kissing the most sensitive area of my neck. His teeth scrape against my earlobe as he inhales deeply.

"Carly," he whispers into my ear. His soft voice and breath relaxes me completely. His tenderness is overwhelming me. "I want you. I want us." He's staring into my eyes, his fingers softly caressing my face as he slowly pushes into me. I gasp in pleasure at the sudden fullness inside of me. He devours my moans with his lips, tongue, and mouth. I can feel every inch of him inside me as he drives deeper.

"I love you, Carly," he says. His hips swirl and this incredible movement begins to push me over the edge again. I tense and pulsate around him just as another mind-numbing orgasm ravages my quivering body.

"Kyle!" I moan into his mouth.

His pace quickens as he pumps deeply into me. His body tenses and his chest heaves. "Carly," he moans. I can feel him throbbing inside of me as his release overtakes him.

He slowly pulls out of me, gets up, and walks over to my sink. He cleans himself quickly and returns to my bed. I feel a warm wetness pressed between my legs as he softly cleanses me. His tender gesture causes me to suck in a quick breath. His eyes never leave mine.

My heart continues to pound in my chest. I'm overcome by my emotions as my chest heaves. "Kyle," I start to sob.

"No, Carly, please don't cry," he pleads.

"They're happy tears, Kyle. I'm happy crying."

He slides into bed next to me, cradling me in his arms. "Only happy tears from now on, Carly," he says as he places soft kisses on my cheeks over my rolling tears.

*Dear Emily*

"Promise me," he asks.

"I promise, Kyle. No more sadness. Only happiness." I smile as his lips once again find mine.

We stop kissing as he nuzzles his nose into the side of my neck.

"And I *promise* to love you with all that I am, Carly," he whispers and pulls my body into his so that we're spooning.

Our breathing is in sync as we snuggle into each other.

"I will love you forever, Kyle Finnegan," I say softly as his arms tighten around my waist.

We slowly drift off to sleep when a loud banging commences on my door.

"Carly! We're here!"

Shit. It's Wednesday.

Wine Wednesday.

Kyle softly chuckles into the back of my neck. "We need to get dressed, Car. Your friends want to come in."

I turn toward him so our naked bodies are pressed together.

"My friends can wait, or go away. I'm drunk on you right now, Kyle, so Wine Wednesday can wait." I smile as I lean in and place a soft kiss on his mouth.

The banging on my door continues. "Carly! Open up! We know you're in there!" Manny is yelling as his tone escalates into annoyance.

"Car, they're going to keep knocking," Kyle states.

"Shh, they'll go away." I kiss him more insistently, pushing my tongue into his mouth.

He breathes deeply and rolls me onto my back, keeping our bodies fused together.

"Okay, maybe they will." He smiles and rubs his nose against mine.

"But I'm not going anywhere. Ever."

"Promise?" I ask.

"I *promise.*"

# Chapter 36

## Tabitha

*Philadelphia, Pennsylvania*
**Present**
*Age 21*

THE SUN IS streaming through the windows as I stretch in my bed and feel Seth's warm body next to mine. He has his own apartment a few blocks away, but he is always here. I feel suffocated by his attention and this relationship. I don't know what's wrong with me, maybe it's my hormones, but I'm unsettled. I don't know why I've been going through the motions for so long, allowing him to stay and comfort me. I don't deserve his love or support.

Today is a sober reminder of who I really am. Someone who was discarded, left as trash. An outcast.

It's Halloween.

My birthday.

Emily's due date is one week away.

I'm dreading the next few days.

Seth is sound asleep, so I get out of bed as quietly as a gigantic pregnant woman can. I tiptoe into the bathroom to relieve myself. Emily is firmly pressing into my bladder and I barely make it to the toilet in time.

I finish going to the bathroom, wash my hands, and look at myself in the mirror.

*What have I become?* The dark circles under my eyes are more pronounced and my eyes are sunken into my head. My coloring is gray and my eyes are lifeless. Cold. *Empty.*

I'm already mourning the loss of my child. I'm already feeling the pain that I've earned.

Emily kicks my bladder again and I rush to sit on the toilet. *How can I have this much pee?*

I finish up, walk into the bedroom, and see that Seth is awake. He sits up and says, "Good morning, babe." He smiles warmly and gestures for me to join him in bed.

"I'm going to make breakfast." I say coldly and leave the room.

"Tabitha, what's wrong?" he calls after me from the bedroom as I walk into the kitchen.

I just can't deal with this today. I want to be alone. Away from everyone.

"Tabby, what is going on?" He catches up to me, worry in his voice. He's gotten used to my mood swings by now and I just don't feel the need to explain anything to him again. I just can't.

"Seth, not now. Please. I just want to be alone."

He strides across the room and grabs me firmly by my shoulders, practically shaking me. "Tabby, please talk to me. What did I do wrong? You've been backing away, hiding from me. What can I do to help? Please, baby, let me help," he pleads.

I shake free of his grasp and walk to the other side of the kitchen island.

"I can't, Seth. Please, just understand that I just can't get into it." He won't understand what I'm going through and he certainly won't want to hear what I have to say to him. I've been practicing it over and over again, afraid to say the words. I need to free him from my hell. Let him go.

"Please! What can I do? What do you want me to say to make things right with you? With us? I'll do anything. I just can't take being shut out any longer. For weeks, months you have been constantly pulling away from me." He gets quiet for a second then says, desperately, "Let's get married. Let's keep Emily and have the family that you've always dreamed of."

*What?*

*Fucking hell!*

I start to laugh, almost maniacally.

"Married? Seth, what the fuck do you think I want?" I'm completely shocked to hear the word marriage from his mouth. That's the absolute last thing that I want or need. And I know for a fact that it's the very last thing that he wants.

"I don't know, Tabby. I don't know why I said it. But if it will help you cope with whatever you're going through, I'll do anything. I'll marry you. I'll raise her with you. I'll do anything, please."

He's insane. This conversation just hit nuclear.

"Seth, you never wanted this baby from the beginning. She may not even be yours. Hell, she isn't even mine anymore. She's Carly and Kyle's. She was always theirs, Seth. Always. The day that Alex left me was the day that Emily ceased to be mine."

"Alex? What the hell, Tabby, why bring him up? He walked away from you and never looked back. Dammit! Is that what you want? Alex to be her father? For you to find your happily-fucking-ever-after with him? I was here to pick up the pieces. Me! Not him."

"Pick up the pieces? Seth, I'm broken! How can you possibly think that you can put me back together? No one can."

I start to sob uncontrollably. I'm completely broken and I can't continue down this path. I need to move on – to start completely fresh. He can't possibly understand that.

Seth walks toward me but I back away.

"Tabby, whatever is going on, we can fix it. We always do. Please, baby."

"Seth, I can't do this anymore. I've been fighting this for a long time, but I can't be with you. You've always been a wonderful friend to me, but I just can't do this anymore. *I don't love you.*" His face drops in astonishment. I know that I just stabbed him in the gut and twisted the knife. He really loves me, but I just can't return the feelings and I can't continue to drag him down this painful path.

"Tabby, no. I won't let this happen. Like I said, I'll do anything you want. Anything. Please just let me. Let me in, I'm begging you."

Tears spill down his cheeks as he tries to reach out to me.

"I'm sorry, Seth. I'm so sorry. This isn't fair to you or me. I need to move on and be on my own. I need to learn how to move forward *alone*. I'm a weak person and rely too much on others. I used you. Don't you see that? I used you to fill the void that Alex left. He left a hole in my heart that no one, not even you, can fill."

Shit. I'm an asshole. I can't believe I just said that to him.

His face is now blank, devoid of emotion.

"Tabby, I'm not sure what you're saying, but I think I just heard that you never cared about me." He's broken. I've broken him. What he said isn't true, but I can't admit it. He has been a great friend to me and I have cared about him. I just can't say it. I won't. I need to end this. I need to move on and this is the only way that I know how. Cut the ties; sever the strings. *Set him free.*

"Seth, I'm sorry, I don't know what to say. This is over. I'm so sorry."

I turn, walk back to my bedroom, and gently close the door. I hear him leave the apartment. I know that I won't ever see him again. I just ripped his heart from his chest.

I sink to the floor, cradling my belly. "I'm sorry, Emily. I'm so sorry." I'm not sure what I'm apologizing for. She's going to have an incredible life. She'll never want for anything. She'll have all of the comforts and love a beautiful girl could ask for.

Most importantly, she'll have Carly and Kyle. *A real family.*

I'm *not* sorry for that. She deserves them and all that they can give to her.

I stay curled up on the floor for what seems like hours. I look up at the clock. It's almost noon and I have to get to the bookstore.

I stand up and feel a sharp pain across my abdomen, taking my breath away. I put my hand against the wall to steady myself while moving my free hand to my belly.

Another pain rocks through me as a burst of fluid streams down my legs.

*My water just broke.*

*Fuck!*

I'm alone. Seth's gone and he's never coming back.

I steady myself and make it to my nightstand where my phone is. I press the speed dial for Kirsten.

She answers the phone saying, "Tabitha, where are you? You were supposed to be here twenty minutes ago. Everything okay?"

"Kirsten." I pant and take a deep breath. "The baby. Water… my water just broke. Emily is coming."

"Oh no! What can I do? Where's Seth?"

"That's why I'm calling you. He's gone. *I need you.*"

"Stay put, Tabby. I'm on my way. I'll be there in ten minutes!"

She hangs up and I lie back onto the bed. I brace myself as a strong, painful contraction rocks my body.

*This is it.*

I pick up the phone and hit my second speed dial.

"Hello?" I hear on the other line.

"Carly, it's Tabitha. Can you meet me at University Hospital? Emily is coming." I start to sob uncontrollably. I can't believe the time is here.

"Tabitha! Are you okay? Please tell me what you need. I can be at the hospital within the hour. What can I bring? Do you need anything?" She's stammering and I can tell that she's flustered.

"No, just come soon. Please."

"Okay. Hang in there. I'm calling Kyle as soon as I hang up and then we'll be there right away."

"OK, bye."

I end the call.

I have never felt so alone. Sobs overtake my body and I'm shaking as the next strong contraction hits. I wail loudly, crying and screaming through my pain.

I feel the physical pain of these contractions and the emotional pain of saying goodbye to my daughter.

"Emily, I'm so sorry. I'm so sorry," I cry into the empty room. My tears are streaming down my face as I rub my belly.

"Please forgive me, Emily. I love you."

I hear my front door open and Kirsten calling for me.

*Dear Emily*

"Tabby, where are you?"

I swipe my arm across my face, collecting my tears on my sleeve.

"Back here."

She comes bursting through the door and stops to take in the scene.

"Oh honey. Honey, I'm here. What can I do to help?" She throws herself on the bed and pulls me tight against her chest.

"Get me to the hospital. Fast. My contractions are close together." *Too close.* Another stabbing pain shoots across my belly and I feel tremendous pressure.

"She's coming fast."

Kirsten helps me up and out the door to a waiting taxi.

We're on our way to the hospital.

I'm not ready to say goodbye.

# Chapter 37

## Carly

*Spring Lake, New Jersey*
**Present**
Age 29

"KYLE!" I SCREAM into my phone. "Tabitha's in labor!"

*I can't believe what I'm saying.*

I squeal with excitement.

"Car? Calm down. What hospital is she going to?"

I'm looking into the faces of two zombies, a vampire, and Tweety Bird. I grab gigantic handfuls of candy and dump them into their trick-or-treat bags.

"University Hospital," I say excitedly. "She's on her way there, right now."

"I'm on my way. I'll pick you up in fifteen minutes."

"Hurry!"

"I love you. I promise this is going to be perfect."

*This man always knows exactly what to say.*

"I love you too. And yes, it is. I can feel it."

I hang up the phone and place the giant bowl of candy onto my front porch. I scribble a note that reads, "Take one piece, please. We're out for the rest of the night," and place it above the bowl.

I scramble to find my flip-flops and grab my purse to wait for Kyle outside.

As I sit on the porch, my heart begins to race. I'm watching all of the families and children running around the neighborhood, squealing with delight. I'm picturing Emily in a few years doing just the same thing. Her first Halloween is her birthday. How amazing! For the first time I'll be able to replace the awful memories that I have associated with Halloween and my rape. Emily will forever bring happiness to this day.

I reach into my purse and touch the gift that I bought for Tabitha several months ago. I hope she loves it as much as I do.

Tears well up in my eyes as I think about what she's giving up. I'm so sad for Tabitha and her impending loss. I start to sob as I see Kyle's SUV tear into the neighborhood. Kids are scattering throughout the street as Kyle tries to avoid plowing them down.

I laugh through my tears, jump up and run toward his car.

"Are you ready?" he asks as I slide into the front seat.

He reaches across the center console and grabs my hand.

"I'm ready. More than you know."

I squeeze back as he pulls my hand to his lips and kisses it.

We pull out of our driveway and head toward Philadelphia.

We're about to become parents.

# Chapter 38

## Tabitha

*Philadelphia, Pennsylvania*
**Present**
*Age 21*

SHIT! THAT LAST wave of contractions was so intense. After yelling for pain medication, my doctor finally gave me an epidural so now I feel nothing but slight pressure.

Kirsten left a few minutes ago to go back to the bookstore. She has a signing to host tonight and couldn't stay with me in the hospital any longer. She felt bad, but really, what could she do?

I promised her that I would be fine until Carly and Kyle get here.

Honestly, I need some alone time. I need to prepare myself to say goodbye.

I hear Emily's heartbeat over the fetal monitors.

A deep sob escapes my chest as I place both of my hands on my belly.

Emily.

*Am I doing the right thing?*

I feel her moving beneath my hands as pressure builds again in my abdomen and back. The doctor said I will be transitioning into harder labor soon, but thankfully, I can't feel it. I'm eight centimeters dilated, and I could reach ten any time now. She's almost here.

As tears stream down my face, I close my eyes and picture what could have been if Alex were the father of my baby.

*I see Alex's face clearly and he's cradling a little baby in his arms. She's wearing a pink cap on her head and she's squeezing his pinky finger. He's smiling ear-to-ear as he brushes his nose to hers. He kisses her softly on her forehead and looks up at me. "I love you, Tabs," he whispers. "She's perfect. Our daughter Emily is just perfect. Thank you for giving us this gift."*

*He reaches his hand out to me and pulls me to his side. I touch Emily's warm cheek and smile.*

I open my eyes and snap back to reality.

*What have I done?* I'm taking that vision away from Alex. From Emily. I'm not even giving them the opportunity to know each other. I'm destroying that future. Crushing it with this one decision. It's not fair what I'm doing, what I've done to Alex.

The guilt overwhelms me and I begin sobbing into my pillow. I can barely breathe. Why didn't I make a different choice? I would have never kissed Seth. Alex would be here for me now. If he were the father, we'd be having this baby together. The way that it's supposed to be.

I feel pressure in my belly and another wave of contractions hit me.

I wrap my hands around my baby bump as my grief consumes me.

One of my nurses comes into the room.

"Tabitha, are you OK? Honey, why are you crying? Are you still in pain?" she asks, concern on her face.

I'm sobbing so hard, it's difficult to catch my breath.

"I'm just not ready to say goodbye," I'm able to say. I'm weeping harder now and I just can't seem to stop.

"Honey, are you ready to speak with your social worker? Are you changing your mind? It's okay if you do. You're in the driver's seat here, Tabitha. This is your decision."

I barely hear the words she's saying to me. What does register is that I can change my mind. *There is still time.* I can make my dreams come true. I can stop this adoption from happening and find Alex. I can introduce him to Emily and we can become a family. If he would even want me back. I imagine our family on the road with the band. With dirty groupies throwing themselves at Alex.

I shake my head. "No, I just need some time alone."

She leaves the room quickly. I'm a fucking mess, no wonder she bolted.

*What am I thinking?* Can things possibly get better for me if I do track down Alex? What will he think when he realizes that I kept this from him? And what if he's not the father? He'll hate me even more than he already does. Emily doesn't deserve that. No.

I'm devastated by the magnitude of this decision. All of the lives that I've ruined along the way by making the choices that I have. I've been completely selfish, thinking this is the best conclusion for everyone involved. I've destroyed my relationship with Alex and I shut Seth out on purpose. *I'm despicable.* I don't deserve Emily. I'm never going to be a good mother, lover, friend.

I think about Seth. I grab my chest as a new sob engulfs me. He doesn't want to be a father now. But he'd be a wonderful father. Tears stream down my face as I realize the enormity of what I did to him.

He loved me from the moment we first met at the diner. He settled for my friendship because he knew I couldn't give him anything more. I was in love with Alex and Seth gave me all of himself. He was even going to marry me to keep me happy. In his desperate attempts to keep me, he was willing to compromise everything that he wanted. I'm bawling gigantic, ugly tears now. I destroyed the one person that loved and protected me no matter what. He never backed down, even when Alex was at his throat, threatening him. Seth loved me more than anyone ever has. I just couldn't love him back. Not the way that he loved me. I fucking ruined him. Crushed him.

Would he come back if I asked? Of course he would. He'd compromise himself to make sure that Emily and I had the life we deserved. He would give us everything and too much of himself. He'd wind up resenting me, hating me. I can't do that to him or me.

Then I shudder as I think about Tony. If he ever finds me, I'm dead. I can't put Emily in that kind of danger. Deep down, I know that Tony will find me.

*Fuck!* Pain shoots through my abdomen. The epidural must be wearing off. I wail in pain as I weep for all that I have lost.

Sara.

Alex.

Seth.

Emily.

The nurse comes rushing in. "Tabitha, let's check your vitals, shall we?"

She looks at the monitor and slips on a glove. She feels my cervix and nods.

"It's time to start pushing. Let me get the doctor."

I'm not ready. I don't want to say goodbye yet. I'm choking on my sobs as the nurse leaves room.

"No!"

# Chapter 39

## Carly

*Philadelphia, Pennsylvania*
**Present**
*Age 29*

"No!" I HEAR Tabitha scream. "I'm not ready!"

I tense and whimper as I grab Kyle's hand sucking in my breath.

"It's okay, Car. Relax," he whispers to me.

Tabitha's wails echo throughout the maternity ward, causing my blood to run cold. *I'm terrified.*

Michelle, her social worker, joins us in the hallway.

"Tabitha has been having a very rough time. Her emotions are understandably unstable at the moment. She's been wavering on her decision to give her baby up."

I gasp and feel faint. *No. No. No.* Please, she can't change her mind now. *Oh my God.* I feel as if my world is crashing down around me. Emily is our daughter. I haven't laid eyes on her yet, but she's ours. I start to sob and Kyle wraps his arms tightly around me.

"Oh, Carly, Kyle, I'm not trying to get you upset. I'm just preparing you for what you're about to experience. You need to guard your hearts. She's really struggling with this and will be wavering until the final moments. This is expected. You have to put yourselves in her shoes. How would you be feeling right now if you were about to give up your baby?"

I can't even imagine. My gut clenches as I feel the pain that Tabitha must be feeling. How can she do this? How can she give up her baby? My shoulders begin to shake as tears flow down my cheeks.

"What can we do, Michelle? I'm worried for her."

Kyle rubs my back and says, "We'll follow your lead. Please let us know what we should do next. You say to guard our hearts, but we're far beyond that, Michelle. We're in love with our little girl already." His eyes are glistening and I can tell he's about to lose his composure. I turn and throw myself into his arms.

A nurse joins us in the hallway. "She's asking for you all."

"What? Us?" I ask incredulously.

"Yes! Hurry up, the baby isn't going to wait!"

Michelle grabs my hand and pulls me into the delivery room.

Tabitha is openly crying, sobbing, shaking. She looks terrified.

"Carly," she cries. I rush to her side and grab her hand.

"It's okay, we're here." I reach behind me and squeeze Kyle's hand.

"We're both here for you. For whatever you need."

I start to cry as I smooth her hair around her face.

"I'm sorry. I'm so sorry," she sobs. The pain on her face turns to something else. *Guilt? Fear?*

*Oh no…* she's sorry? My biggest dread is coming true, she's changed her mind. I start to cry and brush her tears from her face.

"It's okay. I can't imagine what you're going through and understand if you can't go through with this." I'm devastated, but I really do understand. I try to mask my devastation with a weak smile.

Kyle comes up behind me and holds my shoulders steady as my sobs threaten to overtake my composure. He rubs my arms and whispers into my ear, "It's okay. It's going to be okay."

I then repeat the mantra to Tabitha as I continue to smooth her hair. The more I say it, the more I want to believe that it will be okay.

"Carly, I need you to stay with me while she's born. Can you stay?" Tabitha begs me, pleading.

"Of course. I'm not going anywhere."

The nurse chimes in, "She's ready to start pushing. The baby's head has fully crowned. I'll go get the doctor and we should have a Halloween baby shortly."

Tabitha starts sobbing again. "It's my birthday today, too."

"What? You're kidding!" I exclaim. "You and Emily will share this special day. That is so wonderful."

The doctor comes rushing in.

"So, who's ready to have a baby?"

He settles on a stool at the end of the bed and instructs, "It's time to push. Are you ready?"

She looks up at me with wide eyes, squeezes my hand, and bears down.

After doing this same routine several more times, the doctor exclaims, "And we have a healthy baby girl." Her cry is almost immediate and he places Emily onto Tabitha's chest.

She looks down at her daughter and calm envelops her face.

"Hi, beautiful girl," she says as her eyes light up, proud of what she just produced. Emily is looking into her mother's eyes.

"You're so perfect, Emily." Tabitha exclaims as she nuzzles her nose into Emily's.

I begin to back away so I can give her privacy with her little girl. Their lives together are beginning in this moment and it's time for me to fade away.

The nurse asks, "Who's cutting the cord?"

I look away, certainly not me. This is Tabitha's time now. She made her decision and it's time for Kyle and me to move on.

"Kyle?" I hear Tabitha ask.

I turn around and look into her eyes. They are glistening with tears and she puts her hand over her mouth to hide her sobs. Her shoulders are shaking with her cries.

"Kyle, please cut the cord," she says between sobs. "It's customary that her father do this."

*What? Her father?*

"But Tabitha, I thought…"

She stops me and says, "Carly, Kyle. You're her parents. You always have been. Please Kyle, cut the cord."

I let go of Kyle's hand so he can do as he is asked.

"Tabitha," I'm able to say, somewhat coherently. "Thank you."

I lose it and completely break down. I put my face into her hair and watch as Kyle cuts the umbilical cord. He reaches over and places his palm over the crown of Emily's head. Tears are now streaming down his face as he says to Tabitha, "Thank you."

The nurse takes Emily from Tabitha's arms to weigh her and clean her off.

The three of us are holding hands and crying. It's beautiful but so tragic.

Tabitha is giving up her beautiful daughter. To us. How can she do this? She's met Emily. She's seen how perfect and beautiful she is. How is it possible that a mother is able to give up her child?

"Tabitha, are you okay?" I ask.

She pulls her hands from Kyle's and mine and begins to wipe away the tears from her face. She keeps her hands over her face for a moment, removes them, and looks up at us.

"No, I'm not. But I will be. It's all because of you that I will be. I'm going to strive to have what you and Kyle have someday. I'll find my happily ever after. It just isn't now."

She looks over at Emily who is crying as she's being cleaned up.

"Emily has always been your daughter. Always. She deserves you both and the life that you're going to give her. Just like you deserve her."

Her sobs return. "You're the perfect family."

She lowers her head into her hands and starts bawling again.

The nurse brings a freshly swaddled Emily over to us. She motions to Tabitha who shakes her head, tears still flowing down her cheeks.

"Please give Emily to her mother," she says through her sobs.

I contain my own cries as I reach out for Emily. She's sleeping again as I cradle her in my arms.

"Tabitha... she's just perfect." I smile as I stare at my daughter.

Kyle is suddenly next to me and he wraps his hands around my waist. "She's beautiful, Tabitha."

We're all silent for what seems like hours. I can't stop staring at this beautiful creature. My daughter. Emily.

The nurse comes over to me and gently takes Emily.

"We have to run all of her newborn screens. We'll be back shortly, so you can feed her, Daddy." She indicates that Kyle is on deck for his next fatherly duty.

I sit next to Tabitha and reach for my purse.

"I have something for you. It's just a small token of how eternally grateful we are to you."

I take out the small jewelry box and hand it to her.

She looks up at me through her tear-streaked eyes and face.

"You didn't have to get me anything, Carly. This is too much. You've already done so much for me."

"You just gave us a piece of you. This is so small, insignificant even. Please, open the box."

She does.

Her eyes find mine as a tear rolls down her cheek.

"It's beautiful."

She removes the heart shaped locket from the box and holds it in her fingers.

"We'll send you special photos of Emily for your new locket. You'll always have her close to your heart." I smile.

"Wow. It's perfect," she says softly.

Michelle speaks up. "Okay, Tabitha needs her rest, now. Carly, Kyle, you can go next door. We have a private room set up for you to bond with Emily. Kyle, you should get ready to feed her." She smiles as she gestures toward the door.

I turn to Tabitha.

"Are you sure?" I ask her. I feel that I need to ask, just one more time.

"I've never been more sure of a decision. Emily is your daughter now. Please love her as much as I do."

I throw myself into Tabitha's open arms and sob into her chest.

"Thank you, thank you, thank you, thank you…"

Kyle comes up behind me and gently pulls me away from her.

"You have no idea what you've done for us," he says through his own tears. "Thank you."

She closes her eyes and lowers her head as we turn to leave the room.

"Goodbye," she whispers.

I hear her soft sobs as Kyle and I leave the room to bond with our new baby.

# Chapter 40

## Tabitha

*Philadelphia, Pennsylvania*
**Present**
*Age 21*

IT'S BEEN FOUR weeks since I gave birth.

Since I gave Emily away.

I reach up and grab the locket around my neck. Carly and Kyle sent me the first picture of Emily just days after they got home. It's a photo of Emily sound asleep in her cradle. She looks so peaceful. *Perfect.*

I rub the heart as I hear the door chimes.

I turn quickly to face the door. It's just Kirsten. I don't know who else I would be expecting.

Alex?

Seth?

I can't believe that it's been four weeks.

I feel empty.

"Hey honey, how are you?" Kirsten sees my distress.

"I'm okay," I lie.

"How can you be okay, Tabby? You gave up your baby girl a month ago. It's fine if you're not."

Truth. It's fine to break down several times a day. It's normal. At least that's what my therapist tells me.

*Dear Emily*

However, for me, my grief is double.

I've lost two babies.

I've lost two loves.

I have to learn how to live again.

I pick up the box of new books and move toward one of the shelves along the wall. I breathe in the scent of the books and this calms me.

"I'm going to be all right, Kirsten. I promise I will. Dr. Randall tells me that as each day passes, my pain will be less and less. I'm hoping to replace the pain with new memories."

I don't know where these new memories are going to come from, but it's worth a shot at something.

Kirsten plops down on the couch.

"We'll make memories together. You and me, Tabby. We can be each other's family. You know that I'm always here for you. I love you, girl."

She reaches out and squeezes my hand.

"Thanks, Kirsten. I love you too."

It feels great to have an actual girlfriend.

And now I look forward to starting the next chapter in my life.

Wherever it may lead.

I wipe the last tear from my cheek and grasp my locket.

I smile for the first time in months and finally allow myself to feel.

*Hope.*

# Chapter 41

## Carly

*Spring Lake, New Jersey*
**Present**
*Age 30*

KYLE RUSHES INTO the house and exclaims, "It's time, so bundle up Emily and come outside."

He's absolutely giddy and this makes me so happy.

I take a sleeping Emily from her cradle and place her into her one-piece pink snowsuit. Once she's tucked safely inside, I carry her out the front door.

Kyle is standing on the front lawn with his hands on his hips, admiring his handiwork.

I reach him, then turn to face the house. I gasp as I see the beauty that's before me.

Kyle has outdone himself this year. Our Christmas lights are spectacular.

Thousands and thousands of white twinkling lights adorn our windows, porch, and shrubs. I smell the pine from the fresh garland that he has expertly strung around our porch.

"Kyle, it's perfect!" I exclaim.

And it is.

It is so perfect that I start to cry.

*Dear Emily*

I do that a lot lately. Cry happy tears.

He pulls Emily and me into his chest.

"Nothing but Christmas perfection for my girls." He softly places his lips on mine.

We make our way back inside the house and settle next to our warm fire.

"I'm not sure what could make this Christmas any more perfect than it already is."

I place Emily back into her cradle. She looks so peaceful. So tranquil. She's just flawless.

I turn to him. "You promised me this would be our future. Thank you."

He wraps his arms around me and kisses my neck. "I'll always promise you, Carly. I promise to love you and Emily until the day that I die. I promise to give you a life of twinkling lights and Christmas trees. I promise to keep you both safe. This has always been our future; it just took us a little while to get here."

More happy tears stream down my cheeks.

I'm thankful for all we have gone through to get here. I'm even thankful for the pain. For without it, we wouldn't have found our future.

Our Forever Family.

# Epilogue

## Tabitha

*Philadelphia, Pennsylvania*
**Two Years Later**
*Age 23*

I ARRIVE HOME to my new apartment. My two jobs and diligent savings over the past two years have paid off. I'm now in a nice complex in a much safer part of Philly. It feels great to have this new, fresh start. I've finally made something of myself, on my own.

I bend down and pick up the package in front of my door, enter my apartment and flop down onto my couch. What a long day. I worked at the bookstore today and Kirsten invited me back to her place for dinner. It was nice and simple. We had macaroni and cheese and split a beer. It was perfect.

Kirsten is so genuine and caring. She wants to see me happy and helps me as best as she can. She understands my need to be independent and doesn't pry too much. But she knows that when I'm ready, I'll tell her all about Emily and her family. And tell her all about Carly and Kyle. She's my best friend and it feels so awesome to finally say that I have one.

It's been almost two years since I gave up Emily.

And I've been on my own.

*Completely.*

*Dear Emily*

I'm actually so proud. For once, I don't hate myself. I learned that jealousy actually does breed hate and disease. I don't want to hate any longer. I want to heal. I'm no longer jealous of others and what they have. I'm no longer jealous of Carly.

I love her.

I love her for keeping her promise and for giving Emily a chance at a wonderful life. Even though I'm in a better place, Emily always belonged to Carly and Kyle. I knew it the moment I realized that I couldn't keep her. They wanted her from the very beginning and she deserved to be brought up with a complete family. And they are complete in every way.

For the first time in my life, I have no regrets.

The package in my hands is from a familiar address. I receive a package from the adoption agency every six months like clockwork.

I dump the contents onto my lap and immediately start to look through them.

A large photo album is on top from the Finnegans: Carly, Kyle and Emily. I'm so happy that they choose to keep me involved in Emily's life. I also receive frequent emails and pictures and keep in touch through Facebook. I love watching Emily grow and she is always smiling from ear to ear in every single picture.

The photo on the cover is taken in front of their fireplace mantel. It's gorgeous! Christmas decorations are plentiful. They're sitting on the hearth and Carly is holding Emily in front of her. Emily is wearing a red and black plaid skirt with a red turtleneck on top. She has red tights and shiny black patent leather shoes. Her curly brown hair is in pigtails fastened with red bows on either side. Her smile is huge. Her teeth are still scattered throughout her mouth, as she has been a slow teether. Her hands are in front of her as if she's about to clap.

Kyle is sitting next to Carly with his arm around her back. Carly is leaning into his side and her head is resting on his shoulder. Their love for each other jumps off of the page. I can feel the purity and the immenseness of it. Carly's smile is huge and infectious. I smile as I look into their eyes. This is one truly happy family.

I slowly look through the book, living each photo as if I were there.

I feel blessed that they choose to share these beautiful memories that they're creating. I smile as I turn to the last page. Attached with a paper clip is a heart-shaped photo of Emily smiling. Carly has these unique photos made for me every year sized just perfectly to fit my heart-shaped locket.

I remove my necklace, open the locket, and place the new picture on the right side. I keep the left side empty for my Sara. Even though I have no photos of her, she will always have a place in my heart. She deserves to share this space with her sister. I smile as I remember the sweet little baby that I was forced to give up. I can't go back to change what happened. I can only move forward.

And I am.

Moving forward.

I place the album onto the bookshelf next to all of the others that the Finnegans have sent me over the past two years.

Tears spill over my cheeks as I think warm thoughts about the wonderful family that is giving Emily the life she deserves.

I hear a soft knock on my door.

I glance over to look at the clock on the wall. Seven thirty. It must be Kirsten coming to pick me up to go work the book signing at the shop.

I quickly swipe away the tears from my cheeks as I open the door. "Kirsten, I'm ready–" I stop abruptly. It's not Kirsten.

My heart races. I step back and stumble away from the open door.

I choke on a sob as I slowly shake my head.

He can't be here. No.

Why? *Oh my God!*

How did he find me?

Tears are now streaming down my face as I become rigid, anxious. This can't be happening.

My hands start to shake and my breathing becomes irregular.

I swallow harshly as my throat begins to close.

I raise my hand to my lips as panic sets in and I say his name.

*"Alex."*

# The End

"Dear Emily"
Forever Family Series
Book 1

# Dear Tabitha

**The Forever Family Series**
**Book 2**
**Tabitha's story continues**
*Available everywhere*

# Note to My Readers

If you or someone you know has been raped or abused, please urge them to seek help. Please beg them to tell someone.

No means no.

Do something and say something.

For more information about how to help yourself or a loved one, please visit one of these important websites or call the toll-free hotlines.

RAINN (Rape, Abuse & Incest National Network)
www.rainn.org
1-800-656-HOPE (4673)

Safe Horizon
www.safehorizon.org
1-800-621-HOPE (4673)

# Acknowledgements

I have so many people to thank and I know that I'm going to inadvertently leave someone out so please forgive me.

I have to thank my family first since they suffered through the writing of this book along with me. However, instead of enduring the same emotional rollercoaster that I was on, they had to endure getting dressed in the dining room where the mountains of laundry piled up for weeks on end. Everyone that knows me knows that my husband is a saint. I love you, Mr. Trudy. You are my Kyle.

I'm very thankful for the wonderful adoption community. Through our own personal adoption experiences, we've met some incredible people and families. Most importantly, I want thank all birth parents for the completely selfless decisions that you make to be sure your children have a wonderful life. We are forever grateful to our own children's birth parents for giving us the wonderful gifts that they have. Our lives are forever changed by their choices. We have two beautiful children today because of four very special people and an incredible adoption agency that connected us.

I hope that all of my readers have friends like Becca, Callie, Manny, and Kirsten. I know that I do and I wouldn't be the person that I am today without them in my life. We have all been through so much together and I'm so thankful for you! I love you guys so much and cheers! *Trudy raising her wine glass to you*

My family is a constant source of support and love. Thank you for helping shape the woman that I am today. I'm proud to be a part of my crazy family, rotating Christmas tree and all.

I'm in complete awe of the indie community! I'm an avid reader and frequently escape into the fictional reality that so many of my favorite authors create. I have been welcomed with such huge open arms by so many authors and bloggers it's absolutely incredible! Thank you to the authors who immediately embraced me into this awesome club: Harper Sloan, Jade C. Jamison, Shantel Tessier, Charlene Martin, T.H. Snyder, R.D. Cole, Lola Stark, Amanda Maxlyn, Mia Fox, Michelle Polk, Brooke Page, and so many others! (Again, I'm sorry, I'm sure I've overlooked some.) I absolutely loved the writing sprints that we've shared and look forward to many more.

Thank you to the following partners who helped make this book what it is today:

Murphy Rae – thank you for helping breathe new life into my books. You helped me become a better writer and I'll forever grateful.

Kathryn Crane – my wonderful editor. When Harper Sloan suggested you, I knew that I had to bang down your door. Thank you for all of the support and your fine skills. You helped make Dear Emily something that I'm extraordinarily proud of. Thank you.

And thank you, Katie, for assembling the best beta team a girl could ask for:

Jennifer, Jodie, Julie, Jennifer, Mindy, Christina and Tabitha. You girls are all so amazing. I'm thrilled that you connected with my characters and helped provide such amazing feedback along the way. I'm glad that we all got to share these characters together along with some laughs and tears. Love you girls.

To my personal beta team, friends who have known me for a long time. Thank you for reading along as this story unfolded. Many of you know the emotion that went into this book and some of the events that inspired it. You know how hard this book was for me to write and I thank you so much for coming along for the ride. I love you guys from the bottom of my heart. Barb, Chloe, Donna, Kathy, Karen, Sharon, Michelle, Melissa, Melanie, and Lindsey – thank you.

Steph's Cover Design – Wow! You totally nailed it. Your cover design is truly gorgeous for Dear Emily. Stunning. Flawless. I could go on and on. It's just so perfect and I thank you. You were an absolute pleasure to work with.

Emily Mah Tippetts – What can I say? You took an unformatted word document and turned it into a work of art. I'm so thrilled with what you were able to do and truly feel that you added beauty and depth to my story. Thank you.

Brandee's Book Endings – Brandee, I LOVE YOU! You did an amazing job on all of the logistics from my cover reveal to blog tour. Thank you for coaching me through the process and for helping spread the word about Dear Emily. You are seriously one of the sweetest people out there and I love that you were so willing to work with me on my debut. Thank you so very much.

I need to give a huge shout out to ALL of the bloggers that took a chance and supported my debut by posting my cover reveal, social media links and reviews. There are over one hundred of you and you all ROCK!

Steve Adams from More Than A Memory Photography. Thank you. I had such a fun day with you and Jeff in Red Bank doing my headshots. Thanks for helping capture the look that I wanted for my professional photos. You are the best!

Finally, thank you to all of my new readers and friends! I hope that you continue to follow the story of these beautiful characters. They have all become a part of me and I can only hope that they touch or inspire you in some way. Stay tuned as Tabitha's story continues.

The Forever Family series will explore the many characters that you've met throughout this book.

# About the Author

Trudy Stiles is a New Adult author, mom to two beautiful children, and married to the love of her life. She's the author of the bestselling Forever Family series including "Dear Emily," "Dear Tabitha," and now "Dear Juliet." She plans to write many more stories about some of the characters you've already met, and maybe a few new ones. The Epic Fail series will begin in the Summer of 2015.

Trudy is a music junkie and you'll know that she's writing when you see her plugged into her laptop with her earbuds in. Her playlist is unique and is a must for her writing sprints.

When she's not writing, she's carting her children to their various activities while avoiding any kind of laundry or housework. She also loves to run along the boardwalk of the beautiful New Jersey shore.

She celebrates Wine Wednesday almost every day.

Email:authortrudystiles@gmail.com
Facebook: www.facebook.com/authortrudystiles
Goodreads: www.goodreads.com/trudy_stiles
Twitter: @trudystiles
Instagram: https://instagram.com/trudystiles/

CPSIA information can be obtained at www.ICGtesting.com
Printed in the USA
LVOW10s2151230516

489637LV00012B/218/P